Beyond Betrayal

Created by
Therese M. Willis

Illustrated by
Robert S. Willis

Wordswork
Philadelphia, Pennsylvania

For my family

Teddi, Judd, Robert, Wendy, John, Charlie, Lisa, Nina and Craig
Cassidy, Summer, CJ, Sophia, Clay, Ike, and Charley

Acknowledgements

I would like to express my gratitude to my family and to each and every person who has inspired me to complete this journey I started many years ago.

To my first readers, Sissy McGrann, Beth McGrann, and Chris Bloom who encouraged me to continue.

To Frankie Lawson and her daughter Jenny Benjamin who met with me on a continual basis to listen to and comment on my progress.

To Bill Kent, author and instructor at Temple University, who provided purposeful feedback.

To Carol Plum-Ucci, author and workshop leader at Peter Murphy's Winter Prose and Poetry Getaway, who painted a realistic picture of the writing/publishing community and provided the push to persist. Gratitude also for feedback from workshop participants Mary Fox and Margaret DeAngelis.

To Peter Murphy for drawing me into the world of the writer and inspiring me to accomplish the impossible, especially in his Wales Workshop.

To Janet Benton of The Word Studio for a thorough analysis that provided purpose, direction, and motivation for my work.

To Daniel Moise for a final edit which streamlined my prose and removed inconsistencies.

To Robert Willis, Pennsylvania Academy of the Fine Arts, who created flawless illustrations to embelish the prose.

We don't see things the way they are.
We see them the way we are. - Talmud

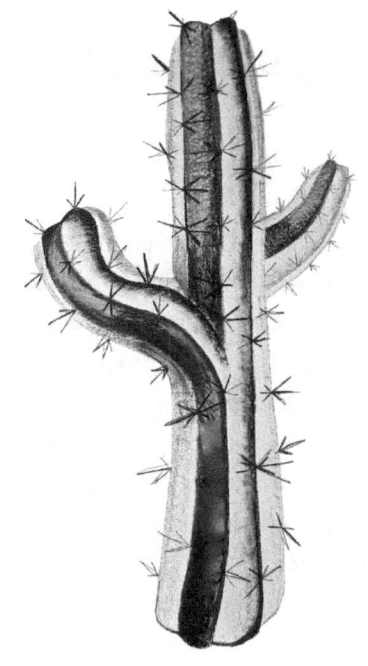

1990

Apprehension

Fran fidgeted in the rented Chevy. She stared out the window looking at the gravestones, sure that Mike's grave wouldn't be marked by a five foot marble cross with beveled edges and a scroll design on the cross bar. She knew beyond a doubt that her brother's marker would be much smaller, that is, if he had one.

She fished through her black leather bag, fingers searching for rosaries, handmade by the cloistered Carmelites. Glancing at her daughter, Carrie, who had the map of the cemetery in one hand and the steering wheel in the other, she asked, "Do you think we already passed the grave? We've been driving around Holy Martyr for about twenty minutes."

"We have plenty of time," Carrie assured her. "We don't meet Rosa until later this afternoon."

Fran forgot about the rosaries, shut her eyes, and shook her head. "Please, don't mention that name. This cross-country trip is not about that woman; it's about my brother, your uncle the priest, and paying our respects." Fran couldn't understand why Carrie insisted on meeting Rosa, the Mexican woman who claimed she was a daughter of Father Mike O'Brien. After all, her brother was a priest and would never look at a woman, let alone have her child. It was as impossible as a snowstorm in Texas. She glanced furtively at Carrie and frowned. She certainly didn't want to meet that imposter, but she felt she should go along with Carrie, seeing as how her daughter was kind enough to travel with her.

"Okay, okay," placated Carrie. "We're almost there. Look, Mom, I think it's ahead. Just beyond that circle. Can you see?" Carrie pointed, then handed the map to Fran.

Finally, they stopped at E Street, Block 23, Row 4, Lot 33. Fran surveyed the plot through the car window, approved of the green grass and the bushy old white poplar, its silvery leaves catching the sun and casting lacy shadows on the grave. Carrie turned off the ignition, sat for a moment in the uncomfortable silence, and then opened the car door. Immediately the heat enveloped her, steaming the creased pleats in her cotton skirt. She stepped out onto the cracked asphalt road, quietly closed the door and walked around to help her mother. Slipping her arm around Fran, Carrie guided her toward the grave. "I think Uncle Mike would have liked this space."

They walked over the uneven ground to the bronze plaque that marked the site. Fran read aloud: "Michael Patrick O'Brien, Capt. US Army Air Corps - World War II - July 12, 1911 to August 13, 1990."

Fran looked up, turned to Carrie. "August! And I wasn't even informed until February," grumbled Fran, wiping the sweat from her forehead with a white lace handkerchief. "I still don't understand why his housekeeper didn't call me," she muttered.

"Now, Mom, you know his housekeeper didn't have your new phone number until she opened the invitation to your 75th birthday celebration. As I recall she called you as soon as she opened it."

Fran looked at her daughter, the red curls and faint sprinkling of freckles, so unlike her, dark eyes and graying brown hair twisted into a chignon at her nape. No one would think they were mother and daughter. "If I hadn't included the RSVP with a phone number on my birthday invitation, I still wouldn't know he was dead. And perhaps I never would have gotten the second phone call, the one from that woman, the one that turned my life upside down."

Carrie looked at the marker again. "Mom, don't you think that bronze plaque should mention something about Uncle Mike's religious life?"

"Yes. You're right. In the very least, the title 'Reverend' should be included. It's quite obvious I wasn't asked," she huffed. Fran reached down, brushed away a stray leaf, and straightened the artificial red and white roses at each end of the marker. "Someone with no taste at all stuck these sad excuses for flowers in the ground. Carrie, tomorrow I want to get some real flowers, maybe blue hydrangeas, to replace these cheap plastic things." Fran's anger masked her feelings of guilt, the guilt that lay heavily on her shoulders because she wasn't with her big brother when he needed her most.

"Sure, Mom. Whatever you want. Hydrangeas would be nice."

Once again, Fran reached into her bag. This time she pulled out her beads and took Carrie's hand as they knelt to pray the five decades of the rosary. She bowed her head, closed her eyes, moved her lips in prayer, started the Sorrowful Mysteries, and thought again of her brother. She hadn't seen him as often as she would have liked in the past few years, for travel had become more difficult for a widow with arthritic knees. She thought of the last time she saw Mike offer Mass at least 15 years ago. He radiated holiness when he put on his vestments; he became Christ recreating the Last Supper. Fran dabbed her eye with her rumpled handkerchief and shoved it in her pocket. As she finished the final decade, she reached for Carrie's hand and slowly stood.

They walked to the car in silence, satisfied to find the gravesite well-manicured and content that they paid their respects, but a bit disgruntled about the inscription on the marker. Carrie settled Fran into the Chevy and slid into the driver seat. She put the car in drive, checked the rearview mirror and moved over the bumpy road, her destination their motel and a meeting with Rosa.

Fran peered out the window seeing nothing. She turned to her daughter, "I don't know why you insisted on meeting that imposter. There is absolutely no truth at all in Rosa's claim. You know that. It is unlikely, almost impossible, that my brother the priest would violate the most important vows of his office." Fran's voice rose as she became agitated. "He was the most devout, the most dedicated priest I knew. No one could steal him from the church. He would rather jump into the burning ash of Mount Saint Helens than betray his vow of chastity." She glared at Carrie, willing her to agree, but Carrie's eyes were glued to the asphalt.

"Uh-uh" she murmured. "I know it's hard for you, Mom." She reached over and patted her mother's hand.

Fran realized she could never make the trip from Philadelphia alone; she softened a bit and gave Carrie's hand a squeeze.

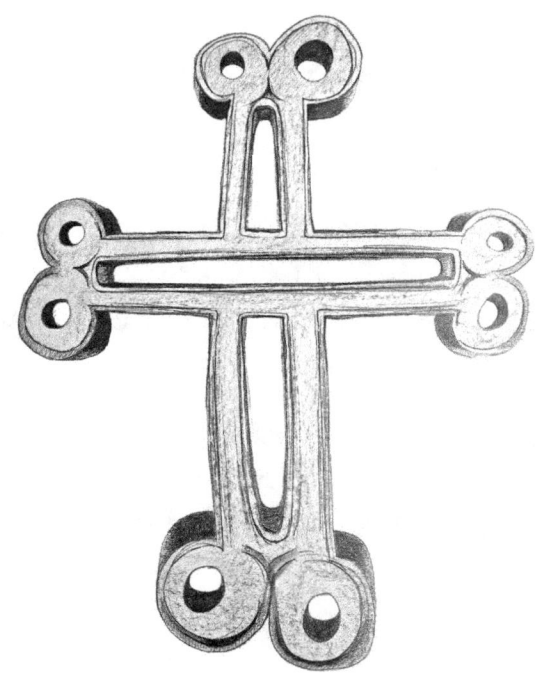

1917-1951

Becoming

From his early years, Mike was attracted to the church. It wasn't just that daily Mass afforded him alone-time with his mom, but it was also the magic of the colors, the singing, the ringing of the bells. Every day as he and Agnes approached the huge stone building, he marveled at its size. Once inside, he loved the colors in the stained-glass windows, the flickering candles on the altar, the heavenly dome, and the life-size statues of the saints. After Fran was born, he no longer went to daily Mass with Agnes, for both he and his sister stayed home with Dad, but he often played priest and never forgot his prayers.

———

"God bless Mommy and Daddy and Tom and baby Fran. In the name of the Father and of the Son and of the Holy Ghost." As Mike got up from his knees and plopped on the bed, he scrunched under his favorite green plaid blanket and looked up at his mom. She was a tall woman but very delicate, almost too slender. Her bobbed hair rippling with waves framed a pale but joyous face. She had changed into her faded blue flowered house dress that complemented her eyes, and she still wore the pearls she had worn to the Communion, the ones Bill gave her on their wedding day, the ones she never removed.

"Mike, I was so proud of you this morning." She tucked the blanket under his chin and smoothed back his curls, then sat on the edge of his bed and looked into his eyes. "When you received Our Lord in Holy Communion, you looked just like an angel. I hope you said a prayer for me."

"I did. I asked God to give you and Dad everything you wanted: a new dress for you and cigars for Dad."

"Thank you, Mike, but I just want my health, and I want you to grow up strong and happy and successful." She picked up the borrowed navy blue jacket and the short pants, folded them carefully, and smoothed them into the box to return to her next-door neighbor. "You looked so handsome in that suit, Mike, walking up to the altar to receive your First Communion. You bowed your head, lowered your eyes, and folded your hands. But as you got closer to the altar, your eyes were wide open and you just stared at the priest as you moved closer and closer."

"Mommy, something happened when the priest gave me the bread. I could really feel God inside me. That's what I want to do when I grow up. I want to be a priest. I want to make people happy by giving them our Lord in Holy Communion. I prayed for you and for Daddy. I felt so good. I prayed for everybody, and I know God will take special care of us."

"Good night and God bless you." Agnes blew him a kiss as she turned off the light and closed the bedroom door.

———

In that little white clapboard house in Camden, Mike's favorite pastime was playing priest, not cars or trucks or cowboys and Indians.

He wrapped the green-and-white plaid blanket around his shoulders. He checked his reflection in the mirror, turning slightly so he could see the back, and nodded in approval. "Priests wear long robes like this, but you'll have to wear a veil, Fran." He swirled around in his blanket expecting to mesmerize Fran, still in her faded blue hand-me-down Dr. Dentons.

She took her thumb out of her mouth long enough to ask, "What's a veil?" Fran had lost much of her baby fat by now, but not her love for her big brother.

"You know. It covers your hair, and it's white, and it's pretty. It's what girls wear when they make their First Communion."

"Oh." Fran had no idea what he was talking about, but because she adored playing with him, she went along with anything he said.

"Now, what can we use?" He searched his bedroom: *Peter Pan* still open at the foot of his bed, pajamas in a pile on the chair, underwear rumpled on the floor. He looked no farther. "This is perfect for you, Fran." He stooped down and grabbed a smudged undershirt.

"Is that a veil? Yuck, don't like it," complained Fran, hands on hips. "No, no, no." Her pigtails flew as she shook her head, "No, it smells." She tossed the undershirt on the floor and headed for the door.

"Please, Fran," he coaxed. "Just pretend. It's not really a veil, but it will work. I'll even give you my favorite green glass marble."

"You will? Promise? Maybe Mommy has a veil."

"She's still at church. You can ask her when she gets home, but for now just pretend. Okay?"

Fran just couldn't resist his pleas. "Okay." Like a cocker spaniel puppy wanting to please her master, she walked back and let him drape the smelly undershirt over her hair.

"Perfect," he clapped, "just perfect." He could tell by her body language that she thought it was pretty far from perfect.

"Now, I'm going to give you Communion. Are you ready, Fran?"

"What's that?

"Well, it's…Fran you're too little. Just do what I say, okay?"

"Okay," said Fran hesitantly.

"Now kneel down."

"Where?"

"Right here. I'll move the marbles." He kicked the marbles aside, even his favorite green glass one, then gently put his hands on her shoulders as she knelt on the floor. "Great, now put your hands together. Good, only point them up, up to heaven, Fran."

"Doing right?" She looked at his hands and put her chubby little fingers together. "Perfect." She smiled and looked up at him, her brown eyes sparkling. "See, not too little."

"Good, now close your eyes and stick out your tongue."

"Don't want to."

"Don't worry. I'm just going to say some prayers to change this cookie into the baby Jesus, and then put it on your tongue."

"Yuck, don't want baby Jesus. Want green marble."

Roots

Although the O'Briens were hard-working and rich in the love of God and family, Agnes and Bill dreamed of one day returning to Newfoundland, their roots. For years they put aside as much money as they could each week until finally they had the fare for third class. To them, this trip was better than finding the Holy Grail. Seventeen years had passed since they left their home in St. John's, Newfoundland, and they still missed their family left behind, but more importantly they wanted to introduce the children to their uncles, aunts and cousins, and walk the land of their ancestors. After much discussion, they hired a trustworthy gentleman to run their small grocery store in Camden and booked passage on the *Pomeranian* for the whole family.

———

The gulls squawked as they swarmed over the stern of the *Pomeranian* on the return trip. The trans-Atlantic steamer had the signature red funnel, black top, and white band. All passengers had boarded and she was ready to leave port heading to Philadelphia. All five of the O'Briens, Agnes, Bill, and the children: Tom, the oldest, Mike, and Fran, now four, stood on the deck leaning against the rail to search for their Canadian relatives in the mass of waving people on the dock. "I see them! I see them!" yelled Mike.

"Where?" questioned Tom.

"They're right where we left them, in front of the fish market. You can see Aunt Nell's red hat." He began to wave frantically.

"Can't see." Fran stood on tippy toes and grabbed the railing trying to pull herself up.

"Here you go." Tom hoisted her over his shoulders. "Is this better?'

"I see! I see! I see her red hat." Fran's pigtails swirled in the wind. She reached up to anchor them.

The engine rumbled, a billowing cloud of smoke exited from the red funnel, the horn exploded in booms and the steamship began to move.

While in St. John's, they stayed with Frank, Bill's brother. Frank had found employment in the fishing industry and decided to stay in Newfoundland. Bill, on the other hand, was forced out of the country by the cooper's union when they discovered he had flouted their rules and taught a non-union member the skill of barrel making. Bill always lived by his own rules and saw absolutely no harm in teaching his good friend a trade. The union, however, didn't agree with him.

The winters in Newfoundland were cruel: ice-like stinging snow, bitter wind, and stormy seas buffeting the rocky coastline. But the summers were idyllic. The two families formed new ties as they swam, fished and hiked through the balmy summer weeks.

After dinner, they would sit around the table and tell stories far into the night. Mike barely said a word but listened as his relatives laughed and cried remembering their past. One story he would never forget was one of Aunt Nell's. She told about an O'Brien general in the English Army who retired to Newfoundland when given a grant of land, Harbor Grace, by the king back in the 17th century. Aunt Nell also said that generations back, "Presbyterian priest hunters" would travel miles to catch a Roman Catholic priest, try him in a hastily convened kangaroo court and then sentence him to death. Rumor had it that this particular General O'Brien, a staunch Presbyterian, joined quite a few of those hunts. Much later in the 1700s, one of the O'Brien Protestants fell in love with a Catholic woman. One night as she was sitting in front of the fire praying on her wooden rosary beads, her husband came in. He was so furious that he grabbed the beads and threw them into the blazing fire. The next morning, when the husband was raking the cold ashes, he found the beads unharmed. The O'Briens have been Catholic ever since. The story made a big impression on Mike who already made his First Communion and anticipated making Confirmation in the near future. His thoughts lingered on this story as the ship inched away from the dock.

Despite the heavy wind, the O'Briens waved to Aunt Nell and Uncle Frank until they became specks in the distance. As the ship steamed further away from the banks of Newfoundland, Agnes grabbed Fran's hand and they all made their way down to third class to stow their luggage. "Fran, you will bunk with Dad and I; and you, Mike, will sleep with Tom." Fran looked up at Agnes and pouted while Mike jumped with joy and pounded Tom on his shoulder. "Yippee!" he yelled.

Tom unlocked the metal door to the small berth, hardly large enough for the bunk bed. The boys quickly shoved their duffle bags under the bunk and joined the rest of the family to explore. Mike held Fran's hand as they ran along the narrow cream-colored corridors and skipped down the central staircase carpeted with a rose Oriental rug. "Now, now, children, slow down. Don't run into the other passengers." Agnes held the banister as she tried to keep the children in her sight. "Tom, please run ahead with the children. I don't want to lose them."

They passed the main dining room and stopped at the community room. Bill and Agnes stood at the doorway, watched the crowd for a bit and decided to enter. Within a matter of minutes they joined a bridge game in progress. Fran cuddled up on a nearby couch and fell asleep. Mike sat nearby playing marbles and watched Tom wander all the way across the room to a group of teens singing around a piano.

Cigarette smoke swirled around the mid-deck hall. Mike rubbed his eyes, tired of playing by himself; he pulled at his mother's sleeve. He could see that look of concentration on her face as she stared at the cards and drummed her fingers on the card table. He tried again to get her attention. Agnes didn't take her eyes from her hand as she mumbled, "Later, dear, later." She glanced at Bill and led the ten of hearts. Mike tried interrupting his mother again. "Mom, I want to go over there with Tom to listen to the singing."

"Where?" Mike pointed to the group of twenty-somethings clustered around a piano singing 'By the light of the silvery moon....'"

Agnes scanned the room looking for Tom. After spotting him next to a young brunette, she said, "All right, but stay with him. Don't leave his side now, dear." She watched Mike scamper over to the group, glanced at Fran napping on the sofa, then returned to the bridge game. Smiling when Bill returned her hearts, she triumphantly covered his nine with her ace and captured the opponent's king and jack.

Mike lurched through the crowd toward Tom until he finally tugged on his cable-knit sweater. "Mom says I can stay with you."

"Are you sure?" he replied, a bit crestfallen.

Mike didn't like the way his brother looked at the girl in the green sweater with the long brown hair curling down her back. He watched Tom inch next to her, squeezing in until his brown knickers almost touched her gray skirt.

"One more time," yelled the piano player, and the room swelled with the refrain, 'By the light, of the ....'"

In an instant, Mike forgot all about Tom and the girl with the green sweater. He noticed only the fingers of the piano player moving up and down the white and black keys of the scarred upright. He tried to mimic the movement of the fingers, but they were flying over the keys so fast, he couldn't keep track. Finally he resigned himself to keeping the beat tapping with his fingers on Tom's sweater. Then his foot started. Mike was fascinated with the music making; he had never been so close to a piano. Soon his head was swaying back and forth with the rhythm of the notes, his eyes glued to the dancing fingers. He wiggled his way closer to touch the magic keys, but Tom yanked him back.

"Tom, I just want to touch the keys," he whined.

The brunette watched the interplay. "Is he your brother?" she asked, eyes flirting. "He seems totally immersed in the music."

"Yes, to your first question, and yes, I think you're right!" He turned to Mike whispering, "If you don't behave, I'll send you back to Mom." Mike shrugged himself free and scowled at Tom.

"When you finish babysitting, come on up on deck. There's a full moon tonight. See you later." The brunette waved as she walked toward the narrow staircase.

"I don't like her. I'm not a baby." Mike stared as she turned and smiled at his big brother.

Tom and Mike lingered at the piano until the grand finale, "God Bless America." Mike looked up at him. "Someday," he said, "I'm going to play the piano like that." Then he scooted back to Agnes, who was still engrossed in the bridge game.

"Hi, Sweetie. Did you have fun with Tom?"

"Not exactly. But I did have fun watching the piano player. Tom barely said 'hi.' In fact, as soon as I left, I bet he chased that girl with the green sweater up to the main deck to see the moon. When I grow up I'm never going to look at girls like Tom does."

"What do you mean, dear?" This time she turned away from the cards.

"You know, all dreamy eyed, and smiley faced." He crinkled his nose in disgust.

"Well, we'll see what happens ten years from now when you're 19."

That summer was one each of the family would remember far into the future, each for a totally different reason.

Maturing

True to his word, Mike began piano lessons in school that fall the family returned from Newfoundland. He didn't care that there was no piano in that white clapboard house in Camden. Each day at lunchtime or after school, he hurried to the Assembly Room to practice, willing his fingers to dance on the keys. Hard work paid off, for when he reached high school, he often played "The Star Spangled Banner" before assemblies.

Despite the difference in ages, Mike and Tom remained close through the years. Tom studied diligently and had been accepted as a scholarship student at Temple University Law School. Because he still lived at home and helped out at the grocery store on the weekends, his needs were few and he had the time to be a friend to Mike. The brothers had an ongoing competition at the chessboard.

"Tom, the director of the musical *H.M.S. Pinafore* asked me to accompany the cast. How swell is that, huh? "Mike moved his bishop to attack Tom's king, then ran his fingers through his chestnut curls.

"Wow, do you mean the big spring production that involves the entire school?"

"Yep! That's exactly the one I mean. What do you think of that?"

"I'd say pretty swell. I'd say I'm pretty proud of my little brother." Tom reached over to shake hands.

Mike almost toppled the board as he jumped up, hand outstretched. "I have the score already, and we start rehearsing in two weeks."

"Are you trying to interrupt my concentration, capture my king, and checkmate me, you rascal?"

"No, I'm just really excited about the operetta. I only hope I can learn the score in time. Gilbert and Sullivan is not so easy, especially when we don't have a piano at home I can practice on." He leaned on his elbows to watch the board more closely, hoping he had stumped Tom.

"I hear you, brother. But if anyone can do it, you can." Tom drummed his fingers on the board.

"Tom, your time is just about up. You need to make a move."

Tom checked his watch. "I want to catch *Amos 'n' Andy* on the radio tonight. Let's see if we can end this match soon." He peered at Mike, grinned, then tumbled the white bishop with his knight.

"How did you do that? That's not fair! I didn't see that move."

"Concentration, Mike, concentration. Now what were you saying about Gilbert and Sullivan?"

"It's just that I have to learn the score in two weeks, and I only know one number, 'Drink, Drink, Drink.' But learning the entire operetta in 14 days and doing all my homework besides—that's pretty hard, especially without a piano."

"I've been amazed with your progress, Mike. Mom said your piano teacher even called last week to tell her you were her best pupil. When I start practicing law, I'll buy you a new piano, but for now maybe we should try to find a used piano somewhere. When I go to the grocery store tomorrow, I'll tack a note on the bulletin board."

Mike jumped up, his eyes brighter than his cat's eye marble. "I've been praying for a piano for a long, long time."

"Be careful of what you pray for. And, remember, I'm not promising anything, Mike, but I'll ask around."

"Holy cow! You're just the swellest big brother that ever lived."

"Checkmate." Tom chuckled as he captured the white king with his rook. "Now don't look so sad. You beat me the last time, remember?" He reached across to shake hands.

———

Mike didn't get a piano in time for the school play, but he was a persevering teen and used a neighbor's piano when he was unable to practice at school. He played his heart out and was thrilled when the conductor recognized him before a sold-out house. That was probably the moment he decided to make music his life, forgetting, for the moment, that he wanted to be a priest.

College

When Tom graduated from Temple Law School, he started to work at a prestigious firm in Philadelphia on Broad and Walnut streets. Soon he established a reputation as an astute estate attorney as well as an eligible bachelor. Finding a date was never a problem. The girls swooned over his blond buzz cut and powder-blue eyes, but he was dedicated to his family and gave most of his salary to his parents. Of course, he kept his promise to Mike and surprised him one Christmas with an upright Cunningham.

In his senior year, Mike was accepted at Villanova University with a double major in Music and Education. With Tom's help financially, Agnes and Bill were able to afford the tuition. Although he and Agnes seldom made the trip from Camden to visit, Bill sent him a letter every week with a one-dollar bill enclosed. Tom, on the other hand, visited on a regular basis, but hadn't been to campus for several weeks because he was working on a complicated tobacco case. Finally, his schedule cleared, and he headed to Villanova.

———

"Hey, Mike! Wait up? You going to the Gamma Pi party tonight?" asked Joe, his roommate, as he fell in step with him.

Mike shifted his books, shivered, and pulled his hat down over his ears. "Haven't decided yet, Joe. Are you going?" It was the first cold day of winter, and Mike wasn't quite used to it yet.

"Yeah! Wouldn't miss it. Supposed to be lots of girls from Rosemont, and of course, the keg will be perking. Why don't you come along?" Joe's saucy grin and outgoing ways always attracted the girls. They would hover around him, giggling at his ridiculous jokes and admiring his athletic build. Mike, on the other hand, could take or leave the girls, except for Julie, who was more of a friend than anything else.

"I'll give it some thought. The football game is a definite, though. My brother went to Temple, and he's been ribbing me about the game all week. In fact, we have a big bet on—Tom will take me to dinner tonight if we win, and I can already taste the filet mignon."

"Hope his wallet is full. By the way," Joe paused, "is Fran coming with him?"

"Not this time. She's studying for a big test in geometry." Mike thought he saw a gleam in Joe's eye. He remembered the last time Fran visited campus, Joe teased her unmercifully and Fran seemed to enjoy the attention.

"Just wondering. Well, I'm heading down to the gym, going to shoot some hoops."

"Lucky you. I'm headed for class. As much as I hate these Saturday morning classes, I'm glad I got Bolton, and I still have time to practice the piano and get to the football game."

"Well, hope to see you later tonight. So long." Joe veered off to the right as Mike continued past Cromwell Hall and through the Student Atrium to St. Augustine Center for Philosophy 301.

Mike shifted his thoughts to the tenets of Thomas Aquinas, certain Professor Bolton would give them a pop quiz. He reflected on Thursday's discussion, dominated by the quote: "Three things are necessary for the salvation of man: to know what he ought to believe; to know what he ought to desire; and to know what he ought to do." It had plagued him ever since. He wondered how people knew what they wanted to do. Ever since Joe was a freshman in high school he knew he was going to be a doctor. Mike still didn't know exactly what he wanted to do after he graduated. He promised himself to talk to Tom about it after the game this afternoon. He checked his watch, picked up his pace, and pulled his collar up, his hat down.

As expected, Bolton started with a pop quiz, which Mike aced. The discussion focused on more words of Aquinas. "Good can exist without evil whereas evil cannot exist without good." Philosophically it intrigued him as a complicated, debatable idea, but it just didn't hit him personally the way Thursday's discussion did.

After wolfing down a quick hamburger at the café, Mike bundled up again and headed to the Arts Center. Practicing the piano was no longer a problem, for all music majors had keys to the practice studios and selected their own time slots. He unlocked a practice room, unwound his scarf—the blue and white one his mother knitted for him last Christmas—removed his matching woolen cap and leather jacket, and then sat at the upright. He rubbed his hands, blew on his fingers. Finally, he warmed up with the minor scales. Before long, he was lost in the adagio movement of the *Pathétique Sonata,* eyes closed, humming softly as his fingers teased passion from the keys. When he reached the end of the movement, he returned to the beginning, put brackets around the measures he had trouble with, and played each one at least 10 times. Satisfied, he tried them from memory, first slowly and then faster and faster, changing the tempo on the metronome each time. *Good,* he thought, closed the book, placed it on the shelf, wrapped himself up against the cold, locked the studio, and dashed down the stairs heading to the stadium—all the while visualizing the steak he knew Tom would be paying for later on.

He waited at the gate, hunched over to preserve his body heat, bracing himself against the wind, stamping his feet to keep them from getting numb. He vowed that he would never live on the East Coast in the future if he could help it. Suddenly, he felt a tap on the shoulder. He turned. "Tom!" he smiled. "Hi!" He gave his older brother a big bear hug. "Hey, it's been a while."

Tom grinned, "Hope you've been behaving yourself."

"Sometimes you sound more like my dad than my brother."

"Well, I do like to look after you. Want to keep you from the mistakes I made."

"I never saw you make a mistake, Tom. You're my role model."

"Thanks for the compliment. By the way, I'm sorry you had to wait in the cold so long. I had to park all the way at the end of the lot, and then I almost lost my life crossing Lancaster Avenue; they really have to put in a traffic light someday soon. Well, let's go into the stadium. It's going to be tough to find good seats; I don't want to be way up in the nosebleed section."

"Neither do I. Let's huddle in the middle of the stadium where we're protected from the cold wind."

"Good idea, Mike. You lead." He patted him on the back as they walked through the turnstile. The stadium erupted in a loud roar. "Must be Temple scoring another touchdown."

"I doubt it. Villanova is unbeatable this year."

"Holy cow! You're right. Look at that scoreboard: 18 to 3."

Mike spotted Joe halfway up in the bleachers on the 50 yard line and waved. "Hey, Mike," Joe yelled, "Come on up. Plenty of room." The brothers climbed the bleachers, jostling people as they moved to the center of the row and squeezed in next to Joe.

The temperature dipped lower and lower as Villanova scored touchdown after touchdown. By the end of the third quarter, the score was 28-9 in favor of Villanova. "What do you say, Tom. Still think Temple will pull it out? Ready to admit defeat? I'm so hungry, my stomach is growling, and besides, my toes are icicles. I'm not sure I can still walk."

"Okay. I really thought Temple would burn Villanova. Seems like I always lose anymore." The brothers bid Joe goodbye and made their way out of the stadium to the parking lot.

"Did you drive up in your new Plymouth sedan?"

"Sure did. I opted for the extra-cost hydraulic shock. Wait till you feel how smooth it is. It's right over there next to the black sedan. I made it all the way from Camden in an hour and a half."

"Holy smokes, Tom, that car was on the cover of *Cruisin Magazine* just love all that chrome. The lawyer business must be pretty good in Philadelphia."

"Let's just say it's not too bad. Where to, Mike? You call the shots."

"I heard that Phillips has a pretty good steak. It's in Ithan, just down the road a couple of miles. Joe ate there with his parents a couple of weeks ago. He gave it a thumbs up."

The flowered wallpaper, candle-lit tables, and roaring hearth created a warm, comfy atmosphere. Within minutes, the men felt toasty and eagerly perused the menu. When the waitress approached, Mike smiled, "I've been dreaming all day of the filet mignon smothered in béarnaise sauce. I'll take it medium rare with the French fries and string beans. What about you, Tom?"

"I'll go with the flounder, fried, and also the French fries and string beans. Oh, and I'll have a Manhattan please, on the sweet side; and for Mike, I believe, a Glenlivit up, rocks on the side."

Mike handed his menu to the waitress and leaned back in his chair. "How are Mom and Pop? I still miss home." He rested his arms on the table and leaned toward Tom.

"They're doing pretty well. I'm really happy that I'm making a decent salary and can contribute to grocery bills and so forth. Mom still makes the best rice pudding around, and Pop is busy listening to his radio programs. Almost every night he builds a fire and turns the dial to *Jack Benny,* or *Fred Allen,* or *Fibber Magee and Molly.* Not too much has changed."

"How's Fran doing?"

"She's become quite the athlete these days. She goes to the Y a couple of times a week to swim, but she's studying hard, too. She has a good head on her shoulders, wants to go to Temple next year, just to keep it in the family. By the way, she says 'hi' to your roommate. I think she's keen on him. But, more importantly, Mike, how are things with you? I mean really. I want to hear it all—the good, the bad, and the ugly."

Mike ran his fingers through his curls, pursed his lips, sighed, and said, "Well I do need some advice. Maybe you can help me sort through some options. I graduate next year, and I don't know exactly what I want to do. I feel time closing in on me." His brow furrowed.

"Have you thought about the law? It's quite satisfying intellectually and socially. I feel like I'm making a difference. Besides, I've made some very good contacts in Philly, and I know I could introduce you around." Tom slowly sipped his Manhattan and nodded approval.

"I have thought about it, Tom, but I don't think I'm cut out for that. I just wouldn't be happy with all that research. Sitting in a library day in and day out— all that reading and all that writing. It just doesn't interest me."

Tom considered what his brother said. He rubbed his forehead. "Well, now, what courses do you like? What gives you pleasure?"

"Probably not anything that would suggest a career. I like my music, my God, and my family. Like this afternoon when I was practicing the *Pathetique,* I got lost in the music exactly the way I get lost when I pray. I mean, when I stop by St. Thomas Chapel in the early morning or after classes when the church is empty, I go up to the altar rail and kneel down. When I am all alone with my God, and I start to pray—all of a sudden a half-hour has passed, and I don't know where I've been." The waitress interrupted with dinner. "Holy cow, this smells great, Tom. I've been visualizing this all afternoon while watching that blowout."

"Hey now, careful with that language. Just remember who's paying for dinner. But to get back to our conversation—I just want you to know that whatever you decide to do, I'm there for you. I'm making a decent salary, and if I can help in any way, I'd be most happy to. I wonder though, if you ever thought of the priesthood. You did mention that you find solace in prayer. That would sure make Mom and Pop happy."

Fork poised in mid-air Mike replied, "You know I have often thought of the times when I was young and I would play priest with Fran. And I know Mom especially would be thrilled, but I don't know if I could take a vow of celibacy. I mean, I'm not crazy over girls, and I'm certainly not dating anyone special right now except maybe Julie, but I'm not sure I would want to abstain from women for the rest of my life." Mike valued Tom's opinion and wanted his approval probably more than he needed his parent's approval. He always looked up to his big brother and admired his ambition and drive.

"Mike, I can't answer that question for you. Actually, between studying so intensely for school, then the law boards, and now keeping up with my case load, I don't have much time left for women. I'm afraid I can't be of much help in the female department. But I do know that choosing between Julie and God needs a lot of deep thought. That's something you have to decide for yourself. Don't worry about it. It will come in time; don't force it. Keep your options open. But, it wouldn't hurt to talk to Father Reilly the next time you come home."

"Thanks, Tom, I always feel better after I talk to you. But now, for the important things: What's for dessert?" He motioned for the waitress.

"By the way, how is Julie? I haven't seen her lately."

"She's good, she...."

As the waitress cleared the table, she asked, "Just what can I get you gentlemen for dessert?"

"I'm tempted to say 'rice pudding,' but I know nothing can compare with Mom's. I think instead I'd like some cherry pie with a big scoop of vanilla ice cream. How about you, Tom?"

"Sounds tempting, but I think I'll just have a cup of coffee." He turned to the waitress. "Bring the check with the dessert, please."

Choice

After that conversation with Tom, Mike spent most of his free time thinking of his future. He had a serious conversation with Father Reilly and also consulted several of the Augustinians at Villanova. At the same time, he continued to date Julie, the vivacious brown-eyed blonde he met dancing the Big Apple at Rosemont College in sophomore year. Jitterbugging to Bill Haley and the Comets was the glue that held them together. But, in January of his senior year, Mike applied to St. Bonaventure Seminary and just before graduation learned that he had been accepted. He considered Julie a friend, a very good friend, but still wasn't sure how she would react to his plans. Therefore he avoided telling her until the last few weeks of the summer. That summer in Cape May would be remembered for Mike's life-changing decision.

———

"Hey, Fran!" Mike waved as he jogged across the beach, squinting into the noonday sun. He loved the gritty feel of the sand on his toes, the smell of the salt air, the gentle breeze ruffling his hair, and the heat of the sun on his back.

"Mike. Is it really you?" Fran shaded her eyes from the sun glare. "I didn't think you were coming down until tomorrow."

"The big cheese, otherwise known as Tom, gave me the week off. He just finished a difficult case and decided we earned some vacation time."

"Now, now, Mike! Be nice. Remember he's the only reason we're here. It's amazing when you think of it—that he would rent that little cottage just so we could summer here."

"Believe me, I'm grateful! Grateful for the cottage and grateful for the paycheck he gives me every week." Mike hopped up on the stand and plopped down next to Fran. "But, more importantly, how's the lifeguard business?"

She looked at him and rolled her eyes behind her sunglasses. "No action. I think they gave me this isolated beach just because I'm a girl. Matt, a real flat tire who guards three beaches down, had five rescues so far this month and I had none."

"You've got to admit, little sis, it's a bit unusual to have a female lifeguard. I doubt you would have gotten the job without Tom's intervention."

"But I deserve the job; after all, I was the strongest swimmer in the trials at the beginning of the summer."

"Okay, okay, simmer down. The important thing is no one has drowned yet. By the way, my roommate is driving down in his old jalopy tomorrow."

"Joe? Peachy keen! He's fun to have around."

"Do I detect a sparkle in those eyes? I do think you might be carrying a torch for him. In fact, I would say you were blushing—but then again, it could just be sunburn."

"Mike, don't tease! I'm just trying to be friendly. After all, he doesn't know anyone in Cape May Point."

"He did ask me how you were measuring up against all the guy guards."

Fran blew her whistle, motioned a swimmer in, stood up, shaded her eyes, and watched until he got his footing. Then she relaxed a bit, adjusted the towel that almost fell from the wooden bench when she jumped up. She pulled her hair back, sat down, and resumed the conversation. "Mike, did he really ask about me? I mean, do you think he was just being nice, or do you think he really could be interested in me?"

"I wouldn't kid you, Fran. I think he might be stuck on you."

"Say, a bunch of us are putting on our glad rags and going to the movies in Cape May tomorrow night. Do you think he would want to go? It's a new film, *Laugh, Clown, Laugh* starring Lon Chaney."

"Probably, but how about me? Don't I get an invite? After all, Joe is my roommate."

"Sure, sure. I'm taking you for granted. What about Julie? Think she would want to go, too? She was here on the beach earlier, but she went home to make a sandwich for her grandmother. Have you told her about your plans yet?"

"No, I'm not looking forward to that. You haven't said anything, have you?"

"My lips are sealed. I would never spill the beans, especially about something so serious. But I do think you have to tell her soon. It's really not fair to her. I think she really likes you. In fact, I think it's downright mean to lead her on."

Mike turned away frowning. Sometimes Fran could really be a pain, he thought. He leaned back on the bench, getting as comfortable as possible on the wooden seat. Being with Julie was lots of fun and he knew the fun would end once he told her. He just wished he could be a priest and continue his relationship with her. He knew Fran was right. He had to tell her. "Okay, Fran! I'll do it soon. I promise. But honestly we're just good friends."

———

After Mass on Sunday, they walked home from St. Bernadette, the tiny stucco chapel nestled in the pine trees by the circle marking the center of town. The sun warmed more than the hearts of Mike and his mom and pop. Agnes opened her pastel flowered umbrella to protect her pale skin from the sun. Mike, walking slightly ahead, turned to talk. "Just think, Mom! Someday, I might be preaching the sermon at St. Bernadette. Then, I will stand outside the chapel and shake everyone's hands and thank them for worshipping with me. Would you like that?"

"You know I would love that, Mike. Nothing would please me more. But I hope you haven't made your decision just to please me." "No, no, Mom. I agonized over the decision. I've been thinking about it for a couple of years. I had several conversations with Father George from Villanova who helped me prioritize my goals. And of course Father Reilly back home was a big help; he steered me toward St. Bonaventure and agreed to sponsor me there. Everything seemed to fall into place." Mike glanced at his dad, but he couldn't read his face. He was a man of few words, but his approval was important to him. "Pop, what do you think?" "Mike, if this is what you want, then it's what I want as well. What about the cost? How will we manage that?" Bill reached for his white handkerchief and wiped the sweat from his brow.

"Pop, I've already talked to Tom. He promised to help out. I've also applied for assistance."

Agnes put her hand on Mike's arm. "What about Julie? She'll be devastated. Have you told her yet?"

"That is going to be tough." Mike rubbed his forehead. "I'm working up to doing that tonight. I'm not looking forward to it. If only there was a place in the church for her. I often wonder why Catholic priests can't marry the way Episcopalians do."

———

That night, Mike hoisted himself onto the sunken concrete ship, shook his head vigorously, rubbed the salty seawater out of his eyes, and breathed deeply. The ship, a large concrete vessel used in WWI had been partially sunk off Sunset Beach at the tip of the point as a first step toward building a dock. However, the funding didn't come through so construction halted, and now the kids mainly used the ship as a diving board during the day and crowds gathered at dusk to watch the sunset. Swimming the mile from the beach to the ship always invigorated Mike. He loved the cool velvety touch of the ocean as it coated his skin. He took a minute or two to balance himself on the slanted deck; then peered into the fading eight o'clock light searching for Julie. He watched her swim the last few yards. "Just a few more strokes," he shouted encouragingly. Swimming out to the ship was not a spur of the moment idea. He considered several other places first. He thought about walking along the beach or taking her to the ice cream parlor, but he knew he needed a place where she wouldn't run away from him before he could explain. He wanted someplace special where they would be alone, just the two of them. For what he had to tell her tonight wasn't going to make her happy.

As she glided effortlessly as a mermaid to the ship, he reached down to pull her aboard. "Wow," she exclaimed as she leaned against him to steady herself and felt his arms about her waist. Before she could snap off her bathing cap, his lips brushed hers, gentle as butterfly wings. "Julie, he whispered, "Let's sit down. I have something important to tell you tonight. I hope you can understand." They sat on the edge of the cement and dangled their feet over the side.

He watched her take off her bathing cap and fluff her hair, the blonde curls he liked to run his fingers through. When she looked at him again, her eyes were empty. She wondered what could be so important, why he looked so sad. "What's wrong, Mike? You seem so serious."

He took her hand, laced his fingers in hers. "Julie, this doesn't have anything to do with you. I mean, I really like you. I mean really. I like to talk with you. I like to dance with you. I like to kiss you. I like to swim with you. I like to play the piano with you. I like to sit here on the sunken ship with you. I really just like to be with you."

"But why, then, are your eyes so sad?" She squeezed his hand.

"I've made a decision. A very difficult decision. And I don't know how to tell you." He stared at the ripples in the Delaware Bay, wishing he didn't have to tell her, wishing they could just continue forever like the endless ripples, wishing priests could marry. But he knew he had to tell her.

———

Breathing heavily as he neared the end of his run, Mike flopped on the grass. The early morning dew soaked the back of his shorts and T-shirt, and the air was chilling fast. Shivering, he gazed at the clouds. They skimmed by, growing darker and darker with every second. He knew he should get home and help Mom with the windows and the shutters before the nor'easter started. The run helped clear his head. "I know I made the right decision," he muttered. "Why don't I feel good about it?" He sat up, rubbed his arms, smoothed his hair, untied and retied his black canvas high-tops. Finally he unwound his arms and legs and stood. At a much gentler pace, he headed to the rented cottage, hoping Fran was awake—she had a knack of putting "stuff" in perspective.

"Fran," he called as he slammed the screen door.

She turned at the sound. When she saw Mike, she continued to ladle oatmeal over the bananas in her bowl. "Holy cow! What happened to you? You look like a wraith. And you're sopping wet. It's not raining yet, is it?"

"Whoa, back up. To answer your questions in order: I just finished a five-mile run. After which, I passed out on the wet grass. And no, it's not raining yet. But I don't think you'll have to work on the beach today."

"But you didn't really answer my question. I want to know exactly what's troubling you. You're pale and you have big black circles under your eyes. You look as if you didn't sleep at all last night."

"You're right. I didn't get much sleep." He mopped his face with a dishtowel.

"Why not? You weren't out late. By the way, didn't you have a date with Julie last night?"

"Yep, that's the problem." He was ready to confide in his sister. They never could keep anything hidden from each other.

"What happened? I know she thinks you're the cat's meow."

"Well, I told her I was going to be a priest."

"Oh, I bet she was upset." Fran rolled her eyes.

"Pretty much, yes. But my problem is that I feel lousy. I thought I would feel like a big weight had been lifted off my back. But I feel like I'm weighed down by half a ton. I'm not happy."

"Not happy because you're going into the priesthood?"

"No, I'm pretty sure about that."

"What then?" She waited patiently while he labored to find the words to describe what he meant.

"No, I think I'm not happy because I upset her so much."

"Well," Fran bit her bottom lip, "How do you think God feels about the whole situation?"

"I hope he's happy with me. But you're right, Fran. I guess that is the only thing that matters. I knew you would help me put everything into perspective. Thanks."

Change

The only sound was the ping of forks as the seminarians speared the meatloaf, the clink of glasses touching the bare wooden trestle, an occasional cough or clearing of the throat, or the drone of the lector's voice as he read from the Book of Psalms. Even though he averted his eyes, Mike visualized his tablemates, willing them to make eye contact. He missed the long debates and the philosophical conversations he had with his Villanova classmates, the laughter,and the good-natured fun.

Although he savored the quiet in the library as he explored the thoughts of St. Augustine through his *Confessions* and the early mystics through their treatises, and the times in the chapel when he felt at one with God, the lack of communication with his fellow seminarians stifled him. It pervaded not only the library and the dining hall, but also prevailed in the lecture hall, the corridors, and the bedroom. He felt wrapped in a cloak of invisibility with only his mind, his books, and his listening for the voice of God. He wanted to escape, to run all the way back to Villanova, to Camden. Instead, he left the dining hall, grabbed a sweater from his cell, and walked down the hall, through the double doors of the red brick building, Devereux Hall. As he followed the path toward the woods, he fingered the rosary in his pocket, enjoying the comfort it provided. He eyed the mountains in the distance; the birds and the crickets sang softly. Perching on the stone wall isolating the seminary from the college, Mike closed his eyes and leaned back to feel the warmth of the spring sun.

Almost a year had passed since he drove through the gates of St. Bonaventure. Now he needed to hear more than the numbing quiet. He listened for the voice of God, but his ears detected only the distant voices of co-eds on the far side of the wall. He could just about detect their giggling and imagined them discussing the hot jocks, arguing about grades, and debating the merits of Byron over Wordsworth. Even though they were only on the other side of the wall, he felt separated from them and their world—stifled by silence in his. He wanted to join their conversation, to follow them down the path, to touch their hair, hold their hands. He thought again of Julie, running with her on the beach, body surfing in the cool waters of the Atlantic, playing duets on the piano, jitterbugging with gusto to *Pennsylvania 65000*. He had that dream of her again last night: he was walking on the boardwalk when he saw her; he ran toward her as fast as he could, called her name, and just as he approached her, she disappeared. He wondered if he made a mistake eight months ago when he decided to leave the secular world, to channel his zest for life into prayer and sacrifice in service to God and his community. He thought he had settled his doubts back then.

Often he walked through the woods—his beads in his hand, his mind on his God—surrounded by pines and poplars, brushing away stray branches, his footsteps crunching dead twigs below. Usually a 45-minute meditation in nature calmed his restless spirit. He spent some of his happiest times in these woods and the chapel when it was deserted, for it was then he could hear God speaking directly to him. He often wondered if the other seminarians felt the same temptations and what they did to relieve them. He wished he could break through the wall of silence and discuss it with them. He hoped for answers during his conference with his spiritual advisor later that day.

The bell tolled, calling him to the chapel for Vespers. All throughout Vespers, Mike's mind wandered. He wanted to make sure he phrased his doubts so Father Frank would understand him and offer appropriate solutions. After Vespers, Mike walked to the administrative wing and knocked on Father Frank's door.

"Ah, Michael, my boy, you're a faster walker than I," said Father Frank coming up behind him. "Come inside, please." He unlocked the door and indicated one of the simple wooden armchairs while he took the other. Mike was surprised to see a cell much like his own: a tiny room with one window, a plain wooden bed covered with a brown woolen blanket, a desk under the window, and a simple crucifix hung above the bed. A bookcase crammed with books on the opposite beige wall was the only difference between his room and his superior's. Of course, Father Frank's desk was different as well, with piles of papers scattered pell-mell across the dusty maple veneer.

Father Frank removed his glasses and, taking the large linen handkerchief from his robe, wiped off the smudges, then settled them on his nose. "Now, my son, what's been bothering you? You seemed quite preoccupied when you walked into chapel for Vespers."

Although Mike hadn't planned to, he blurted out his worries. "Well first of all, all of this quiet just doesn't bring me closer to God. I hear all of the clicks and the shuffles and the sniffles and the sighs and the scraping chairs instead of the voice of God. And second, even though I try not to, I keep thinking of Julie, a girl I used to go out with every once in awhile."

"Hmm, I see." Father Frank adjusted his rimless glasses, picked some imaginary lint off his brown robe, and folded his hands around his voluminous waist. Finally, he started. "Now Michael, it seems to me that you are resisting the silence. You seem unwilling to immerse yourself in it. It's not sound you should be focusing on. You must concentrate on God, not silence or lack of silence. Just let yourself sink into it. Lose yourself in the vacuum, wrap yourself in the spiritual, open yourself to God. Then, He will come. Have you read *The Cloud of the Unknowing*, my son?"

"Not yet, Father. I've been studying St. Augustine's *Confessions.*"

"Very good. Very good, my boy. But you must read *The Cloud of the Unknowing*. Let me think now." He got up, walked over to his bookcase, perused the shelves, and removed a well-worn copy of *The Cloud of the Unknowing*. "Even though it was written in the 14th century, this book is directed toward young monastics. I think you'll find this little volume very helpful. Yes, this is the passage I was thinking of." Father Frank settled his bulk in the chair again and read a passage from the text.

"… if all dreams and imagined visions grew silent, and every tongue and every sign and whatsoever is transient - for indeed if any man could hear them, he should hear them saying with one voice: We did not make ourselves, but He made us who abides forever: but if, having uttered this and so set us to listening to Him who made them, they all grew silent, and in their silence He alone spoke to us, not by them but by Himself: so that we should hear His word, not by any tongue of flesh nor the voice of an angel nor the sound of thunder nor in the darkness of a parable, but that we should hear Himself whom in all these things we love, should hear Himself and not them: just as we two had but now reached forth and in a flash of the mind attained to touch the eternal."

He closed the text, looked at Mike. "Does that help at all?"

Mike rubbed his forehead, then cupped his chin, and bit the inside of his lip. "I would definitely have to read it over again. But does it mean I should forget about silence and sound and just connect to God?"

"Well, that's one way to say it. Try it, my son. Here, take my copy. The author might speak differently to you. Now, about your other problem, the Julie problem. Just how involved were you with this young lady, Michael?"

"We were really good friends and always had a great time together. I met her at a Rosemont mixer. We would go dancing or to the movies or to the beach sometimes. But we weren't going steady or anything like that. That's why I can't understand why she keeps popping into my mind instead of God." He sighed and waited for Father Frank to respond.

"Michael, Julie keeps popping into your mind because you are human. You are a man imbued by God with passion. As long as you live, you will wrestle with this problem. After all, if it were easy to live a celibate life, it wouldn't be worth very much. Remember, it is not only Catholic priests who aspire to celibacy; Buddhists, Muslims, and Hindus also believe that celibacy is necessary for a religious life." Father Frank paused; he looked at Mike with sadness in his eyes, for he knew that his struggle with his humanity was never ending. "Michael, my lad," he continued, "Don't think of giving something up. Think instead of what you will gain. It's not the sacrifice, the giving up, that's important, but the dedication, the devotion. Open yourself to the spirit, my lad. Do you understand?" Father Frank rose, signaling the end of their meeting.

"Thank you, Father, I feel a little better knowing it's normal to have these feelings." Mike followed him to the door.

They shook hands. "Let's meet next week after Vespers. And Michael, keep reading *The Cloud of the Unknowing* and Augustine as well. I'm sure you'll find some answers there."

———

Mike followed the advice of Father Frank. He skimmed St. Augustine but absolutely pored over *The Cloud of the Unknowing*. Somehow it spoke to him. He began to meditate, and it soon became a habit. With his reading and his weekly consultations with Father Frank, he was able to funnel his emotions into dedication and devotion to God. As ordination approached, his zeal intensified.

All Mike's family and his best friend, Joe made the trip to Buffalo for his ordination at St. Bonaventure. None could be prouder than Agnes and Bill. Everything seemed worth it—Bill's labor as a cooper and Agnes's hours in the corner store—for today their son would become a priest. Tom had taken the two of them to John Wannamaker's in Philly to purchase new outfits. Agnes selected a navy blue suit, a pink silk blouse, sensible navy-blue shoes with a matching purse, and a pink hat with a band of tiny pink roses, which complimented her now-white bob and delicate complexion. Bill chose a gray suit from Jacob Breeds with a matching vest and a navy blue and white striped tie. They made the six-hour drive the day before, stayed at the Parkside Hotel in town, and were well-rested and eager to attend Mike's ordination. For the last four years they had scrimped, saved money from the grocery proceeds and the weekly allowance Tom gave them, and were able to buy a silver chalice and ciborium for Mike inscribed with "All our love, Mom and Pop." They hadn't seen Mike yet, so they were itching to get to the chapel.

They followed Tom as he led the way on the final leg of their odyssey. They walked under the apple blossoms and beside the pale purple tulips lining the path. Agnes noticed every detail: the manicured green lawn, the statue of Our Lady in the center of a cluster of lilies of the valley as well as the stately gray stone buildings. She wanted it emblazoned in her mind forever.

They were early for the ceremony and able to get pews in the front of the cathedral. As she glimpsed over at Tom, her heart softened. How sophisticated he looked in his three-piece tan suit and brown-and-gold figured bow tie, so sure and cosmopolitan on the outside, but a lovable teddy bear on the inside. Agnes knew he made a sizeable donation to the Franciscan seminary prior to Mike's being accepted. What an exceptional son he was. She prayed he would marry and have a family one day. Turning around, she looked for Fran. When she spotted her sitting next to Joe, she smiled then waved.

She wished some of her friends were able to attend the ordination, but the trip was a bit too far. Besides, Father Reilly had organized a big celebration for Mike next week in his Camden parish. Everyone would be there, even the archbishop and the cardinal.

———

The organist intoned Pachobel's *Canon in D* and the processional began. At the head, the cardinal, wearing a white chasuble and silk miter trimmed in gold, held his crosier aloft. The president of the seminary followed, trailed by several professors which included Father Frank and visiting prelates, and then finally the seminarians, soon-to-be priests. The congregation rose.

Mike's head was bowed; he seemed very solemn, very devout. He had studied indefatigably for this day. In addition to his Bachelor of Arts from Villanova, he had four years of study at St. Bonaventure. His courses included Theology; Sacred Scripture; Dogmatic, Moral, and Pastoral Theology; Homiletics; Church History; Liturgy; and Canon Law. He also spent many hours assisting Father Maloney at the local parish church, St. Francis of the Fields, where he visited the sick and dying and served at Mass. But as intense as the coursework was, the most difficult part of preparation for Mike was accepting a life of celibacy. He spent many hours poring over the research on clerical celibacy, especially the Corpus Christi Campaign and the Call to Action organization. In addition to reading all of the literature, he had discussions with his confessor and fellow seminarians. He knew about the movements in various parts of the world to make the celibacy requirement optional for priests. He also read about all of the ordained clerics who resigned from the priesthood to marry and subsequently lost their sacramental authority.

He knew the pros and the cons. In the end, he realized he loved his God above all else. Knowing it might be extremely difficult at times, he felt called to relinquish all thoughts of marriage and family and devote himself to the service of his God. Mike was happy, almost delirious, with his decision. He was certain beyond a doubt that he could control his sexual drive.

As the procession approached Agnes, Mike was so focused on his spiritual transformation that he missed her beaming at him as he passed. He was completely enraptured with every second of the two-hour ceremony: the incense, the music, the singing, the Latin prayers, and sermons. When the cardinal laid his hands on Mike's head and prayed that the Holy Spirit would descend upon him, tears streamed down his cheeks. Mike felt transformed, intensely connected with God. Later as he lay prostrate on the cold marble before the crucifix, he pledged his obedience to his bishop and dedicated himself to celibacy.

The entire congregation erupted in applause when the seminarians, now priests, walked from the sacristy in their clerical vestments.

A happy throng of people milled around outside the chapel. As soon as Mike saw Agnes, he ran over, hugged her, picked her up, and spun her around.

"Michael, you put me down!" she demanded. Mike did no such thing knowing she secretly relished the attention.

Mike shook Bill's hand, hugged him.

Then he turned to Tom with a big bear hug; they patted each other's backs. "Tom, do you remember that career conference we had when I was back in Villanova? That was when you planted the seed; I hope you're happy with the way it grew."

"Couldn't be prouder, little brother."

Father Mike pummeled Joe on the shoulder.

"Congratulations, roomie," shouted Joe.

Mike noticed Fran standing very, very close to Joe. "Maybe, someday, I'll be performing a marriage ceremony," he said as he looked at the two with approval.

He grabbed Fran so tight, she squealed and laughed until she cried, "I am so happy for you."

Mike checked his watch. "We have a luncheon in half an hour where we'll have a group picture taken. Then I'm free until I celebrate my very first Mass tomorrow morning, which I hope everyone will attend."

Together

After ordination, Mike was sent to Deming, New Mexico, as an assistant in a poor parish near the Air Corps base. He was the right hand to Father Jones, who had been the pastor for the last 25 years. In addition to his duties there, he said the noon Mass at the base and heard confessions as well. Letters flew back and forth from Deming to Camden at a rapid pace.

In the meantime, Joe received his MD from Jefferson Medical College and asked Fran to be his bride. One of the first things Fran did after Joe proposed was grab a pen and share the news with her big brother. They were both determined that Mike marry them.

———

Fran heard the voice as she bounded up the porch steps and opened the front door. "Hey, Mom. Who are you listening to?"

Agnes sat by the radio mesmerized by Kate Smith's rendition of "God Bless America." "Hush! She's almost finished."

Fran dropped her tap shoes on the floor, put her sheet music on the hall table, and plopped on the couch next to Agnes. For a year now, Fran taught tap dancing at the YMCA in the center of Camden. Her bubbly nature and high energy had doubled her class size.

Agnes put her finger on her lips to signal silence. The two of them listened as Kate Smith belted out "God Bless America" for the first time to a radio audience.

"She's really the 'cat's meow.' No doubt about it."

"I could listen to that voice all night, Fran." Agnes turned the radio off. "How did tap class go this afternoon?"

"Pretty good. I was able to rent the high school auditorium for the annual review." Fran absently twisted the gold band with the half-carat diamond on her left hand ring finger and automatically thought of Joe. The diamond might be tiny, but their feelings for each other were immeasurable. "By the way, did any mail come for me? I'm dying to find out if Mike can marry us."

"Oh, I'm glad you asked. I almost forgot. You did get a letter from Mike. I put it on the kitchen table."

"Mom, why didn't you tell me?" She jumped up and headed for the kitchen.

"I just did."

Fran ripped the envelope, pulled out the letter and quickly skimmed the contents. "Oh horse feathers! His pastor won't give him the time off! Father Jones says he just can't do without him. I guess it's nice to be indispensable, but I refuse to get married if he can't perform the ceremony. What will I do? Wait till I tell Joe."

"Now, now, Fran, don't fret. We'll think of something."

"But this is major stuff, Mom. Do you think Tom could call Father Jones and influence him a bit." Tom had always been the go-to guy for Fran and Mike, too. He had a knack to make things happen.

"I doubt if Tom's influence reaches all the way to New Mexico."

Fran balled up the letter and threw it on the coffee table. "Then what can we do?"

"Hmm, I wonder. If Mike can't come to us, why don't we go to Mike?"

"What do you mean?"

"Exactly what I said."

"But how far is it?"

"About 2,000 miles, I think. A couple of hours by plane, about four days by car."

"Way too expensive to fly."

"Well, what about driving?"

"Do you think we could do it?"

"I don't know why not."

"That might be fun. Tom could drive his Plymouth and Joe could use his old jalopy. Do you think his car would last the trip?" Fran didn't even pause for breath. She expressed her thoughts rapid fire as they whorled through her head. "We could follow each other cross country, have picnic lunches, and stop at night in some pretty little roadside places. Let's do it, Mom. I can't wait to tell Joe our new plan! Oh, Mom. It will be so hotsy totsy; everybody will want to go."

———

And that is exactly what happened. The O'Brien and Wills families motored all the way to Deming, New Mexico, for the wedding ceremony with no mishaps.

Fran found the perfect wedding outfit at John Wanamaker's of Philadelphia: a light, lovely lavender flapper dress with tuxedo style pleating on the bodice and a full-pleated skirt ending just below the knee with shoes dyed to match. She carried it safely in the huge Wanamaker's box on her lap all through the trip and carefully hung it in the various motel closets every night of the trip.

There was only one thing she asked of Joe: a huge bouquet of irises, van Gogh purple. *No problem*, he thought. The day before the wedding the old Villanova roommates piled into Joe's jalopy and visited every florist in Deming. Because it was January and Deming had little call for irises in the middle of winter, there were none to be found. As a last resort, Joe purchased a tiny violet nosegay hoping Fran wouldn't be too upset, after all it was only a couple of shades paler than the van Gogh purple and a bit closer to the lavender of the dress. He decided to wait until just before the ceremony to surprise her with it, hoping that she would be too excited about the ceremony to get upset.

Joe's hunch was right. The violets were the exact hue of her dress, and Fran couldn't have been happier. It is the one story from that wedding in the middle of winter in the town of Deming that has been passed down from generation to generation.

———

The young couple moved to Philadelphia near Jefferson Medical Center where Joe was employed as an anesthesiologist. Before long, they became the parents of a son who favored his father with his sandy hair and hazel eyes. For their first, the only name under consideration was Michael, the center of the O'Brien family.

Separation

Life for Tom was not as idyllic; the asthma he suffered as a child returned and demanded attention. He unlocked the door to the Camden homestead, slowly walked into the kitchen, unwrapped his scarf, and hung his jacket on the back of a chair.

"Mom!" He stood behind her, placed his hands on her shoulders. She was always slight, but seemed frail tonight. "I think I have to move. Dr. Tasker says that my asthma will only worsen if I stay in this climate. I have to live where it's warm and dry. It would be best for my health if I moved out West."

"Oh, Tom, I was afraid Dr. Tasker would say that."

"He's right. All this sickness is beginning to affect my work. Gus Wilson, senior partner, called me into his office today and had a heart-to-heart about my health. He's concerned about my recent absences because he respects the quality of my work. But he said, and I think he's right, that I need to be in the office or the courtroom five days every week. This was a warning. But I know there are many days when I just can't breathe. The writing's on the wall. He'll probably ask me to leave the next time I'm out sick."

"Oh, I don't think he would ever ask you to leave; you're just too valuable. But you're right, nothing is more important than your health." Agnes checked the roast chicken, pulled it out of the oven to sit for 10 minutes so the juices would run back inside.

"Hmmm. That smell tantalizes my taste buds. Let's eat!"

Agnes reached up into the cabinet for the everyday china.

"Let me help." Tom opened the utensil drawer and finished setting the table while Agnes rummaged around for the masher and started on the potatoes, adding milk and margarine.

Tom entered the living room to catch the war news on the radio. The Germans were advancing and the news became more stressful every day. He wondered what Wilson would do.

Soon Agnes called Tom, pushing a stray lock of white hair back into her bun. "Turn that radio off. Your dinner is getting cold." He ambled in and took Pop's place at the table, his usual seat since Pop's death the year before. The whole house seemed empty and quiet without Pop and Fran.

Agnes shook out her napkin and placed it over the lavender and blue cornflowered housedress. "Tom, I've been anticipating the news that Dr. Tasker gave you. And I've been thinking that this place is just too big, what with Joe and Fran over in Philly and your dad gone. We just don't need this old house anymore. Now that I'm older, the cold weather makes my bones ache and my joints are beginning to swell up. I've been thinking about selling the house and moving West with Mike myself."

"Don't you want to be here to watch Mikey grow up?" interrupted Tom.

"I'll be fine. I'll go out to New Mexico with Mike."

Tom picked up the fork to serve Agnes and then took a large helping of chicken for himself, and heaped the mashed potatoes and string beans on his plate.

"First of all, Fran's little family needs their own space; they have their own lives to live." Agnes said. "Joe has a wonderful job, so I'm sure they would fly out West on a regular basis to visit."

Agnes must have been thinking of this for a long time, Tom figured.

"Well if you're really sure, we'll both go West."

"I think that settles it," said Agnes. "I would be left here by myself anyway. We'll put this house up for sale. The money we get should be enough to buy a small place out West and also leave enough for us to live on for a few years. Tom, you can go out there first, scout around for a smaller house, maybe Gus Wilson has some contacts out there. Fran can help me with the sale of the house and the packing and I'll follow."

"Okay. I probably could stay with Mike while I get situated. But, Mom, that's going to be a lot of work for you."

"Do you forget, Tom, that I have moved a several times in my life already? The first from Newfoundland to New Jersey. This time I just might get it right. I might look like a frail old woman, but I'm a Bunsen burner underneath. I bet Fran would love to have the Queen Anne parlor-room set and maybe the dining room table and chairs. We could advertise the rest of the furniture for sale and take only what we absolutely need."

"Is that a knock at the door?" asked Tom. "I'll get it." The door opened before Tom reached it. Joe, Fran, and the baby tumbled inside. Mikey ran first to Agnes who gave him a big bear hug. Then he squealed as Tom grabbed him and threw him up in the air, thrilled with his giggles.

"We had to stop by with our good news," announced Joe. His smile bounced off the floor and ricocheted around the room. "Fran had an appointment with old Doc Burns at Cooper and after he examined her, he informed us that baby number two was on the way." Another round of hugs and kisses commenced in the room full of euphoria.

"We have to drink a toast to that!" Tom exclaimed. He rose to get glasses. After searching the fridge for wine, he yelled, "I guess it's beer all around." Joe and Fran dropped their coats on the counter and took their old seats at the table. They raised their tumblers of Schlitz beer and drank to baby number two. "Cheers!" "Hear, hear!"

"We have some news, too," Agnes proclaimed proudly. "We're moving out West."

"Whoa," Joe said, "You're moving out West just like that? Don't you think you should give it a little thought! Weigh the pros and cons. Sleep on it for a while."

Fran put her glass down abruptly. "Mom, how could you? The baby just adores you. Don't you want to be a part of his life? And me—I would miss you horribly. I rely on your support."

"Well your brother has to move because of his asthma."

"But you don't have to move with him. He can certainly take care of himself. You could move in with Joe and me. Isn't that right, love?"

Agnes reached over and touched her hand. "That's generous of you to offer, but I've made my decision. The cold weather makes my winters quite painful. Besides, you and Joe and the baby need your space."

There was no changing Agnes's mind.

Trouble

Mike could hear Father Jones' voice bellowing from downstairs. In the three years Mike lived in the rectory, the pastor barely spoke above a whisper.

"Mike," he yelled. "Can't you hear me?"

"Yes, Father, what is it?" Mike ran down the stairs like he was sprinting the last few inches of a 50-yard dash, Blackie, his black cocker spaniel, followed, tripping after him. He rounded the corner and peered into the den.

Father Jones was sitting in his recliner, head in hands, leaning as close to the radio as possible without falling, his normal grin turned downward into a scowl. "Son, grab a seat and listen. The Japs bombed Pearl Harbor this morning."

Mike dragged a chair over and the two huddled by the radio. Blackie ambled over and settled down between them, poking the pastor's slipper with his nose. Father Jones moved his foot. "Listen, Mike."

Franklin Delano Roosevelt's voice came over the radio. "This is a day that will live in infamy. The United States of America has been suddenly and without provocation attacked by the Empire of Japan. Folks, this is a day our children and their children will remember through the ages. The military forces of Japan have attacked Malaya, Hong Kong, Guam, the Philippine Islands, Wake Island, and Midway Island."

Father Jones looked at his subordinate. "This is trouble, son. Real trouble. Roosevelt will have to declare war." He turned up the volume on the radio. "I'm afraid it will bring the bombs to our shores."

They continued to listen. "Father, don't you think we should pray the rosary?"

"Right now, I want to hear what our president says. There will be time for prayers later."

Mike couldn't sit still. He ran his fingers through his hair, cracked his knuckles, tapped his feet. Finally, he rose. "I'm going over to the church. You can tell me what happened when I come back." He motioned to Blackie to stay and headed out.

After he unlocked it, he pushed the heavy oak door open and entered the sacred house of God. He headed straight for the altar, ignoring the stained-glass windows and statues of saints, which usually attracted his attention. He knelt and prayed—not for success should the Americans enter the war, but for the strength to handle the problems that would transpire.

On December 8, Sunday, parishioners lined the aisles and overflowed outside onto the church steps. Fear was written on their faces, but overpowering the fear was a willingness to defend their country. Mike sensed it, felt it, saw it from the pulpit. He knew that he, too, must serve.

Later in the day, he approached his pastor. "Father, I've been thinking and praying a lot about the war for quite a while now. I feel it's my duty to answer Roosevelt's call. In fact, I've been anticipating this and have already received permission from the bishop to attend the chaplain's school at Harvard. I leave at the end of the week."

"Now, Mike, don't be hasty. You are needed here too, you know. I waited almost a year for your appointment. I don't know how the parish can function without you. With the increase in the number of parishioners attending Sunday Mass, we surely can't omit any of them. Besides, you've just started that program to feed the poor. It answers such a need in the parish; I would hate to see it fold."

"Father, when the men start to be called for the draft, I think there will be quite a few empty pews in the church. As for the food program, Adrienne and Jim Benchley can run it blindfolded. I think the parish will thrive with or without me."

"What about your mother and your brother? Aren't they arriving next week?"

"They'll understand! Besides, my brother is perfectly capable of settling in without any help from me."

"Well, what about me? I've gotten used to you hanging around. Who will I play chess with?"

"Now, now, Father, you'll be fine. I'll leave Blackie with you for company."

"Oh no! I don't think so. That mongrel and I don't usually see eye to eye. Wherever you go, he goes—whether it be Boston, or Guam, or the Philippines. We would kill each other if you left him here."

That was a problem Mike would have to deal with later. First on the agenda was getting to Boston and completing the requirements of the six-week cram course to become a chaplain.

———

Fran switched the phone to her left hand and wiped her right on her flowered apron. "Hi, Mike, it's so good to hear your voice." She had been expecting Mike's call. He had recently completed chaplaincy school and was driving down from Boston with Blackie to celebrate with her and Joe.

"That's good news, Mike. It seems like you just started your studies. We can't wait to see you." Since he hadn't seen their row house in Philly, she was especially thrilled about his visit.

"Not already! You're being shipped to the Philippines on Monday? But that's too soon!

"I hope you'll still be able to come for dinner tonight. We are all so excited to see you again.

"Good. Good. The kids will be so happy.

"You're kidding, Mike. You can't really mean that. You know I already have Lassie, my little black and white spaniel.

"No, she doesn't need a boyfriend, especially not Blackie. The last time I saw that dog he had no hair on his back, the poor thing. He would constantly lick and scratch until his skin just oozed.

"Mike, the answer is no. I just can't do it. I have a baby to take care of, one on the way, and a dog, and a husband.

"What do you mean he's already in the car?

"Mike, just go back to the car, open the door, and take that mongrel out. Leave it with a friend. That's my final word." Fran slammed the receiver and sighed.

Joe, his arms flecked with tiny bits of cut grass, sweat dripping into his eyes, T-shirt stuck to his back, feet tracking in bits of mud and freshly mowed grass, sneaked behind Fran and gave her a squeeze. "Oh, Joe, you're a mess," she protested, squirming away from him.

"Is that brother of yours being cantankerous again?"

"Well, he has orders to leave for the Philippines on Monday and—can you imagine—he wants to leave Blackie with us."

"Well, he can't take the dog with him, that's for sure, and I doubt if he can leave him at Harvard. Hmmm, do you think the kids might enjoy having two dogs?"

"Now, Joe, don't tell me you're on his side."

"Mmmmm! Do I smell garlic, rosemary, and oregano—your special culinary delight, tomato sauce and meatballs?"

"Don't change the subject. But, yes, special request of Mike for his 'last supper.' He's about ready to leave Boston, so he should be here by dinnertime."

"You know, I'm surprised Mike decided to enlist. As a priest, he could have been deferred."

"Haven't you figured it out yet, Joe? He's unlike the rest of us. He's passionate about serving, about doing everything he possibly can to make the world a better place for we mere mortals—namely, you and me."

"Well, in that case, maybe you should volunteer to care for that poor mutt until he safely returns."

Service

On a white sand beach fringed with palm trees in the Philippines, General Thomas, Chief of Staff of the Air Corps Hospital, was on a mission. He charged through the hall, all six-foot-five-inches of him, looking for answers. He heard through the grapevine that Chaplain O'Brien had been hospitalized and he was determined to locate him and discover the extent of his injuries. In the six months Father Mike had been on base, he had made a reputation for himself and the general relied on him to keep up the men's morale. General Thomas approached the nurse station to find answers.

"Father Mike O'Brien? They brought him in this morning, General," the orderly said, looking up from his paperwork. "He collapsed while saying the eight o'clock Mass. He's itching to get out of here, says it's just a mild case of the flu."

"Thank the good Lord for that."

"But, we're still a little concerned; he's exhibiting symptoms of malaria. He's sweating yet complaining of chills. He's nauseated, vomiting, feverish one minute and freezing the next. We're pretty sure it's malaria. We're running some tests and should know in an hour or so. If that is the case and it's in the early stages, we can control it with medication. In a day or so he should be up and back in operation, General."

"That's good to hear. Some of the boys feared Father Mike was caught in the raid last night on the Tacloban Fields and wanted me to check on him. Where is he? I'll stop by when I finish my rounds."

"He's still in the ER, General. As soon as a room opens up, we'll switch him. Some of our wounded from the Japanese air attack have heard he's in here and are asking for him."

"The naval attack on Leyte must have infuriated those Japanese generals. Can you believe they strafed us 12 times in one night?" He scratched his brow under his surgical cap. "You know Mike really has a way of keeping the morale up, and that is so important to recovery. If he is ambulatory and not infectious, let him roam around, visit the men, try to make them see some positive in the sacrifices they made."

The general finally finished rounds, stopping to chat with each of the men who were conscious. He despaired over the tragedies he witnessed: limbs blown off, heads with gaping holes, fire-singed bodies. He sighed and wondered, but just for a second, if it wouldn't have been better if some had died in the attack. He knocked on Father Mike's door and entered quietly. "Father Mike, they told me you were in here. How are you feeling?"

"Embarrassed more than anything else." Mike adjusted the sheet over his legs. "I don't belong here taking up a bed; some of our boys who were hit hard last night need it a lot more than I do. I don't know why they have me hooked up to this machine."

Checking his chart, the general explained. "Now, Mike, your doc thinks you have malaria. If that's so, you could go into convulsions and slip into a coma without the proper medication. We wouldn't want that to happen to our favorite chaplain, now would we?"

"Malaria? How could that be? I've taken all the suggested precautions; I even sleep under a net every night, for gosh sakes!"

"Well, I heard you weren't sleeping under a net last night. Corporal James told me you sneaked out to the fields and were comforting the wounded, hearing confessions, and giving Communion. What are you trying to do, win the 'Philippine Liberation Medal' or a free trip to heaven, for Christ's Sake?" His exasperation was evident as he spit out his thoughts. "Oh excuse the language! But really, Mike, we want you alive so you can comfort the men. Dead you're no use to us at all. Who would say Mass every morning? Who would listen to the tragic tales of our boys? Who would give them the spirit and spunk to get out there every day to protect the folks at home? Mike, I don't mean to lecture, but we need you. Don't put your life on the line, please."

"Okay! Okay! General, I hear you. I guess I needed that, but I heard those planes buzzing overhead and then the guns, and even though I wasn't close enough, I heard the groans, the moans, the calls for help. I feel so inadequate sometimes. I just had to do whatever I could to help."

"You're right. It was bad last night, but not as bad as the Bataan Death March."

"My Filipino cook, Juan, told me his story of escaping from the March, after witnessing the brutal beheadings and slashed throats, the bayonet stabbings, the rapes, the disembowelments, and rifle-butt beatings. The horror of the whole thing gives me nightmares. It tortures me. I feel I can't do enough to help these men.

"By the way, Mike, on a lighter note. I hear there was quite a bit of singing in the canteen last Saturday night and that you were in the center of it."

"Yeah, that old upright looked so lonely in the corner, and I thought the men could use some cheering up. Beethoven is usually my choice, but he didn't seem appropriate for that beer-drinking crowd, so I changed my style a bit. I think we all had a good time, forgot what was happening all around us. Did you get complaints about the noise?"

"No, just the urge to leave my bunk and join the crowd." His mouth turned up in a smile.

"While we're on this subject, General. Would you mind if I use the upright to practice during the lulls? I find my fingers are getting a bit rusty."

"Of course not, Mike. It's yours whenever you find a spare minute. But back to the malaria: you will probably be prescribed quinine. The drug does have some side effects: mild hearing loss, possible erratic pulse, so you must be monitored, and most importantly, you must remain on quinine for the rest of your life. However, the side effects are minor compared to convulsions, coma, and death."

"I hear you, General. Thanks for the advice and for the visit."

"Get some rest now. I'll stop in tomorrow." The general returned Mike's salute and walked out the door.

Following that conversation, the chaplain and the general became good partners for several more years ministering to the spiritual and physical needs of their men in the Philippines.

———

When his tour in the Philippines ended, Mike re-upped for four more years… even though he swore he wouldn't. He simply couldn't refuse the promotion to captain, the accompanying pay raise, and the charge to rebuild Germany—Bavaria, to be exact. After several weeks of intense preparation, Mike spent time with Fran, Joe, and the kids before departing for the American Zone in Bavaria.

Although the weather was colder than he was used to in the Philippines, he discovered he missed the changing of the seasons. However, he was saddened that the great museums, the art, the opera had been silenced, but hopeful he would be instrumental in restoring them. Walking through castles and medieval towns surrounded by rolling hills and lush green forests would have to wait for a future visit. Now he was determined to do his part in the larger effort to feed the hungry, fight disease and crime, restore cultural artifacts, re-establish industry, restore electricity, telephone, and water. Solving a myriad of problems involving currency, housing, education, elections, and displaced persons were all in the scope of work for the men deployed to Bavaria. The Germans welcomed the Americans, for they considered the "Yanks" salvation. Rebuilding started rapidly and in no time the Wochenmarkt (weekly market) was back in some kind of operation. Each day brought a new challenge.

Although not lavish by any stretch of the imagination, Mike's quarters were comfortable. He had his recliner, a small kitchen with a stove and refrigerator, and a bedroom. He said Mass in the chapel on base, and worked with the local parish to establish schools and to administer the sacraments. The work was difficult both physically and mentally. He spent every waking hour ministering to all the enlisted men in addition to aiding the poor Germans displaced by the intense bombing of the Allies. Mike's only form of relaxation was a running chess game with Father Don Monahan.

He and Father Don arrived in Bavaria the same day. It was Father Don's first tour of duty and Mike was his role model, despite being opposites in both physical attributes and personality. While Mike was an extrovert and at ease meeting new people, often the center of attention in a room, Don was more reserved and very humble, yet possessing an admirable inner strength. Don was a big man, muscular rather than flabby, with a shock of salt and pepper hair that flopped over his black, piercing eyes. The two chaplains often worked with the committee reorganizing the educational system according to General MacArthur's philosophy, and soon became best of friends.

———

One day, Mike was walking back to his quarters from the Wochenmarkt when his neighbor, Harold, interrupted him. "Say, Mike, wait up," called the staff psychologist housed next door. "I've been meaning to talk to you. I thought you might be interested in something I'm involved with. I've been communicating with amateur radio operators all over the world, especially in the states. Would you like to see how it works?"

"Sure," said Mike, "I get so darned busy, I barely have time to sneeze. Now what are you talking about? Some kind of radio station up and running here in Bavaria?"

"Come on in for a couple of minutes." Harold introduced him to the amateur radio station, whereby a trained licensed operator could communicate with another licensed operator on a designated radio frequency. Mike was fascinated. He recognized it as an inexpensive way to connect to home. Immediately, he thought of the enlisted men on base. Depression or homesickness plagued at least half of them. He wondered if the ham radio could help. He asked Harold question after question until midnight. Harold lent him a couple of books, and Mike was hooked. After some focused study, he was able to qualify as a ham operator with his own call sign. Then, using war surplus radios, he converted one for his own use.

He used the radio to keep in touch with his mother and brother, who by this time had relocated to Deming, New Mexico, and also to talk to Fran and Joe. Even though it took some planning to set up the logistics and locate another ham operator in close proximity to the party he wanted to communicate with, it did wonders for lifting his spirit: it was a lifeline to home. Soon word spread and many of the enlisted men asked Mike to contact home so they could congratulate a wife on the birth of a child, or talk to their kids, or merely say, "I love you" to a sweetheart.

———

Even in Bavaria, despite the destruction and despondency, Christmas was a special time to rejoice. The enlisted men were huddled in the ruins of the cathedral singing the familiar carols a cappella. The voices weren't the most melodic Mike had ever heard, but they were the most fervent. "Silent night, holy night all is calm…" The men, every one of them, sang from the heart. The familiar melody lifted them out of Germany, took them home to Texas, to Idaho, to Vermont. Wisps of memories of Christmases past when they were home with the people they loved pervaded their minds. Mike noticed the glazed eyes, the faint smiles. Their voices rang in the chapel, filled it with the sounds of Christmas.

Mike was no different from the men who stood before him. He too lapsed into the distant past. Julie was standing next to him, holding his hand, gazing into his steel- gray eyes. After all these years, he could still smell her hair—that combination of roses and heather. They sang together in the tiny crowded church in her Delaware hometown. He knew she had expected a ring that Christmas long ago, but in his pocket was a necklace with a pendant, a Villanova charm. He wondered how different his life would have been if, indeed, a ring had been in his pocket.

The carol ended and the silence scattered his thoughts. He rose, walked to the lectern. The men sat and looked expectantly in his direction. They needed encouragement, especially tonight, and Mike never failed them. His mouth turned up in that ever-present grin. "Boys, that was absolutely the most passionate 'Silent Night' I have ever heard."

The men chuckled, knowing how pitiful they sounded. Mike looked into each one of their faces, identifying with their loneliness, their isolation, and their need for human contact.

———

One day, as Mike and Don left the meeting, snow stung their faces like BB pellets as they leaned into the wind. Mike pulled his scarf tighter; he never liked the cold. The military-issued scarves were never as warm as the ones his mother used to knit for him. "Don, I really feel that we're making a difference here. The general is a smart man and really passionate about rebuilding Bavaria. I think we accomplished a lot."

"I agree. Your idea about starting classes as soon as we can find available rooms rather than wait until reconstruction is completed is a viable one. These poor displaced people need some semblance of routine, of normalcy."

"MacArthur is right; we can't wait. We have to get things done yesterday. Just look around, on this block alone only two buildings are habitable. I wonder what it all looked like before this destruction."

"Fortunately, the cathedral is still standing. Even damaged, it is a perfect place for classroom space. Maybe even four or five classes. We must start the ball rolling."

They trudged through the snow in silence. Mike thought of Carl, the young corporal who had a wife and two youngsters in California. Carl cornered him before the meeting asking for advice. He worked very closely with a civilian liaison, a beautiful, intelligent, compassionate German who lost her husband in the bombing. They were working late one night trying to set up a food bank and, as Carl explained it, one thing led to another and before he knew what had happened they were in each other's arms. Guilt was destroying him far quicker than the long hours and the heavy workload. He didn't deny his physical attraction to Katrina; he explained that it seemed more real than his relationship with his wife. Every passing day, he seemed to drift further and further away from his stateside family.

Carl wanted advice. He wanted to know how to control this physical longing that almost made him crazy. He didn't want to hurt Katrina, but above all, he wanted to remain faithful to his wife. Mike wished he had a magic formula for Carl. He sympathized with his predicament, but felt inadequate to help, for he had little experience with women and family life since first entering the priesthood. He certainly felt attracted to Julie, but their hugs and kisses were chaste.

Right now, to help Carl, he was working on a call through the ham radio thinking that some contact with his wife, even though limited to conversation, might help strengthen his resolve. He wondered how Don handled these problems.

Don broke the silence, "How about a short game of chess? I feel lucky tonight!"

"Come on! You know there is no such thing as a short game of chess. I think it was about one in the morning before I captured your king the last time."

"Let's put a limit on the time."

"Eleven, not one second more."

"Okay—but this time, I take *your* king." Don unlocked his door and the friends escaped the snow.

————

As the clock struck three, they were still huddled over the chessboard studying their moves. Mike still had his woolen scarf wrapped around his neck. The wind howled, rattling the windows. "Say, Don, one of the men asked me for advice on keeping his marriage together. I was wondering how you deal with these questions. I just feel so ill-prepared to help the men with these personal problems."

Father Don looked up at Mike as he completed a strategic move into Mike's territory. "I'll tell you what I often do. I often consult a psychology text I have, *Putting God into Marriage.* Would you like to borrow it?"

"Sure, I'm grasping at straws right now. I would welcome anything that would help. I managed to contact this fellow's wife via a ham operator. I'm not sure how it's working. I'm just keeping my fingers crossed and, of course, praying for him."

"The book is right over there on the shelf. Pick it up on your way out after I whip you."

Mike looked at the bookcase and nodded. "Thanks, Don, I would appreciate that." He rubbed his cold fingers together, blew on them, and bent over to study his next move.

The coal burned slowly in the cast iron stove. Despite the chill in the room, neither man wanted to stop until a victor was apparent. After Mike moved his bishop to safety, he mused. "Don, I've been thinking of using my leave to explore a bit of the countryside, rather than return to the states. I hear the Alps, with its vegetation and unusual rock formations, are startling, and the lakes, especially the Eibsee near Edelweiss, are deep and clear. The destruction here in the city can really be depressing."

"That's a thought. But if I were you, I would concentrate on the game at hand. Checkmate, my friend."

Mike's tour of duty passed quickly. He left Bavaria with pride in his accomplishments, a renewed respect for the enlisted men, and an admiration for the displaced Germans he helped. After his discharge from the Air Force, he was assigned to the parish of St. Ignatius in El Paso, Texas. There, he would assume the duties of pastor and was charged with building a school. He was looking forward to seeing Agnes and Tom who were relocating to El Paso. He had spent a lot of time selecting a gift for Agnes and finally chose a delicate Bavarian china pattern rimmed in gold with a band of tiny yellow daisies.

As they said their final goodbyes, Mike and Don shook hands and promised to renew their friendship in the states.

1952-1967

Changes

As soon as Mike returned stateside, he flew to El Paso and went straight to St. Ignatius. José DelGado, a welcoming committee of one, was waiting as Mike's cab pulled up to the curb. The muscular Hispanic with sparkling dark eyes and a broad grin extended his hand as Mike stepped out of the cab. "Welcome, Father. Happy to have new pastor. Please, call me José. Help with bags?" José's English was not perfect, so he was relieved when Mike responded in Spanish.

As he looked at José, Mike noticed the church behind him. It was a love affair before he even stepped inside. Everything else vanished—the cab, the luggage, José—as Mike stood and marveled at the modern edifice, this sacred house of God. He scrutinized the circular shape, the chiseled stone, the dome roof, and the colorful windows.

"Beautiful, eh Father?" José's words interrupted Mike's trance.

Hurriedly, he reached for his wallet and paid the cab driver. "Can I go inside, José? Now? Right away?"

"Sure, sure. Here key."

As Mike opened the metal door, he was bathed in a kaleidoscope of light reflected through the multitude of stained glass windows. The unexpected phenomenon startled him. He froze. Finally, he noticed the Stations of the Cross along the stucco walls, the simplicity of the oak pews, and the terra cotta tiles leading to the altar. He walked down the central aisle and knelt at the altar rail. Raising his eyes to the large wooden cross behind the altar, he vowed to dedicate his life to bring love, hope, and honor to St. Ignatius and the parishioners.

———

Soon after Mike settled in the rectory, his mother and brother arrived from Deming. They found a small cottage nearby and usually spent Sunday at St. Ignatius attending Mass, helping count the collection, and later staying for dinner. Life was just about perfect for Mike, although he couldn't help but worry about Agnes; she had aged noticeably and had a difficult time adjusting to the relocation. She was rather frail to begin with, and Mike was shocked by the change in her physically as well as spiritually. Her long wispy white hair was pulled back in a plaited bun. She had lost that spark in her eye, and she was so thin he could see the blue veins beneath the pale skin when he circled her wrist with his thumb and forefinger. But what concerned him most was her general lack of energy. So he was especially delighted when her face lit up as she removed each piece of the Bavaian china from its packing and asked Tom to put the kettle on for a cup of tea.

The brothers were happy to be together again and soon settled into a comfortable rhythm. Tom helped out at the parish, ushering on Sundays and lending his legal expertise when needed, especially in reviewing contracts for the new school. On Sundays Mike often played his prized piano, one he bought second-hand from one of his parishioners in need of cash. Agnes would sit in his recliner, eyes closed, listening, while Tom prepared dinner.

Getting to meet his parishioners, building the new school, saying Mass, and ministering to the sick and dying became Mike's passion. The spare minutes he had were filled with music. Daily practice of scales and arpeggios became as routine as prayer, and attending concerts by the El Paso Symphony became a habit.

―――――

One night, across the Rio Grande, another pupil of classical music, a young Hispanic woman with curly brown hair and laughing chestnut eyes was also preparing to attend the very same Beethoven concert.

Maria rushed through the streets of downtown El Paso, zigzagging through the foot traffic. She had lived all of her 34 years in Juarez, and it wasn't often that she crossed the bridge into the U.S., but tonight the symphony was performing Beethoven's *Ninth Symphony,* a piece she played as the lead cellist in her high school orchestra. Attending the performance was a must. The smell of tacos and burritos was heavy in the spring air. Horns, whistles, vendors, and crying babies made it all but impossible to think. She hurtled past a bent, graying woman pushing a stroller. "Con permiso." She nodded as she moved onward.

Reduced price tickets went on sale exactly one half-hour before the concert began. Maria hoped to be one of the first in the queue. Then, if she was lucky and there were still unsold tickets, she would watch Eugene Ormandy, a guest conductor, coax magic from the El Paso Symphony. She dashed up the steps of the concert hall, pushed through the heavy door, and immediately turned right, relieved to see that she would be the second in line.

"Hola." She smiled, caught her breath, and nodded to the middle-aged woman in front of her. All afternoon at the library, she had practiced how to say "one ticket, please." A few months ago, she had started as head research assistant at the Ben Franklin Library built by the U.S. for Mexico. She was hired on the provision that she learn English, but she hadn't time to practice much lately.

After a fifteen-minute wait, Maria approached the ticket window and easily completed the transaction. As she walked away from the window, she paused to check her seat number, DD-102. She couldn't believe her luck and glanced at the ticket again, DD-102. Most often, she sat near the end of the alphabet, not the beginning. Maria was overjoyed.

Grasping her ticket, she walked down the aisle toward the orchestra. The sounds of strings and horns tuning up spoke to something deep inside of her. She checked the letters on the arms of the aisle seats: "F," "E," "D." *This must be it*, she reasoned, as she looked at her ticket one last time. Maria adjusted her shoulder bag and smoothed her brightly colored skirt as she slid into the upholstered seat. She settled into 102, looked around as empty spaces filled, then paged through the program and looked at the photographs, resolving to study English a little better. Suddenly, she was aware of someone standing directly in front of her.

"I think you're sitting in my seat," Mike O'Brien said as Maria looked into his steel-gray eyes.

Glancing up at the curly haired gringo, she shrugged. "En espanol, por favor?" Her happy face turned to a frown as Mike explained in Spanish that he sat in D-102 every second Tuesday of the month. Maria studied her ticket again, then glanced back at him as she thrust her ticket into his outstretched fingers. When he examined the ticket, he realized that Maria's ticket, DD 102, was in the balcony, not the orchestra section. He motioned for the usher, but changed his mind when he saw her crestfallen expression. "I have a better idea," he said. "Why don't you sit right here? After all, you were here first. Let's swap. I'll give you my ticket, and if you give me yours, I'll go upstairs and find DD 102. I always wondered if sound rose as heat does."

Before Maria could thank Mike, he disappeared as deafening applause muted conversation and signaled Ormandy's arrival on stage. *What a nice guy*, she thought. She raised both hands high and clapped longer and louder than anyone else around her. Then the strains of the Ninth Symphony erased everything from her mind but Beethoven. She became 17 again, straddling the cello, fingering the strings, teasing from them the same melody that now swirled throughout the amphitheater. The force of the finale, "Ode to Joy," swept through her like a magnificent thunderstorm. She closed her eyes and felt its pulse.

As the final flourish died and Ormandy acknowledged the virtuosity of the orchestra, Maria remembered the kind man with the steel-gray eyes and turned to scan the balcony. Their eyes met. Their hands waved. *Adios.*

Mike soon forgot the young Hispanic woman, but he was never completely absent from Maria's mind. He was always lurking just behind the surface, ready to pop into focus.

———

The overhead lights dimmed, creating a romantic glow throughout the elegant room. Candles flickered on the tables for two in the intimate dining room of one of Juarez's premier hotels, the Lucerna. Maria and her sister sat by the sliding glass doors where they felt the cool breeze flutter the palm fronds, saw the moonlight shimmering on the pool, and admired the gaily decorated lanterns casting gold, ruby, and amethyst shadows. "Alma, you shouldn't have, but I'm so glad you did." Her favorite cobalt blue silk blouse with a matching blue and yellow flowered skirt accentuated Maria's dark hair and chestnut eyes.

"Now, Maria, you only turn 35 once. Let your big sister sing happy birthday to you in style."

Floodlights circled the room then spotlighted the band as they took center stage. Maria liked the Tex-Mex sound of Leonardo Flacco, the combination of the accordion and the deep bass always sent a dance message to her feet. She and her sister swayed to the music. Maria's toes started tapping.

She scanned the room until her gaze stopped at a familiar face. "Alma, I think I know that gringo. I've seen those steel-gray eyes before. See the two men sitting over there? Right over there, to the right? He's the one with the curly brown hair, with the sport jacket." She took another sip of coffee and glanced back at him. He turned and their eyes met for a second. Quickly, she averted her gaze. "I wonder why he's not dancing," she mused.

Maria had a reputation as an excellent dancer. For the next half hour she was on the floor constantly, but none of her partners seemed to interest her. Several times her eyes met Mike's. She sat down again as the band took a break. "I wonder why he doesn't dance!"

"Well, why don't you ask him?"

"Oh no. I just couldn't." Being coy was not one of Maria's characteristics.

"I never knew you to be shy."

Mike looked their way again.

"I think he really wants to dance with you, but is just too shy. After all, if you ask him there are only two things that can happen. He will dance with you, or he won't. Just go ask him as soon as the band comes back."

"Only if they play 'The Twelfth of Never.'"

"Oh great! What are the chances of that? We're in Juarez, you know."

"That's exactly what I mean. Chances are one in a million. But it is my favorite."

"Here they come. They're warming up. Get ready, Maria. I think I hear a very familiar tune."

Maria, per usual, didn't need much encouragement. "Is my lipstick okay? My hair?"

"You couldn't look more beautiful in that blue. Now go!"

Maria tucked her blouse into her skirt, pushed her chair back, and slowly started toward Mike's table.

———

Mike reached into his breast pocket for the contract from DelGado & DelGado, the contractors who won the bid for building St. Ignatius' new school. He trusted José DelGado, general manager, implicitly: he was the first parishioner he met as well as an upstanding member of the community and a very good friend. However, understanding the technical language of a contract and building a school were new territories for Mike and he needed his brother's legal advice. Tom suggested they meet at the Lucerna since he was already there on business. As Mike unfolded the contract and handed it to Tom, Maria interrupted. Surprised at the staccato beat of her heart, she said in her melodic Spanish tongue, "Excuse me, I don't mean to be rude, do you remember me?"

Mike rose and in fluent Spanish replied, "I thought I recognized you." He looked at the brown curls, the chestnut eyes. The conversation continued in Spanish. Tom looked from one to the other mystified.

"I stole your seat last week at the Beethoven concert."

"Ah yes, it all comes back. Well, that concert was just as exceptional in the balcony as it would have been in Row D. Ormandy is a real magician." He noticed a faint blush spread across her cheeks.

"I agree, but isn't Leonardo Flacco excellent as well? He makes my feet move and my hips sway and my head nod."

Tom continued to observe the exchange, trying to gauge their connection as well as the conversation.

"Please, have a seat." Mike pulled out a chair and motioned for her to sit down. "Let me introduce..." he began.

"No, no. I just came over to...that is, my sister dared me to...I mean would you like to dance?" *There*, she thought, I've *done it*.

"I... well... I..." he noticed the sparkle disappear from her eyes. *What harm can come from one dance*, he thought. "Of course," he said. Then noticing the startled look on Tom's face, he began to introduce Maria. "Tom, this is...this is..."

"Maria, me llamo Maria," she stammered and offered her hand to Tom. "Hola!"

Mike pushed the chair back under the table. "Well then, Maria, can I have this dance?"

"I'd be delighted." She felt his hand encircle her waist. His fingers lightly touched hers as they glided onto the dance floor. The butterflies inside surprised her.

They swirled through the other couples like Fred Astaire and Ginger Rogers. As they floated through the crowd, Maria hoped the music would bind them together until "The Twelfth of Never."

As the song wound down and Mike pulled away, Maria grabbed his hand and propelled him to her table where Alma waited, unable to hide her approval. Maria had not been very successful in past relationships, and Alma hoped to see her meet someone who treated her with respect.

"Mike, meet my sister Alma. She's to blame for sending me over to invite you to dance."

Mike noticed the similarity in their eyes. As much as he would have liked to join the sisters, he knew he couldn't. He shook hands and started to walk away, but Maria continued the conversation.

"I'm staying here in Juarez with Alma for a bit until I get settled in my job and find my own apartment. She brought me to the hotel tonight to celebrate my birthday. Can you stay and chat a while?"

As quickly as he could without being rude, he excused himself and returned to Tom and the contract. Tom put his martini down and folded the contract. Before Mike even had a chance to sit down, Tom began to grill him. "Mike, I haven't seen you dance for quite a while. What was that all about?"

"It's like riding a bike: once you learn to dance, it's rather easy to get back into it," Mike wiped the sweat from his forehead.

"That's not exactly what I mean. I am referring to your partner. She is rather attractive and seems smitten with you. I caught her looking at you a couple of times."

"Oh she was sitting in my seat at the symphony a couple of weeks ago. It was completely innocent. There is nothing to it," he reached for his cerveza.

"But there could be parishioners here," Tom warned him. "They might misinterpret what they saw. Can you imagine the gossip that would sweep through the parish? You really should wear your Roman collar when you go out."

"Tom, you know me better than that. There's nothing to worry about. Nothing could be more important to me than my priesthood. I wouldn't jeopardize it for anything. God, and my music of course, satisfy me completely. And why in the world would any of the parishioners come over to Juarez anyway? Besides that collar is really itchy. Can we return to the contract? I really need your understanding of legalese."

"Sure." Reluctantly, Tom picked up the papers. "It seems to be pretty straight forward. There's just one section that needs a bit of clarification. On page five, 'Change Orders' and 'Inspection Issues' should be addressed. Suppose I take the contract with me and send you the changes tomorrow." He folded the contract again and stuffed it in the manila envelope.

"That would be helpful. I appreciate it."

"Mike, she's looking this way again." Tom put his hand on Mike's arm.

"I'm a little tired of this. If it will make you happy, let's just leave."

"Okay, I really think that's a good idea. You didn't tell her your name, did you?" Tom motioned to the waiter for a check.

"For Pete's sake, Tom. Get off my back, will you?"

Tom reached for his wallet and handed the waiter a a couple of Tens. "Thanks. Keep the change," he said.

The only way to the exit was past Maria's table by the sliding glass door. As the brothers approached the table, Maria caught Mike's eye. "Thanks for the dance, Mike." He paused momentarily.

"Will I see you again?" she asked, looking up at him wistfully.

"I'm not really sure. But I did enjoy the dance." He could feel Tom's frustration, not only for the Spanish he couldn't understand, but also for the impropriety of the situation, so he started for the door. Maria gently put her hand on his arm to restrain him.

Mike couldn't help noticing Maria's eyes, round and brown as a sunflower center. "Oh," Mike finally muttered as an afterthought. "Alma, this is my brother Tom."

"Hi." Tom nodded in Alma's direction as he took Mike's elbow and steered him toward the sliding glass door.

"Adios, amigos." Mike followed Tom outside, still thinking of Maria's eyes. It was a two-block walk to the car, past the grand entrance to the hotel, several storefronts, a taco place, and a closed dress shop. A few people hurried along the otherwise empty sidewalks. Traffic was light. The brothers were quiet: Mike still visualizing Maria, and Tom anxious to get Mike home. Even though he knew he shouldn't, Mike recalled the dance, the closeness of Maria, the light in her eyes and the scent of her lavender perfume. It had been a long time since he danced with a woman.

"I'll drive," exclaimed Tom as he reached for the door of his sleek black Lincoln Capri.

The brothers didn't say another word as Tom drove back to El Paso over the bridge, almost empty this time of night. Although Juarez was only about 20 minutes from El Paso and the U.S., it seemed a continent away. It wasn't just the foreign tongue; it was a completely different culture. Barefoot, brown-eyed, brown-skinned children playing in the dust, cowboy boots and sombreros dotting the sidewalks, shops selling brightly colored blankets, serapes, and pottery—it was a magical place, a make-believe place. Tom slowed as he approached customs, wound the window down, and showed the officer his license. In minutes he was waved through crossing to the USA and reality. The Lincoln soon stopped at the rectory. Tom made a left into the driveway, waited as Mike opened the door and slid out.

"Thanks, Tom. I really needed that night out."

"So long." Tom nodded. "See you Sunday." He turned the wheel and eased out into the street toward home.

Mike opened the side door of the rectory, entered the kitchen, ignored the pile of dirty dishes in the sink, looked in the fridge for a Coke, popped it open, then walked over to the baby grand in the living room and sat down. He combed his fingers through his hair, took a swig of Coke, set it on the console, rubbed his hands together, and started the scales, one after the other: the majors, the minors, then the arpeggios. He paused. Instead of the Bach fugue open on the piano, he closed his eyes and started "The Twelfth of Never." He hummed the notes and started to sway. All of a sudden he stopped in mid-phrase, rubbed his eyes, left the piano, and flicked on the TV.

As he sank into his recliner, he glanced over at the plaque on the wall above the TV that listed his citations from the Air Force: the Presidential Unit Citation, the Asiatic Pacific Campaign Medal with three Bronze Service Stars, the Philippine Liberation Medal with one Bronze Service Star, a World War II Victory Medal, a Service Lapel Button, an American Campaign Medal, and a National Defense Service Medal. It seemed like a whole lifetime ago instead of a few years. *Life was so simple then,* he thought, Maria's perfume still lingering on his shirt. He willed her eyes away from his thoughts and concentrated on The Late Night Show. Jerry Lester always amused him. In a minute or two he was laughing out loud at the monologue.

Finally, he turned off the TV and picked up his breviary on the side table, *Oh God,* he thought, *I have been blessed all my life in your service. With your help I was able to save many men and talk them through their demons in both the Philippines and Germany. I can remember countless parishioners from Deming, where I first served as a rector to the present who put their trust and faith in me. I have prayed with mothers and fathers who have lost a child, with women who have been abused by their husbands, with husbands whose wives have had affairs, with children whose fathers have abandoned them. I have grieved with those who have lost a parent, a spouse, a friend. I have fed the hungry, given a helping hand to the poor. With your blessing, I have increased the revenue of the parish and am building a school. I have indeed been blessed. But, God, I do feel somewhat inadequate when it comes to helping husbands and wives solve their problems, especially sexual problems. It seems to me that if I were married, as several of the early popes were, I would be a better priest.* He opened the breviary to Friday, March 18, and bowing his head began reciting the psalm.

———

Although Mike wouldn't admit it to himself, he looked forward to his next concert, not only to hear Mozart conducted by Rafael Frubeck de Burgos, but also in case he would see Maria again. For some reason, he couldn't eradicate her from his memory. As he tucked his ticket in his breast pocket, he thought about the woman who sat in his seat at the Beethoven concert, her chestnut curls and laughing eyes.

And see her, he did. In fact, he almost collided with her as he exited the concert hall. Maria insisted that they stop for coffee so she could properly repay him for allowing her to experience Beethoven in his orchestra seat at the last concert. Worrying that he might be seen by a parishioner here in El Paso, he promised, instead, to meet her in Juarez.

———

As time slipped by, Mike and Maria became friends, good friends. He always insisted they meet in Juarez, to separate his friendship with Maria from his relationship with his church and parishioners.

Mike was taking no chances. After he buttoned his gold and royal-blue flowered Hawaiian shirt and smoothed back his hair, he took one last glance in the mirror, then, whistling, he hopped into his old sedan. Even though his mind told him not to, his heart gave him the go-ahead. He left the rectory and headed toward Juarez and Maria, not entirely guilt-free. Some day, he thought, he would tell Maria he was a priest, but definitely not today.

The last time he met her, they went to see *David and Bathsheba*, Maria's choice. The film mesmerized both of them, and afterward when they stopped for a cup of coffee, Mike was more amazed at Maria's knowledge of the Bible than he was at the electricity that ignited his heart when his hand touched hers accidentally as he reached for his sweet Mexican coffee. They discussed the accuracy of the film in its portrayal of the biblical story, about the acting prowess of Gregory Peck and Susan Hayward, about the love story, and about the power of film to influence people.

"Now, Mike, perhaps the film does dramatize the Old Testament story, but imagine how many people who see the film then might open the Bible to read other stories."

Mike liked the way Maria looked when she concentrated, the way she tilted her head to the side and bit her lip. He couldn't stop gazing into her hazel eyes. They were operating on a different frequency than her words, and he had no difficulty reading them.

"A possibility, of course, but a pretty slim one." He wanted to prolong the night. "How about another coffee?" Maria nodded. He motioned for two more to the waitress.

Maria sipped the residue from the rough clay mug, then placed it on the table for a refill. "How do you think it compares to *Quo Vadis*? I read that it was nominated for a few Academy Awards."

"Peter Ustinov was certainly outstanding as Caesar. Maybe he'll win an award, but the film itself seems to use religion to increase the emotional appeal. I think the story of Peter is used arbitrarily as a foil to set off the love story of Marcus and Lygia."

Maria was thrilled to meet a man as interested in religion as he was the movies. If, however, she was honest with herself, she was probably more attracted to his eyes, his steel-gray eyes, and the curly brown hair, that gentle laugh which punctuated every other sentence, and the ease with which Spanish rolled over his gringo tongue. She had waited a long time to find someone like him. "Where do you live, Mike?"

The perfectly innocent question caught Mike completely off guard. He knew he couldn't tell her he lived at St. Ignatius rectory. He picked up his mug and sipped the warm sweet liquid slowly while his mind raced through numerous possible answers and consequences.

"Mike," she prompted.

"With my brother. I live with my brother, Tom. He was with me when we met a couple of weeks ago at the Lucerna."

"Oh, yes. I remember him. Tall and fair with blue eyes, not the same blue-gray as yours, a bit lighter, more of a robin's egg blue. But, do you live here in Juarez?"

"No, Tom has a home in El Paso. It's a small home, but comfortable enough for the two of us." This was the first of many misleading facts Mike would tell Maria. He was surprised at how glibly the lie rolled off his tongue.

When he was with Maria, Mike wasn't a priest. He was just a man, a man interested in a woman who was sitting across from him. Neither watched the clock, nor noticed time passing. Finally though, their mugs empty, their minds full, Mike gave the waitress diez billete de dólar, and the couple walked to the door.

As Mike was about to push the door open, he recognized a stocky man across the street, José DelGado, the general manager of the construction crew building his school. Jose was more than a hired worker; he was a friend. Mike had been a dinner guest at his house several times, especially after a round of golf or before a game of poker. His wife Ana's chicken quesadillas were the best he had ever tasted. Often Mike had a quick game of catch with the DelGado's son after dinner or helped their daughter Pilar wash the dishes.

Mike knew instinctively that it would be a mistake to be seen. Thinking quickly, he told Maria he needed the daily paper and immediately made a U-turn back to the coffee house. With his back to the window, he hid his face in the folds of the newspaper and perused *El Diario, del Norte* and the *Guadalajara Reporter* for as long as he thought reasonable. Maria, very impressed with his interest in Hispanic affairs, felt he was really simpatico to her culture. Finally, he selected *El Diario*, paid for it, and for the second time, they exited the coffee shop.

"Maria, I apologize for my behavior back there in the coffee shop. You must think it a bit strange." He looked about to make sure no one was within earshot, moved a bit closer, then explained. "You do remember when I told you about my covert missions with the military, don't you?" Maria's curls bounced as she shook her head. "Well I thought I noticed a military operative across the street just as we were leaving the coffee shop, and I couldn't take the chance of being discovered." He reached for her hand and studied her face, relieved that she seemed satisfied with his explanation. Even though he assured himself there was nothing wrong with meeting Maria, he knew instinctively that he shouldn't put himself in a place where he and Maria could be seen together. Despite the fact that he believed their relationship was completely innocent, Mike resolved not to make the same mistake again.

———

A couple of weeks later, early on a Saturday morning, Mike rolled out of bed, dressed, and hopped in the car eager to begin the day, for he was spending it with Maria. This time their destination was Chihuahua, a couple hours away from Juarez, from El Paso, and, most importantly, away from St. Ignatius—yet close enough that he could make the round-trip in a day and be back in time to say Mass the next day.

As soon as he made the left-hand turn, he saw Maria waiting for him behind the cyclone fence surrounding her sister's tiny stucco cottage. The neighborhood was a modest one, homes spaced one after the other lined up in a row. She waved, fumbled with the gate, and dashed out to meet him. Before he could open his car door, she was sitting beside him.

"Hi, Mike, I'm crazy to find out where we're going this afternoon." The breeze felt wonderful; the air smelled sweet. "I can hardly stand the suspense. Where are we going?" She leaned her head back, turning her face to the warming May sun.

"It's a surprise, one I really think you'll enjoy." Mike pulled away from the curb.

"Don't tease me. Just tell me." She flashed her eyelashes, looked coyly over at him.

"But it won't be a surprise anymore if I tell you."

"Mike, come on now."

"Okay! We're on our way to the Fiesta de Santa Rita in Chihuahua." He stepped on the gas as they entered the highway, happy Maria was sitting beside him, forgetting about his parishioners, forgetting about his church.

"Oh, Mike, I loved that fiesta. When I was just a little girl, around ten, I walked in the procession, not once, not twice, actually many times. I remember holding the colorful red ribbons flowing from the banner depicting a life-sized portrait of the saint. I wore a white dress, a white veil, and white shoes. I can remember walking through the park, palm trees lining the path. My eyes closed tight, my lips praying to Saint Rita."

"The procession must have made a big impression on you? What else do you remember about it?"

"I remember the bishop in his rose-colored robes and miter carrying the relic encased in a gold monstrance. I can still hear the adulations and petitions of the faithful as we passed by. I just wish I still believed with such intensity and innocence. It's part of my past I treasure."

Maria grew silent for a while, lost in her thoughts, as they rolled by the cactus and the barren fields. "But, Mike, Chihuahua is not close by, it's quite a distance from here, isn't it?"

"It's just a few hours. I thought we could stop along the way and have a picnic lunch. I'll have you back in Juarez before dark."

"You are so organized. You do prepare for everything, don't you?"

The picnic, the palms, the procession, the pageantry—the excursion was perfect and as predicted they returned to Juarez before dinner.

———

Church finally emptied after the last Mass. Mike always enjoyed greeting his parishioners. He shook their hands, patted them on the shoulder, and asked about their families. After everyone left, he returned to the church. The parish was thriving; the congregation was poor but also loyal, giving, and faithful. He walked slowly up the center aisle, conscious of the presence of God all around him, his feet echoing through the quiet. The sun shone through the stained-glass windows bleeding red, blue, yellow, and green hues over the pews and marble floor. Mike was alone in the sacred sanctuary, unaware of the rainbow around him. Kneeling at the altar, he blessed himself.

He looked up at the carved pine crucifix, stretched out his arms. "God," his voice barely audible. "I have a problem, a big problem. I'm locked between two lives, whirling between reality and insanity, my eyes turning inward in deep confusion. Somehow I have gotten involved with a wonderful woman, but then you probably know that. You also must know how much I love you. That I dedicated my whole life to your service. That I accomplished much in your name. You also know I will be faithful to you forever. I will never forsake the vows I took almost twenty years ago. Yet there is something I just don't understand! Why did you introduce Maria into my life? I feel deep within my soul that you led me to her as part of your divine plan, but I am confused. What do you want me to do with this woman?" He turned his head toward heaven, his voice now mute, his mind racing.

"Is this the path you have planned for me? A double life? One foot in the sacredness of the sanctuary, the other in the heart of the family. She is a humble, holy woman, yet the emotion I feel for her is not the same as the love I have for you. I could never leave your service. I pray you will show me the way to resist this temptation and rededicate my heart and soul to you." He looked down, bowed his head, his shoulders heaving in sobs.

He remained for a half hour in the hushed stillness, then slowly stood and walked from the apse to the sacristy. Carefully, he lifted the bright green chasuble embroidered by the women of the Altar Society. He ran his fingers over the gold figures along the edges then slipped it over his head. Opening the closet, he placed it on a hanger, fussing with it until it hung in perfect folds. Removing the stole, he kissed the embroidered cross in the center and draped it over the rod. He untied the cincture and took off the white cotton alb, hung it next to the chasuble; and lastly he folded the amice and carefully placed it on the shelf. Before he closed the door, he surveyed the closet: the bright purple chasuble for Lent, the pale rose reserved for Easter, and his favorite, the pure white emblazoned only with a gold cross in the center. These vestments were a part of his life for a long time. When he donned them, he felt the spirit permeate his being: he became the representative of Christ himself. He knew it was impossible to surrender them, impossible to relinquish his role as the leader of his flock. He vowed to explain his religious life to Maria, for he owed her that much.

He shut the closet, looked around making sure everything was in order, then left by the side door and walked across the street through the white adobe fence, up the path into the bustle of his parishioners counting the collection in the rectory kitchen. Tom was at the stove scrambling eggs and cooking bacon, the coffee already brewed. The camaraderie was evident—laughter and chatter mingled with breakfast smells. Father Mike smiled, raised his hand in salute.

"Father, it was a good collection today, one of the best," called out Emanuel, the head usher.

"I liked your sermon today; it seemed to touch me right here." Eduardo said and patted his heart.

"Do you have more wrappers? There are a lot of quarters today, in addition to all the bills and the checks," yelled Emanuel.

"The second collection for the Mexican missions is already counted and placed in the envelope on the buffet. It totals $2,255. Not too bad!" Eduardo whistled.

"That will certainly buy a few shoes for those poor Mexican children who live in poverty in the mountains," added Susan, parish secretary.

"Wonderful! Wonderful!" Father Mike beamed.

Tom was making the rounds with the coffee pot when he noticed Father Mike's furrowed brow, the distant look in his eyes. He walked over, reached for his arm, "Are you okay, Mike? What took you so long after Mass? Did someone corner you with a problem? You seem concerned about something."

"Oh no, no," he mumbled. "Thanks. I guess I was just thinking of Mom. It hasn't been a year since she passed. I miss talking to her. She always gave me good advice." *Heaven forgive me*, he thought, and quickly changed his mood. "I'm hungry as a bear now though. Hey, how about some bacon and eggs over here."

––––––

The time never seemed right. Weeks passed and Mike still wrestled with his double life. It wasn't that he didn't want to tell Maria he was a priest. The opportunity just never presented itself. Every time he vowed to tell her, the words just slipped away. He came close the day they went to the bullfights.

"Mike, if you never take me to another bullfight again, I won't be disappointed." Maria reached for Mike's hand as they made their way down the stands among the 40,000 others exiting the Plaza Mexico in Ciudad de los Deportes, Mexico City.

"But the bullfight is just like a ballet. Carlos Arruza is without a doubt a world-renowned matador. And this, the Corrida de Aniversario, rivals anything Spain has to offer." Mike was passionate about the bulls. Maria just looked at him, eyebrows raised as she jumped down the last riser, put her arm in the crook of his elbow.

"As soon as I hear the drum roll, and the dance between man and animal on the sand begins, I am entranced. Did you see the way Carlos manipulated the cape to excite the bull? He swirled around and sidestepped the enraged animal with merely seconds to spare." Mike guided her through the throngs of people toward the exit.

"As soon as I hear the drum roll," Maria said, "I close my eyes so I won't see the poor bull suffer—or the matador gored to death. I do like the bullfight music though: it's so dramatic."

Now it was his turn to raise his brows and look down at her.

"Michael, let's walk through the park; it's such a gorgeous afternoon."

Mike wondered what was bothering her other than the bullfight. She only used the formal "Michael" when she had something serious on her mind. Continuing with the crowd, they crossed the street and walked toward the park. He and Maria dodged toddlers chasing each other, dogs chasing after sticks and balls, and teens chasing after their heartthrobs. The sun, filtered by the leaves, formed a grid, a yellow brick road, which led through the path to a vacant bench right next to a brilliant fuchsia bougainvillea. "Let's sit here a while and let the traffic thin out."

Mike leaned back, inhaling the bougainvillea. He watched the Mexicans taking a short cut through the park, jabbering about the matador and his finesse. He looked at the toddlers again, the babies in their strollers.

"Aren't they sweet? Look at that little curly haired child petting the puppy," Maria sighed. "The one losing her sun suit, her face smeared with dirt."

In that instant it pained Mike to know that he would never have a child, that as long as he was a priest, he could not marry Maria nor father her children. He must tell her he was a priest, and tell her now before their relationship progressed any further. He watched Maria watch the child, now shrieking with delight as the puppy licked her cheeks. "Oh! Just look at her. Isn't she precious?" She pointed to the child and looked over at Mike.

"Maria, I have something I have to tell you, and I don't know how to say it."

"You can tell me anything, anything at all. She said still watching the child.

"Well I've been meaning to tell you…."

"Yes…"

Off to the right, Maria noticed a cluster of people gathering. She tried to concentrate on Mike, but the crowd won out. "Mike, what's going on? Look, all of those people by the huge pine tree. Come on, let's go see what's happening." She jumped up and grabbed Mike's hand. He had no choice but to follow. They soon become part of a crowd staring upwards. There on the bough of the old gnarled pine was a parrot, a green parrot with a red head, a hooked orange beak, and bright yellow tail feathers. He preened, groomed himself, looked down at the crowd, and screeched, "Hola, muchachos, hola!"

"How silly," she said and turned her big brown eyes up to meet Mike's. He knew the moment was gone. Maybe another time.

"Let's go," he said, "I think the traffic has thinned out enough."

Commitment

Mike's relationship with Maria escalated rapidly. It became second nature to invent reasons to drive across the bridge to Juarez. Before long he realized he couldn't live without her, nor could he live without his church. As time passed, he became adept at keeping his two worlds separated. Even though Maria thought he had secrets he wouldn't reveal, she never suspected the truth.

She was the happiest woman in Juarez, in Mexico, in the whole world, when they started to plan a life together, a wedding. At first, she wanted a big party with a Tex-Mex band and lots of tamales and tortillas and a huge piñata, but Mike just wanted something simple. He said he didn't want to be distracted by anyone or anything else but his bride. He wanted their wedding day to be all about the two of them. He was so convincing, Maria didn't even resist when he took complete charge. He made all the arrangements, booked a suite at the Lucerna Hotel, contacted a judge to perform the ceremony— even reserved dinner afterward in the hotel restaurant.

———

"I can remember that night so clearly," Maria said to her sister, "the night I first met Michael, our first dance, 'The Twelfth of Never.' You were there, remember Alma? It was a Friday night and we were here in this exact hotel, down in the restaurant. He seemed so shy, so gentle. I remember how my heart beat a little faster as I looked up into those silvery gray eyes. Even though we only danced once, I just knew I would hear from him again. I could tell he was mine." She looked at her sister and smiled, then leaned her head back against the red satin mahogany armchair and closed her eyes reliving the dance. She dreamily got out of the chair and began to waltz, circling round and round. "Do you remember?"

"Sure, I remember, Maria. I can still see the two of you, eyes locked, twirling around in a bubble, oblivious of everyone else around you. It was as if there was no one else on the dance floor."

Maria opened her eyes, walked to the closet, and reached in for her dress. Holding it up, she gently shook out the wrinkles then slipped the silk dress over her shoulders, the gold accenting the brown of her eyes. She fussed with it, straightened the neck, pulled up the zipper, and adjusted the shoulders. She stood before the full-length mirror, twisted around to see the back. "Do you like it, Alma?"

"It's perfect! The slim sheath silhouette really accentuates your slender figure."

"It's the new waltz length."

"You look like you belong in one of those gringo magazines."

Satisfied with the dress, Maria rummaged in her suitcase, open on the bed, for her earrings and necklace. With the jewelry in her hand, she sat in front of the mahogany vanity, unused to such luxurious surroundings. Holding up some turquoise beads, she checked the effect. "Alma, will you please fasten these? Actually, they're mother's—something old, you know. I borrowed them from her this morning."

"Sure, let me help you. There now—what about earrings?" Maria picked up the silver posts with the dangling turquoise teardrops. She slid the posts into her ear and attached the backing. She shook her head watching her reflection, happy with the way they dangled. She turned to face her sister.

Alma stepped back to get the full effect of the outfit. "Why you look even more gorgeous today than you did that night six months ago. Here, let me brush your hair. Are you going to wear it down or would you like me to pin it up for you?"

"Oh, pin it up please. I want to look special. And maybe pull out a few loose curls. I love the way you do that." Maria spontaneously hugged her sister. "I'm so happy you are with me today. Isn't this room gorgeous, Alma? I just love the velvet drapes and the matching blue and gold bedspreads, and the way my toes sink into the carpet."

"It couldn't be more perfect!"

"And I'm truly happy we're having a simple wedding—no crowds, no bands, no dancing, no piñata—I'm glad it's just us."

"What about his family?"

"Unfortunately," she grimaced. "They can't come. He said his mom was too frail to make the trip and it's impossible for Fran with the two boys."

"That's too bad."

"Si, I really would like to meet them. Someday soon, I hope."

"Well, how about his brother? He's not in Ireland like the rest of them. He was at the hotel the night you two danced, remember?"

"No. Mike said his brother had to go to Dublin to take care of his mother."

"You mean only the two of us and mother will be here?"

"And the judge, of course."

Alma stepped back, surveyed her work on Maria's upsweep, smoothed a stray hair into place. "Maria, we don't have time for all this idle chit-chat. Look at your watch. You don't want to be late today. Don't we have to be downstairs at three o'clock for the ceremony?"

"Yes! But—Oh, Alma—this day couldn't be mas perfecto! She examined her reflection in the gilt-edged mirror turning her face to one side and then the other. "I am just so happy. Alma, we are going to have the most wonderful marriage in the whole world."

"Not if you don't get downstairs in time to say, 'I do.'"

"I guess I'm ready. Do I look okay? She stood and pirouetted. Happy with what the mirror showed her, she turned her attention to her shoes. "Where did I put my pumps?" Puzzled, she looked on the floor, on the bed. "Oh here they are, still in my suitcase." Maria sat on the satin comforter and slipped on her "dyed to match" stilettos. I hope Mamá is downstairs. I told her to be here about 2:45. Do you think we should call the lobby to make sure? Oh no—let's just go. I'm ready." The sisters picked up their purses and left the room together.

———

"Querido mio, these are the best breakfast burritos I've ever tasted. The cheese is spicy, the eggs are creamy, and the tortilla is soft and warm. You are spoiling me." Maria scooped up another forkful.

"Anything for my beautiful bride." Mike leaned over the tiled table, curled his hand around hers and guided her fork into his mouth. His hand lingered, his lips touched her fingers. He studied her eyes. "What shall we do today? I want to spend all 24 hours with you."

"Absolutely no bullfights." She smiled remembering their last visit to the arena.

"Okay, I promise." Mike picked up the paper and rifled through the pages until he found the weather report. "Sunshine all day long. How about a walk in the park?"

"Perfect! I'll pack a picnic lunch. And I'll bring Octavio Paz and read some of his poetry to you. I think you'll like 'Palpar' especially, it's one of my favorites."

"Only if I can lay my head in your lap and look up at your eyes and the sky."

"Si, Si."

"Sounds like the way I want to spend every day of the rest of my life. But of course that's not possible."

"Why not? What do you mean?"

"Well, I wasn't going to mention this until later in the week."

"Mention what?"

"I received my orders yesterday. I have to report to duty on Thursday." He couldn't look her in the eye. He was afraid she would sense the lie.

"But, Michael, we just got married. You can't leave so soon. I mean, who will make my breakfast in the morning?"

"Holy cow! Is that all you're worried about? That's not a big deal. I'll show you how I make my special gringo burritos tomorrow so you can have them every single morning I'm gone." He wondered how life got so skewed and took a deep breath thinking the worst was over.

"Oh, I'm not really worried about the eggs. I'm afraid for you. Afraid you'll get hurt." Her eyes watered.

"Now, Maria, I already explained that I'm in Intelligence. I'm not in combat. I won't be near any fighting, any violence. I'll be behind a desk interviewing people, researching information in the library, writing reports. I have to support you now that you are my wife." He willed her to believe him, to trust him. He reached over and ruffled her curls.

"Promise me you'll be safe." She dried her tears.

"Por mi vida."

"Where is your uniform? I want to wash it and press it so you'll be the hand-somest Air Force Intelligence officer in the world."

"That sounds better. I'll go get it for you. Here, look at this article in *El Diario*. Looks as though there's a concert in the park this afternoon." Mike pushed his chair back and handed the paper to Maria, relieved that his story worked this time, but troubled that it was too easy to create such an elaborate charade to maintain their relationship. Returning with his khaki pants, he tossed them on the ironing board.

"Michael, look at this disgusting story right next to the one about the concert. The bishop defrocked a priest after discovering he secretly married his housekeeper and had a family. The article interviews Juan Garcias, the priest. How could any man of God do something like that? Standing in the pulpit Sunday after Sunday, preaching to his congregation while he himself lived a lie. Can you believe that! He broke his vow of celibacy. Thank heavens he was discovered. How two-faced! Why he is the devil himself, pure evil!"

Mike's heart beat a worried tattoo. He looked over her shoulder. "I guess you're right, Maria, that is upsetting behavior; however, in all fairness to Father Garcias, priests don't take a vow of celibacy, they merely promise to live a celibate life."

"Michael!"

———

Thursday dawned too soon for Mike, but he dare not stay in Juarez any longer. The bishop had given him permission to do missionary work in Mexico, but he didn't want to raise any red flags.

Mike's steel-gray eyes were puffy. A tiny muscle twitched in his cheek. He measured coffee into the percolator, a tablespoon and a half for each cup, and turned the gas flame to high. He dreaded leaving so soon, but there was no other way. Because he hated this double life he was forced to live, he tossed and turned most of the night thinking of the pros and cons. More than anything in the world he wanted to introduce his parishioners to his wife, and his wife to his parishioners. He desperately wanted her to know him as a priest, but wondered how she would react to the truth. When he tried before to tell her, the moment slipped away before he could say a word. If he failed to reveal the truth to Maria today before he left, he knew he never would. He remembered her remarks about Father Garcias and was afraid she would label him as the "devil himself."

Maria, still in her nightgown, appeared in the kitchen yawning. "Mike, so there you are. I didn't feel you get out of bed. Why didn't you wake me up so I could give you a morning hug?" She wrapped her arms around him and kissed the wiry curls at the nape of his neck. "I love being your wife and waking up with you in the morning, sharing your coffee."

"I just wanted some silent time. I've got a lot on my mind. I need to figure a few things out."

"Querido mio, you do look dreadful. Do you feel okay? Your eyes are red and puffy. Did you sleep at all last night?"

"Hardly. I would dream of losing you, and then I would wake up and find you sleeping peacefully beside me. Then I remembered I had to leave you soon to go on that secret mission, and I couldn't get back to sleep."

"Don't worry about me, Mike. I'll be fine. Until you come back, I'll be waiting for you, thinking of you every second of the day."

"Maria, you know I love you more than anyone else in Juarez, in Mexico, in the world, in the entire planet."

"I know that, Michael. And I love you more than I ever thought it was possible to love another human being."

"Maria, there is something I have to tell you."

"You look so serious, you're scaring me."

"I've been searching for the right words."

"What is it, querido mio?"

Mike held her, buried his face in her hair. *I just can't do it*, he thought. *She'll never understand, never.* "I, I, I'm worried you won't be here when I return." He closed his eyes disappointed in himself. Disappointed he couldn't tell her. Couldn't tell her the truth. He knew he never would. He turned the burner off, poured a cup of coffee, and handed it to her.

———

Reluctantly, he opened his eyes, one at a time and searched for the source of so much unbearable noise. Abruptly, the sound stopped as he hit the buzzer. Mike patted the other side of the bed reaching for Maria. Finally he rolled over. No Maria. In a flash he realized he was in El Paso in the rectory, not with his wife in Juarez. *Mass,* he realized and immediately threw back the comforter, pushed his toes into his slippers, grabbed his robe, and prepared for Mass. Although he missed Maria, he was excited to see his parishioners and celebrate Mass with them.

He showered and shaved in record time. Hurriedly, he slipped the collar around his neck and buttoned the black cassock, comfortable again in its folds, and rushed out the door.

"Father Mike, welcome back," called Poncho from across the street. He waited for Mike to reach him, shook hands, and patted him on the shoulder.

"Good to be back! Happy to see one of my favorite ushers!" Mike flashed his characteristic smile. "How are Flora and the boys?"

"Pretty good. Flora's on new medication and her back has been pretty good."

"What about the surgery? Is that still imminent?"

"Maybe not. We're playing the 'wait and see' game."

"And Mark? Did he bring his grades up?"

"He did. Only one 'C' this time in history and not even one 'F.' We're pretty happy with his progress."

"Ah! That's good to hear." Mike pulled out his keys and opened the front doors of the church. "Let's talk more after Mass. I want to hear about the progress on the new school." He walked down the middle of the aisle, his footsteps resounding on the tile floor. Proudly, he scanned the building, the familiar Stations of the Cross, the arched windows pulling in the rays of the sun like a magnet, the altar, a simple wooden table directly in front of him, and finally the brick wall behind the altar. He thrilled in the presence of God, knelt down as he reached the altar. With his hands clasped, he bowed his head and poured out his heart to his God, all the guilt, shame, and confusion that became his life.

It was so easy to slip back into the routine of the parish. He missed saying Mass and rallying his parishioners around the plans for the new school. One of his regrets was that Maria and his future children would never know him as Father Mike. They would never know of the good he did here in El Paso. If all went as planned, the groundbreaking on the new school building was scheduled for Wednesday of next week. The bishop would certainly appreciate all his efforts to make St. Ignatius one of the leading parishes in the diocese.

———

As Mike walked over to the construction site, the racket from the hammering, the chain saws, and the radios escalated. "José," he yelled so he could be heard. "José, you've been working very hard." Mike grasped the hand of the general manager. "Good to see you. How are Ana and the kids?"

"They're great. Thanks for asking. Pilar is tops in her class, and her brother isn't far behind."

"Good to hear. It's just amazing to watch the school grow. Each time I return from Mexico, I see such great strides. I hate the way my missionary work pulls me away from the parish, but it is important too."

"Thank you, Father, the men have been working hard. They are happy to get their paychecks, but more importantly they care about doing a good job." José pulled a big red bandana from his overalls and wiped the sweat off his brow, streaking dust across his forehead. "Would you like to get a closer look, walk through the frame? We're almost ready for the cement crew."

"Sure, I want to talk to the men. Are any from the parish?"

"I tried to hire as many as I could after we had that last talk.

"Good, good! I like to help them as much as posssible. What about Manuel, were you able to use him?"

"Yeah, he's right over there, turned out to be one of my best workers."

"That's what I like to hear."

"By the way, Father, since we're talking about salaries, we have enough cash to meet the next payroll, but after that we will need another installment."

"Not a problem, José, I'll see that you get it."

"Thanks! I know I can count on you. Now for that walk-through. Hey, Manuel, get me a hardhat for the Father!"

Mike left the building site thrilled with the progress of the construction crew yet swimming in consternation. It wasn't just the heat of the sun causing his sweat. He knew the parish was reaching the end of the construction funds. St. Ignatius wasn't a rich parish, but the parishioners were devoted to raising money for the new school. The ladies held several bazaars, they scheduled bingo on a weekly basis and ran several taco-and-beer nights. The local banks and most of the businesses downtown had already made hefty donations. He just didn't know where else they could find money. Making a mental note to call his usher, Franco, he hurried the two blocks to the rectory.

Mike drummed on his desk waiting for Franco to pick up.

"Hola! How can I help you?"

"Hi, Franco. Mike, here. I just returned from the building site."

"Looks great, doesn't it, Father?"

"Absolutely. Everything is proceeding according to schedule. There's just one small problem I need some help with."

"Of course. What's the problem?"

"In one word: money."

"Yes, that is a problem, Father. I think the parish and the local community have emptied their pockets. I'm not sure where to turn next."

"Can you explain what happened? I thought we raised all the necessary funds to complete the project."

"You're right. We did. But some of the material was unavailable and we had to substitute a more expensive product. Also there were several delays due to bad weather and, in order to complete the facility on the target date, we had to hire more workers and create additional shifts."

"Okay. So now it's necessary to raise more funds. Maybe together we might be able to brainstorm further ideas." Mike picked up his pen and began to doodle on his desk blotter.

"Well, there is one idea I had, but I didn't think you would give your approval."

"What is it? I don't want you to rob any banks." He immediately stopped doodling and listened carefully.

"No, no, nothing like that."

"Well, what then?"

Franco began hesitantly. "Well, I just don't think you will approve."

"Try me."

"You know, Father, there is a lot of money to be made at the bullfights."

"Franco, we couldn't."

"But, Father, surely the ends justify the means. It would only take a little bit of cash for an investment, and the rewards could be substantial. I've given it a lot of thought, and I just don't know where else to turn."

"Franco, you know the end never justifies the means. Have you contacted the bank again and explained why we have exceeded our initial financial projection?"

"I did, but perhaps if you…"

"Certainly. I'll give them a call right away."

He paused, then added. "If they can't help, perhaps the bullfights would be an answer. We can discuss it again." Father Mike hung up, scratched his head and frowned, deep in thought.

Troubles

The transition into a double life became routine. Mike moved from the parish to Maria effortlessly, that is, until the twins arrived. Coping with the boys while Mike was away, sometimes for a month or more, was tiring for Maria. She wanted Mike home more for moral support as well as for companionship.

After clearing the table, Maria stood at the sink absentmindedly washing the dishes, trying to decide how best to convince Mike that she needed him to take a more active role parenting the boys.

Whistling along with the radio, Mike walked into the kitchen to help Maria. "Ahh, Maria, it's so good to be home again." Mike couldn't be happier. He still tasted his favorite turkey mole, Beethoven's Ninth was on the radio, the twins were asleep.

"I wish you could be home more often, Michael."

Uh-oh, what's wrong now? he wondered. He picked up the turkey platter, grabbed a dishtowel, and began to dry.

When he didn't respond, Maria continued. "Michael, have you ever thought of leaving the military and getting a job in Mexico? A job where you would come home every night. It is very hard when you are away one or two months at a time, especially when I'm pregnant. The twins are out of sorts because you're not here. I no sooner get one to sleep when the other wakes up. I change one and then the other starts to cry."

"Oh, I'm sorry. I've been so thoughtless. Why don't we hire a babysitter to help you out?"

"A babysitter is not what the twins want. They want you. They want you to sing to them, to throw them up in the air and wrestle with them, to take them for walks in the park. They miss you; they don't care about any babysitter."

"Oh," Mike said. He placed the platter in the cupboard. He wrapped his arms around Maria, leaned his chin on her hair. "Suppose we invite Alma to come over the next time I'm deployed on a military mission. She would love to be here with you and the twins."

Maria turned around to face him, gazing into those steel-gray eyes that always mesmerized her. "Mike, don't you understand? I want you to wake up with me every morning, drink coffee with me at breakfast, go to market with me for tortillas, listen to Beethoven after dinner, go to bed with me every night."

Mike kissed her forehead, brushed a stray hair out of her eyes, wondered how to appease her. "Maria, I would love to be here with you all the time, but I'm not trained to do the kind of work that would allow me that lifestyle. I have been trained by the military to handle high-priority items with a great deal of expertise. The kind of expertise that is absolutely useless in civilian life." He paused, hoping he sounded convincing. "I've been thinking about buying a vacation place in Acapulco. Let's drive down tomorrow and see what's available. I think the boys would love to play on the beach.""Michael, you just don't understand, do you? A vacation house on the beach is not what the boys want. Not what I want. We want you here with us at home."

———

The little family did, however, acquire a vacation home in Acapulco as Maria continued to adjust to Mike's absences.

"That's mine," yelled Pancho. He grabbed the fire truck, snatched it out of Eduardo's hand. Pancho paused for a second, looked at his empty hand, then turned to Eduardo and started to howl.

"Now, now, boys. You have to share." Maria tried to keep her voice even. She counted to 10, breathed deeply, and tried again in a firmer voice. "Pancho, why not trade your trash truck for the fire truck?" She wished Mike were home. He knew how to coax the boys out of their arguments until they were laughing and rolling on the floor.

Maria, still at the table assessing the situation, gulped down her taco then sat on the floor with the boys. She pulled Pancho onto her lap and started to tickle him then reached for Eduardo. The boys soon forget about the trucks as they exploded in huge belly laughs.

As soon as they settled down, she dialed her sister. "Hi, Alma. I'm not having a very good day. Your nephews are little devils. Sometimes I feel like such a bad mother. It's different when Mike is here. He's so wonderful with the boys. I asked him to leave the military and get a civilian job, but he explained that it just wasn't an option." Maria ran her fingers through her hair, which really needed a shampoo and some styling.

"I didn't realize you were between jobs. Where are you going to work? At Spa Mayahuel?"

"Are you still doing manicures and pedicures?"

"With a citrus rub, that sounds delightful. I swear, you'll be opening your own shop one day. When do you start?"

"Not for a couple of weeks? I wonder if you would...." She paused trying to think of how to phrase a request for help that couldn't be denied.

"Could I use a little help? I desperately need help, a lot of help. Your nephews also need a lot of help. Alma I could use you 24 hours a day and I haven't even told you the worst part yet."

Maria took a deep breath. She continued, "Mike won't be back in time for the baby's birth. I don't know what I'm going to do." She wiped a tear away with the back of her hand and waited for Alma's response.

"You're going to move in with me? And will you really be with me when your niece or nephew decides to be born?"

"How can I ever thank you enough?" She started to cry and laugh at the same time. The boys looked over for a split second and then went back to their trucks.

"I'll see you tomorrow, early." *What a life saver*, she thought and hung up.

———

Mike opened the bedroom door cautiously, clutching a bouquet of pink roses. He knew Maria would be upset. The shade was drawn, the room in semi-darkness. He blinked to get used to the shadows. He saw Maria curled on the bed breathing deeply, a light blanket tossed over her. He took a step inside and almost tripped on the bassinet. As his eyes adjusted to the dark, the newborn came into focus. He reached down to touch her hand. Maria stirred. "Mike, is that you? Are you back?"

"She looks just like you, Maria: your dark eyes, the upturned nose. She's beautiful. I wish I could have been here to help you." Mike handed her the bouquet, kissed her on her forehead. "You look so tired. I really should have been here. Tell me all about it." He sat on the edge of the bed, reached for her hand.

Maria moved her hand away, moved her eyes away, more hurt than angry. "I wish you could have been here too. I needed you."

"Wasn't Alma here for you?"

"Was Alma here for me? She took me to the hospital. She took care of the twins. She did the wash. She cooked the meals. She brought me home from the hospital. She was much more than a sister. She was a saint. She should be canonized. But, Michael, Alma is not my husband! She is not the father of my children! She is my sister, maybe the best sister I could ever have, but she isn't you, and I needed you!"

"Well, I'm here now and I intend to make it up to you"

"Michael, you've sung that song before. Every time you leave, I'm afraid you won't be back."

"But I always do come back. I always will. I love you, Maria." Mike wanted to tell Maria about his double life, that he was a priest, that he had a parish, that he was building a school, but he was afraid that she wouldn't understand.

"Is that the baby stirring, Mike? Here take these flowers and put them somewhere, Rosa needs me, she wants to nurse."

"No, don't you move. I'll get the baby, change her, and bring her to you."

Guilt

As Mike predicted, Maria, Rosa, and the boys loved the beach. But it didn't matter whether he left from Juarez or Acapulco for El Paso. Each time he left his family, guilt swallowed him. This time he was not only returning to the parish to take care of his parishioner's needs, he was also returning because Fran and Joe were visiting. He was anxious to see them, for it had been a while between visits. Fran had had a miscarriage, and soon after gave birth to a daughter who was just too young for travel. He wished he had confided in her before, for he desperately needed someone to talk to. He resolved to have a heart-to heart.

There were a lot of things on his mind after dinner as he walked the Acapulco shoreline, his feet impressing shapes on the sugary sand as the silver crescent climbed higher and higher in the graying sky. Rosa's "Bona noce, Pappa," reverberated again and again in his mind. As he walked along, a stone jarred his toe. He stooped to pick it up and fingered its jagged edges, the surface ridges, and then looked more closely, recognizing the stone, bluestone mined from the Mount Franklin Quarry, the very stone he chose to build the school. He had watched the stones pile one upon the other until they became St. Ignatius, his parish school. Tomorrow night at dusk, as the silver crescent again rose in the eastern sky, he would be walking in a different place, a more sacred place. He would be walking down the knave of his church past the stained glass windows depicting stories from the Bible, eager to put on his vestments to begin another Mass at St. Ignatius.

His heart was stretched so thin in the tug-of-war between his church and his family he feared it would break as it cried for both. He feared revealing the secret of his priesthood to his wife, and the secret of his family to his sister. He wished he had confided in her before.

He examined the bluestone carefully, rubbed it between his fingers one more time, then raised his arm in the air, hurled it into the Gulf and watched the ripples eddy round and round until they disappeared. Then he turned back to their bungalow on the beach.

Even though he would see Fran and Joe, this time was no different from all the other times he left his small family. Each time, he put on his Captain's uniform, got into the T-bird for the trip north, guilt weighed heavily on him: guilt for lying to his bride, guilt for lying to his sister and brother, guilt for lying to his bishop. He felt encased in a bubble of Venetian glass teetering on the edge of a precipice, for he never knew when his dream existence would shatter. Each time he left his family, he feared he would never return. Each time he put on his Captain's uniform pretending to return to another Air Force mission, he risked everything. He knew that each time he kissed his wife and children goodbye, it could be the last. Parting was always an intense experience.

———

Back East, Fran was preparing for the trip. Against Joe's better judgment, she decided to take baby Carrie along. Fran couldn't part with her now that she was just beginning to walk and talk. Mikey and Joey however were in school and couldn't miss a month of instruction. She was thrilled Kay was able to take care of them. A lot of her friends didn't get along with their in-laws, but she and Kay were more like sisters, than sisters-in-law.

"Sitting on the dock of the bay, watching..." Fran hummed along with the radio. She held up the dress, checking the full-length mirror. *I really do like the effect of the red roses,* she thought. *This one is a must.* Packing for the trip to El Paso was always fun. Carefully, she folded the silk and placed it in the suitcase. Searching her closet again, she checked several outfits, and then pulled out a lime green skirt with a green and pink striped blouse. *Now for the golf outfits,* she thought. She moved to the bureau, opened the drawer with her summer clothes, and searched for the black and white checked blouse with the black skirt, as well as her latest, the tan outfit with the leather belt and deep pockets in the skirt for balls and tees. Folding everything meticulously, she placed them in her Samsonite.

Satisfied, she closed the suitcase then listened for Carrie's cooing, eager to get her dressed and ready for the trip.

Fran couldn't sit down. It had been a while between visits and she missed her brothers. She called Kay again and reviewed instructions for the boys.

Preoccupied the rest of the day, Fran showered, dressed, and waited for Carrie to wake up and Joe to call. She wore the new outfit just purchased at Wanamaker's yesterday, a bright multi-colored skirt with a belted three-quarter length rose jacket and a darling brimmed hat.

She paced the length of the house from the front door all the way back to the kitchen. After what seemed like days, the phone finally rang. "Hi, Joe...Yes, we're ready and waiting for you...A half hour? Perfect." Fran put the suitcases by the door and went to the nursery to wake Carrie.

The cross-country flight was no problem. After an hour of playing clap hands, dancing on Joe's lap, and laughing with the flight attendants, Carrie slept the rest of the journey.

Because Joe said money was no object this year, they planned to spend a couple of days in Mazatlan before they met the brothers in El Paso. Fran booked rooms at the fabulous Pueblo Bonita on the ocean. As they taxied up the coast to their destination, Fran peered out the window looking for the iron gates and the gray stone wall that she remembered from the brochure. "Oh, Joe, just look at this place. The grass is so lush and so well manicured and the weeping willows lining the lake— looks like a movie set! Then she noticed the blue palm and the unusual salmon-colored bougainvillea she loved so much. They entered the lobby; she walked around the huge floral arrangement. The red and pink roses with the baby's breath were the perfect accent for the ochre walls and the pale tiled floor.

From the moment her feet sank into the pale ginger carpet, Fran fell in love with the suite. She ran to the window, pulled back the pale, sand-colored drapes to reveal the Gulf of Mexico, the sparkling blue water and fine white sand. Baby Carrie was no problem. She snuggled into the crib with her favorite stuffed kitten and slowly closed her eyes.

Fran wanted to pull on her bathing suit immediately and take a swim in the tropical water; instead, she flopped on the queen-sized bed, gave her approval. Jumped up and hugged Joe. "I love it! I love it!" she exulted.

They unpacked and changed into more casual wear. Joe mixed Manhattans with a bit of cherry juice. Fran found some Mozart on the radio, and they lounged in the comfortable bamboo chairs watching the ebb and flow of the Gulf.

———

"Do you want cream or sugar for your tea, Fran?"

"You know I like lemon, Mike, I hope you have it. Is this the tea set you brought back from Germany?" She picked up the cup to get a closer look.

"Uh-huh. Do you like it?"

She ran her finger over the design. "It's no wonder Mom loved it. It's gorgeous, so delicate. I love the blue rims and all of the delicate scrolls and the yellow daisies. Good choice, brother." She glanced up and smiled. "It feels so good to see you again, Mike. It's been a while."

"I understand why you didn't want to risk the trip West last year, having a miscarriage and then being pregnant so soon after."

"It was a difficult time."

"How old is young Mikey now? About ten?"

"You're close. He just turned 11. You really should keep better track of your namesake." She loved to tease Mike, watch his face turn red, his eyes light up.

"Now you be careful, or I won't buy you any more lemons for your tea. Seriously, though, how are you coping with the baby after all this time?"

"Joe is a really good dad, so that makes it easier. Besides, I do love her so. Mike, I wish you could experience parenthood. I mean, babies are the very essence of life, genuine miracles. Life without babies is empty, barely worth living. It's like tea without lemon, pretzels without salt, the Earth without sun."

Mike stirred his tea. He felt this was the time to confide in his sister. He and Fran were always close growing up. In the past, she always helped him solve problems. He wanted to bring her into his other world, his secret life. He wanted to discuss the miracle of parenthood with her. He wanted her to know Rosa, to hold her, to talk to her and play with her, to love her as he loved Mikey, Joey, and now Carrie. Mike thought she would understand, especially since she was a new parent. He put down his spoon and looked at Fran. "I have so much to tell you."

"Mommy!" wailed Carrie as she tumbled into the kitchen. Mike was amazed at the resemblance of mother and daughter. She was a miniature Fran, but with blue eyes and red hair that fell in ringlets framing her chubby face. Except for the coloring, she was a replica of her mom.

"How about a cookie, Pumpkin? Will that dry up all those tears?"

"Say hi to your Uncle Mike, Carrie."

Mike handed her an animal cracker. "Just for you, Sweetie." As she reached for the cookie, the corners of her mouth turned up in a big taco of a smile. *They would be such good friends,* he thought. "Fran, there's something I want to tell you, but I just don't know where to start."

"The beginning is usually a good place."

"I'm not even really sure where it all began. I guess the easiest thing to do is just blurt it out. I have…"

"Is that a car I hear pulling up? Is Joe back already?" asked Fran, looking out the window. "It is Joe."

"You sit, Fran, I'll get the door."

"But you were just about to say—"

"It'll keep.

———

Mike shaded his eyes and followed the arc of the ball. "Holy Cow! Right down the middle!"

Fran leaned down, grabbed her tee, absentmindedly put it in her pocket then wiped her hand on her signature golf skirt. She glanced at Mike, pleased that he was impressed with her swing. "It's the club, my Macgregor VIP. It's all the rage. All the girls at the club have them. It was a gift from Joe last Christmas. It really helps. Do you want to try it on the next hole?"

"Now, Fran, do you really think a lady's club would improve Mike's swing? He needs a giant's club, not a lady's. Perhaps driving from the lady's tee would give him more distance." Tom teased his younger brother.

"Just watch me birdie this hole, Tom. If I played two or three times a week as you do, I'd make you look like a 12-year-old."

Fran slid into the cart next to Tom, took a sip of water from her thermos. "I just love these carts, Tom. We don't have them back East yet." She always felt she was in a time warp on the golf course. The minute she picked up her club, she started to relax. It was easy to forget about shopping and making dinner and changing the baby when she swung that club. And playing with her husband and brothers was perfection to her. She loved the gentle teasing, the friendly banter. It made her forget they lived about 2,000 miles apart. Nevertheless, she was worried about Mike. He just didn't seem right, like he was trying too hard. He just wasn't himself. She seized the time alone with Tom to question him about Mike. "You know, Tom, I've been worried about Mike."

"What do you mean?"

"Well, first, I noticed that he hardly ever wears his collar any more. He seems to dress more often in sport shirts and slacks."

"You're right. He does. But I don't see that as a problem. He's probably more comfortable that way."

"Maybe, but more importantly, he seems different somehow, almost like he's somewhere else. For example, yesterday, when we were alone in the kitchen, he seemed preoccupied, like he wasn't there. He said he wanted to tell me something, and then Carrie came toddling in, and he came to life. The mood was broken. Maybe he's just stressed with the new school and everything."

"Well, Fran, I didn't want to say anything because I didn't want to worry you. But since you noticed something too, I guess I might as well confide in you. I, too, think he's a bit distracted, and I've mentioned it to him. He just shrugs me off, saying it's the church, the school, the bishop, his mission in Mexico, mom's death—whatever."

"Well maybe that's exactly what it is. Maybe he just needs a diversion—maybe our visit is the cure he needs."

Tom steered the cart past the palm trees onto the manicured fairway. "No, there's something else, Fran. I'm almost positive there is, but I just can't put my finger on it. You were always so close growing up, maybe you can get him to talk to you."

"Sure, I'll try my best. What specifically are you worried about?"

"Well, I haven't mentioned this to anyone, so please don't say anything to Joe or anyone else for that matter."

"Tom, you know I can keep secrets. Remember when you broke that vase Mom brought back from Canada? The one she loved so much, the one with the band of purple thistles around the base? Well, did she ever find out who did it? I promise, I won't discuss this with anyone else, not even Joe, for that matter."

"Okay! I think, no, I know I can trust you. You know about his missionary work, right. Well, the time he spends in Mexico gets longer and longer. In the beginning, he would spend maybe one week a month there. Now he's gone for a month at a time. And to compound matters, he won't give me a phone number or address where I can reach him. He does call, maybe once every other week. But I'm afraid he's involved with something there, and I'm just not sure what it could be. Maybe you can talk to him, find out what the problem is, if, in fact, there is a problem. Perhaps I could help if he's in any kind of trouble."

"Oh, Tom, I hope he's not in any kind of trouble. I'll do everything I can to help."

As their cart approached the green, Fran studied Mike. She watched him reach for the putter, take his wedge out instead, replace it, and search his bag, checking all the clubs, until he finally removed the putter.

"I'll mark my ball for you, Fran." Joe shaded his eyes and checked the distance of Fran's putt. "That's quite a distance, but not impossible the way you're playing lately."

I hope I haven't lost my focus, Fran thought as she stooped to measure the distance for a par.

———

As Rosa grew older, she wondered about the absent O'Brien family. As plans progressed for her fifth birthday party, she became more and more insistent that the O'Briens attend. "But, Daddy, why can't my Uncle Tom and Aunt Fran and Uncle Joe and all my cousins come to my birthday party? I don't think they like me very much. They never come to see me. Aunt Alma comes to see me all the time."

"Now, Princesa, they love you very, very much. They can't come to see you because they live far far away. Aunt Alma comes to see you because she lives in Mexico where we live. Your Uncle Tom and Aunt Fran and Uncle Joe live far, far away.

"Why can't they get on a plane and fly through the sky?" Mike wished he could tell Tom and Fran and Joe about his family. He was so proud of Rosa and the twins. He almost told Fran a couple of times. Once when Carrie was just a toddler and then again the last time she and Joe visited him in El Paso when he showed them the school. As they peered into the first grade classroom, he wanted to tell them all about Rosa. He did start, but quickly changed his mind realizing they just wouldn't understand. That was the worst part about his double life. He couldn't tell the people he loved the most about the things that were most sacred to him. When he stood in the pulpit to speak to his congregation, he noticed the boys and girls squirming in their pews and wanted to see his children sitting among them. Keeping his secret was becoming more and more difficult. He just read about a married Lutheran priest who was ordained as a Catholic priest in Germany, but he realized that was an anomaly and the likelihood of priests marrying in his lifetime just didn't exist.

He pulled Rosa closer to him. "Rosa, if they possibly could come to see you, they would. I know they love you very, very, very much. Don't you ever forget that."

"Daddy, where is that picture? I want to look at them again. Do you think I look like Aunt Fran? She is such a pretty lady."

He held her face between his hands and leaning close to her, he whispered, "Princesa, you look just like the most beautiful woman I know, your mother."

1968-1994

Discovery

Mike and the kids spent almost all day playing beach ball in the heated waters of the Marco Polo pool in the center of Mexico City while Maria sat under the shade of a striped umbrella reading and dozing. As the sun sank, the family climbed into the Ford and sang all the way home. Mike heard the phone ringing as he pulled into the driveway. The kids tumbled out of the car. Rosa, laughing, ran ahead of the boys. Mike walked inside and picked up the phone. When he heard the bishop's voice, he went numb. The day he had feared all these years became reality.

How, he wondered, did the bishop get this phone number? In a very officious tone, Bishop Rodriguez told Mike his financial report had discrepancies and that he must see him at once. Mike felt threatened. If the bishop knew his phone number, he reasoned, he must also know about his wife, his twins, and his princesa. He was stunned. He hung up and put on a mask. Inside he was sobbing but his face projected calm as he realized that this night might be the last time that he would ever see his precious family. He knew this night must last forever.

He showered, shaved, dressed, and decided that the best plan of action was to send the family to Acapulco where the house was in Maria's name, not his. The bishop would not be able to force her to leave. He figured the family would be able to live there several years, for the bank account in Maria's name was quite large, and the house belonged to her free and clear. The bishop could never take it from her, for only natives of Mexico could own homes on the beachfront.

Dinner was a happy time that night. Maria made the tastiest burritos ever. The cheese oozed out, the juice dripped down everyone's chins. Between bites, everyone sat around the table rubbing the rims of their glasses until they hummed. They even experimented with the notes, pouring water into or out of the goblets until they had five distinct sounds. They doubled over with laughter as they tried to sing "Tres Pequenos Ratones." After dinner Mike suggested that the family move to the house in Acapulco for the rest of the summer to enjoy swimming in the warm waters of the Gulf. Everyone thought it was an excellent idea. "Maria, I'll ask Carl to drive you and the children in the wagon; I have some business to take care of, so I'll follow in a couple of days in the T-bird."

Mike hugged the children especially hard that night when he tucked them into bed, and he told them over and over how much he loved them. He held Maria that night, like he never held her before. He told her how much she meant to him, how much he worshipped her and their little family. "Maria," he whispered," if for some reason we are ever parted, just remember that my arms will always be wrapped around you, holding you tightly just the way I'm holding you now."

"Hmm, hmm," she sleepily replied as she nestled closer.

He gently traced his finger over her forehead down her nose, her lips, and her throat. He lay awake all night memorizing her.

———

Two days later, Mike was in El Paso. The shrill sound of the alarm woke him from a deep sleep. It took a couple of minutes to clear the cobwebs. Then he remembered: Wednesday, the bishop. He slowly rolled out of bed, knelt for his morning prayers, then headed for the shower. He had just enough time to say the eight o'clock Mass and get to the bishop's by 10 am. He took out his best black suit, his clerical shirt, and Roman collar. Quickly, he dressed, brushed his hair, and was out the door without coffee or breakfast. He walked across the street, said good morning to the few parishioners waiting outside the church door, unlocked it, and disappeared inside.

Mass began. When he raised the host, Father Mike seemed inspired, in another world. He swallowed it and drank the wine, genuflected, and bowed his head. He administered Communion to those faithful parishioners who came to daily Mass. When Mass concluded, he left the altar and walked toward the sacristy to change his vestments and prepare to meet his bishop.

Mike wasn't sure if this interview was solely about finances or if the bishop knew about his family. He had often thought about what he would say if his bishop questioned him, so he had spent some time preparing a defense. Since he hadn't spent one penny of parish money for his secret life, he was confident that he had no fears if finances were actually the reason he was summoned to the bishop. He was also pretty confident that his friendship with his superior would bode well for him.

Mike arrived five minutes early, parked the car, walked up the five steps, and rang the bell. He was ushered into a lavishly decorated room: an Oriental carpet in hues of gold, green, rose; a crystal chandelier; heavy mahogany furniture upholstered in gold and green figured silk; gold damask drapes; built-in bookshelves stacked with bibles, lives of the saints, histories of the church, philosophical treatises; several formal oil paintings of past bishops in gilt-edged frames hanging on beige walls. The room was thick with the essence of incense. Mike sat, crossed his legs, drummed his fingers on the arm of the chair, studied the room, locked in silence. For 15 minutes he listened to the tick of the grandfather clock. Then suddenly, the bishop's footsteps startled him. Mike stood as his bishop, dressed in his floor length black cassock edged in scarlet, entered. His shock of white hair contrasted with his piercing dark eyes. Mike took the bishop's hand, ready to kiss his ring. "Your Excellency," he started.

"Please, Mike, no need for ceremony, sit." The bishop took the chair opposite him, placed the rimless spectacles on his nose, and took a sheaf of folded notes from his pocket. "Mike, I never thought I would be sitting across from you to begin a discussion about such an unpleasant subject. I have always admired your ability to get things done for the church. Your parish, one of the poorer in the diocese, has raised more money for charity than any other parish in El Paso. You have built your school from the ground up, hired excellent teachers, and with them developed a viable student-centered curriculum. Your students are thriving, your parishioners are thriving.

"Mike, I just don't understand how you could sin against your God like this, how you could put your whole career in jeopardy. I have always put my trust in you, supported you, helped you. I feel taken advantage of, duped, slapped in the face. I feel personally assaulted. Mike, I'm not stupid. How long did you think you could live like this?" The bishop paused, took a white handkerchief from his pocket, and wiped his brow.

Mike, overcome with the bishop's disappointment, was speechless.

The bishop resumed, looking now at his notes, "Father Morales from St. Martin's, who was covering the parish for you when you were doing your mission work in Mexico, was puzzled by a letter sent to you. It was from LMAC Mortgage

Company informing you of an increase in your escrow account for a property in Mexico City. Because Father Morales didn't have a forwarding address for you, he sent the letter on to me requesting me to send it along. As you can imagine, I was concerned. At first, I thought you must have been embezzling funds from the church, but what I discovered after investigation is far worse; it is unthinkable. I hope beyond hope that you can tell me I'm wrong. I'm looking at notes from a private investigator that tell me you not only own property in your own name in Mexico City and Chihuahua, but that you also live with a Mexican woman who owns a third property and with her you have raised three children, twin boys and a girl." The bishop removed his glasses, "Mike, please tell me this isn't so. Tell me this investigator has confused you with another Michael O'Brien," he begged.

Mike couldn't hide the tears gathering in his eyes. He knew his life had changed irrevocably.

————

He unlocked the rectory door, scanned the familiar living room, and slung his suit coat on the recliner. He walked down the hall to his bedroom, sank on his knees, buried his head on the comforter, and wept.

"Oh, God," he repeated over and over. "God, I was mistaken. I was wrong. I was selfish. I have sinned. I can see that now. I let my family come between us. I never wanted to hurt you."

He had no idea how long he spent on his knees when he felt a hand tap him on the shoulder. "Mike! Mike! What's wrong? What happened? I've been pounding on the door for about 15 minutes. Finally, I took the key from the letter box and let myself in."

"Oh, Tom! I'm dead! I'm dead!" He shook his head, rubbed his eyes.

"It's the bishop, isn't it? Tell me, what happened." He helped Mike up and sat next to him on the bed.

"I have to be out of here by tomorrow, out of the rectory, out of the church."

"Now, slow down, Mike. What do you mean you're out of the church?"

"I'm laicized, Tom, defrocked. Can't say Mass, or distribute Communion, or preach to my people, or help them."

The reality of what his brother was saying slowly dawned on Tom. He braced himself for the worst. "Now, Mike, I don't want to hear you talking that way.

I am still here. Maybe I can help." He put his arm around Mile's shoulder to comfort him.

"No one can help me. I might as well be dead. The bishop didn't care how much I did for him, didn't care that I founded the school, didn't care that my parish was the strongest, the most generous in the diocese. He didn't care about anything I said or anything I did. I begged for a second chance, Tom. I actually begged, got down on my knees and begged." Still sitting on the bed dejected, he shook his head and ran his fingers through his hair. He reached for his handkerchief, wiped his eyes, his nose, his brow, and turned to Tom. "What am I going to do? When I told him that my wife and children made me a better priest, that my family didn't subtract from my parish, that I had plenty of love to share, enough for God, my church, and my family…"

"When you told him what?! Mike, did you say you have a wife and family?" Mike nodded.

"But that's impossible! How did you do this? When did you have time?" His voice grew louder and louder as he expressed his utter incomprehension of his brother's double life. He glared at Mike. "How in the name of all that's good and holy?" He began to pace back and forth, his mind in a muddle. *Why didn't I pick up the clues?* he asked himself. *The beautiful Hispanic woman in Juarez, the missionary trips to Mexico, the phone calls. Maybe I could have put an end to the double life before the bishop got wind of it.* "Do Fran and Joe know about this?"

"No and I don't want them to know."

"But, Mike, maybe they could help."

"No, I don't think they, especially Joe, would understand. You know him, something is right or wrong, black or white, there's no gray, no in-between."

"Mike, this is a very serious situation. You need all the help you can get." He glared at Mike, slammed the bedroom door, and automatically walked toward the kitchen.

Grabbing the old teakettle, he filled it with tap water, turned the burner to high. Then he reached into the cupboard searching for cups and saucers, found the Bavarian teapot and cups Mike bought back from Germany after his stint with the Air Corps. He found the sugar and creamer and placed them on the table as well. He remembered how Mom loved the delicately patterned china. Although he was grief stricken when she died, he was happy she wasn't alive today. *Thank God,* he thought, *Mom and Pop aren't here anymore. They would be devastated with Mike's defrocking.*

Although he was appalled by his brother's double life, he knew he had to support him. After all that's what siblings were for. He walked back to Mike's bedroom, put his ear to the door and listened. He knocked gently. "Mike, tea's ready! Come on in! Get it while it's hot."

Mike shuffled into the kitchen, sat down and poured a cup of tea. He reached for the sugar and creamer, and then noticed the china. "This is the tea set I brought back from Germany for Mom, isn't it? Oh thank God she and Pop aren't here today. My day of infamy! Oh they would be so disappointed in me! What am I going to do, Tom? I just don't know." Reaching for the teacup, he shook his head again.

"Well, I'm not sure what can be done about the bishop. I'm not too well versed in Canon law. I'll make some inquiries."

"What will my parishioners think?"

"Your parishioners? What about your Mexican family? You will still have them, won't you?"

"Oh, Tom, I just don't know. I realize now I made a mistake. I have to think about it. I just don't know what to do."

"Well, the first thing we'll do is pack your clothes and take everything to my place. The day is half over. I guess we need to take your books and your recliner and the TV and the piano. My buddy Harry has an old Chevy truck I can borrow for the bigger stuff. I'll give him a call. See if we can borrow it tonight."

"Forget about the truck. The bishop says that since everything was paid for with church funds, it's church property. So the recliner, the TV, and the piano stay, but I need to have the Air Corps medals hanging over the TV. Tom, are you sure there's room for me at your rancher? But actually I don't know where else I would be welcome. I've let my parishioners down. How can I ever face them again?"

"Don't worry about it, Mike," he said, more confidently than he felt. "We'll make it work until you decide what you want to do. That's what family is for. After we get you settled, we can discuss your options. Go on back to your bedroom and start packing your clothes; I'll start packing the books."

In a daze, Mike walked back to his bedroom, pulled the black Samsonite from the top of his closet, and started to empty his drawers, dumping socks and underwear into the suitcase, from another drawer he threw in his golf shirts. He opened the closet and looked at the black pants, the black suit coats, the black clerical shirts, the Roman collar. *I won't need these,* he thought. *Why bother taking them*. His eyes filled with tears again. *My vestments, the rose, and the white—I guess I might as well leave them too. But my chalice and ciborium that Mom and Pop gave me when I was ordained—I do want them. I'll have to run over to the sacristy and get them.* He thought of the words sung at his ordination. *You are a priest forever, like Melchizedek of old.* He remembered his study of Canon Law and knew that if as a laicized priest (He hated even thinking the vile word 'defrocked.') he consecrated a host, it would indeed be the body and blood of Christ, however illicit; and that he could offer absolution to a dying penitent if the penitent confessed to him. The bishop didn't need to tell him this. He remembered. He also remembered the vows he took that morning 15 years ago. He felt faint, sat on the bed, lay back. "My life is over," he repeated again and again before drifting off to sleep.

"Mike, wake up," Tom shook him gently on the shoulder. Mike opened his eyes, then remembered and closed them again. "Mike, come on now. Finish packing. The books are ready to go. When we get to my place we can talk and make some decisions. Are you sure the bishop said you had to be out of here by tomorrow?"

"Tom, I really thought the bishop was my friend. He told me time and time again how much he valued my work. He always talked about the progress I made with the parish. But, today, he did a complete turnaround. I'm just beginning to understand how he must see me. He must despise me. I am overwhelmed with the shame of it all."

"Mike, I'm not going to say 'I told you so' but gosh! I just can't believe all of this happened. Why, you were king of the mountain." Tom rubbed his eyes, went over to Mike to comfort him. "Mike, we'll find a way out of this. Don't worry."

"Whatever you do, don't tell Fran and Joe. Please. I just couldn't bear it if my little sister knew. She was always so proud I was a priest. I think I would actually kill myself if she knew. I have nothing, my church, my family, my piano. They're all gone."

"Mike, are you forgetting? You still have God and your brother. Come on now. Let's finish packing your stuff and get over to my place."

"What will Maria think of me?" He sighed as he slowly rolled off the bed to finish packing.

———

Mike fell into a never-ending tunnel of self-pity. He saw no reason to live. He had failed Fran and Tom, his wife, and his children. He had failed his parishioners, his bishop, but most importantly he had failed his God. His mind turned in circles flitting from one failure to another. He refused to eat; he couldn't sleep. Numb with exhaustion and overcome with remorse, he struggled to find a reason to go on. He prayed night and day, listened for the voice of God but heard only the frigid silence of rejection.

Finally he realized what he must do. He knew he must punish himself. He must atone for his sins. He must surrender his family, his earthly love, and dedicate his life solely to God. Even thought the church had cast him out, he must mortify himself, sacrifice himself, deny himself any pleasures until he fully atoned for his sins.

———

"Hey, Mike, here's a letter for you. It doesn't look as if it's from the bishop." Tom shut the door and tossed the envelope to Mike, then hung his jacket in the closet.

"Thanks, I've been expecting to hear from Monahan, my buddy from the military." The oppression that moved in with Mike lightened a bit. For the last few weeks he proceeded step by perilous step, sloshing through the mess he made of his life. "I've wanted to ask him for guidance. We solved lots of problems when we were stationed in Bavaria, so I asked him to help me sort out this mess."

"Sounds like a good idea."

"Tom, you know how devastated I've been since my conference with the bishop." Tom nodded and waited for him to continue. "I'm going to try to explain to you exactly what I've decided to do. You have to believe me. I love my parish, all my parishioners, each and every one of them; but I also love my wife and children. I gave my heart to both and both were thriving with my love. They were the best 12 years of my life. But the only one I've wronged is my God. I didn't remain faithful to my priestly vows. I must atone. I must relinquish my family and my parish and live a solitary life in prayer to redeem myself. There is no other option. As difficult as it will be to deny myself the love of my family, I must concentrate on making reparation to my God." Mike rubbed his forehead, looked at Tom, hoping he understood.

"I think I get it, Mike. But, I'm confused, how can you abandon your family if you really love them as you say you do? How will they survive? Don't you owe them something?"

"It will take a supreme sacrifice on my part to purge my soul of sin, and I can think of nothing more precious to me than my family. Therefore I must relinquish them in order to make amends to my God."

"Mike, please, keep an open mind here. Think about it for a while."

"I will, I will. But I've really thought about it for a long time. My family means the most to me, so I have to eradicate them from my life. However, just to appease you, I will think about it."

"Okay. But, I don't understand what a letter from Monahan has to do with all of this."

"I want to be near him because I think I will need his counsel as I move forward in my resolve. One of his parishioners is moving back East, and he is going to check to see if his house is for rent." Mike opened the envelope and quickly scanned the contents. "Thank God! I will be moving to Alamogordo soon." Tom was silent. Mike wondered if the silence was approval or disapproval.

Rumors

Rumors spread through the parish like wildfire. Everyone wondered what happened to Father Mike. Even though José did his best to quell the gossip, Father Mike was the topic of everyone's conversation. Everyone had an answer.

José's daughter Pilar pushed the door open and ran into the living room dragging her boyfriend Rafael behind her. "Mom, Mom, where are you?" Pilar looked around bewildered. She threw her sweater on the hook just inside the door, looked in the mirror, tried to tame her dark windblown hair. "Mom!"

"I'm in the kitchen, dear. What's the matter?" Ana rubbed her hands on her apron and rushed to the living room. "I'm making some pozole for dinner. You sound upset. What's the matter?" The two women almost collided as they moved toward each other. "My, you do look upset. Oh, hola Rafael. I thought you two were at your pre-Cana instruction."

"We were, but we're not! It's just horrible. The most dreadful thing has happened. I don't know what to do? I don't know how Rafael and I can get married. Right, Rafael?"

Rafael raised his eyebrows, "Right! Right!"

She wiped her eyes with the back of her hands. "It's the most horrible thing you could ever imagine."

Rafael put his arm around her. "It's not that bad, honey. I'm sure we can solve the problem."

Pilar had always been emotional. Ana remembered when she got a B instead of an A in Art History; it took a week to calm her down. "Now, why don't you sit down, take a deep breath, and tell me what the problem is."

Pilar pushed the cat off the sofa to make room for Rafael. "Scoot, scoot. This animal is such a pain, mom."

"Here, Angel, come to mama." The cat jumped up on her lap and snuggled in. Ana absently tickled her black ears until she purred, then turned her attention to Pilar. "Now, dear, what's upsetting you so?"

"Well, you remember the last time Father Mike was here?"

"Sure, your dad destroyed him in the golf match and they came here for dinner. I think I made some chili and—"

"Remember how Rafael and I asked him to marry us and he agreed. He seemed really pleased that we asked him."

"Of course, he was thrilled you asked him. He is such a good friend of your dad's, a good friend to all of us. I remember he took out his calendar right then at the dinner table and you scheduled all of your pre-Cana conferences."

"Well, today was our first one. I left right after work and met Rafael at the bus stop at 5:15 pm. We were both really excited to start our preparation for the wedding. The bus came right away, so we were a couple of minutes early for the session. We sat in his office for about 20 minutes, then we started to get worried, didn't we Rafael?"

"Si, I thought he might have forgotten about our meeting."

"Anyway, finally a strange priest came walking in. He was a very old man with white hair and had a bit of trouble walking. He used a cane. Anyway, he told us he was very sorry to inform us that Father Mike retired and that we would have to go to another parish for our pre-Cana conferences."

"What?" Ana was so surprised she jumped up. The cat fell off her lap and started meowing. "Hush, Angel, hush!" She bent down and scooped her up again. "No, that can't be. He never said a word about retiring."

"That's what this old priest told us, didn't he, Rafael?"

"Si! Si! He did."

"There must be some mistake. We'll have to call your father. He'll know." Juggling the cat in her right arm, Ana reached for the phone with her left.

"Wait, mom, there's more."

"What do you mean there's more? What more could there be?"

"Well, the priest gave us a list of the churches where the pre-Cana conferences are being held, and we thanked him and left. We hadn't walked a block when we saw your friend, Carmen. You know, the one who works in the school cafeteria."

"Si! Si! So what does this have to do with Father Mike?"

"We got talking. She noticed we were upset and asked us what was wrong. When we told her about our problem, she looked strange."

"What do you mean, 'strange'?"

"Like she was trying to figure out whether she should tell us something. Then finally, she told us that there was a rumor going around the school. Mom, you won't believe this. She said there was a rumor that Father Mike retired because the bishop sent him away. He was angry with him. Something about money or something like that."

"Now, Pilar, you know that can't be true. Father Mike would never do anything wrong. He loves this parish. And this parish loves him. You know Carmen, she has nothing better to do than gossip and spread rumors. Why then next she'll say that Father Mike is an alcoholic or a gambler or, even worse, that he fathered children. You know you can't believe what she says. I'll just call your father. He'll know what's happened. I think he was working at the school today, something about the plumbing."

"Oh, Mom, is that the pozole I smell?"

Ana dropped the cat again, dropped the phone, and rushed into the kitchen.

———

The rumors not only inundated St. Ignatius, but also spread across the country. News about a fallen priest, a former Camden resident, was big news, not only in El Paso but also in Mike's hometown.

The phone rang. "I'm coming, I'm coming," Fran called out to no one at all. She had been packing for the annual trip West to visit the brothers; this time they were meeting at a golf resort in Mazatlan. She picked up the phone on the nightstand. "Hello? Oh, Joe, I didn't expect a call from you so early. I haven't finished packing yet. Our flight isn't until 3:40....What? But that's impossible! What is the headline again?...'Priest Embezzles Funds.' Are you sure, Joe? Did you see the article yourself? What paper is it in? ...The Courier Post? I don't think I can get a copy here. I'll call Kay. She probably has one. I don't understand why the Courier would even print a story from Texas. Will you call Mike?...Okay. Let me know what he says. Call when you want me to pick you up. So long...Love you too." Fran hung up the phone, sat on the side of the bed stupefied. *Impossible,* she thought. *There must be a mistake. It's good we're going to Mexico for our annual visit. Joe will be able to fix everything.*

She dialed Joe's sister who corroborated the story. Kay even read portions of the story to her. Before she hung up, Fran gave her more last minute instructions about the boys and Carrie, for it was the first time they were leaving her behind.

Preoccupied the rest of the day, Fran packed, showered, dressed, and waited for Joe to call. She paced the length of the house. Because she was anxious to find out what happened, she couldn't sit down. After what seemed like days, the phone finally rang. "Hi, Joe....You couldn't get in touch with Mike or Tom? Oh-no! They're probably on the road. We'll just have to wait until we get to Mazatlan to get the full story…Okay. I'll pick you up at the subway in 15 minutes. See you!" Fran grabbed her suitcase and keys, anxious to be on the move.

Neither spoke very much as they flew cross-country on TWA. Joe was able to get a copy of the article and gave it to Fran to read. He seemed rather glum, disheartened by the news. *What a dumb thing to do, embezzle funds. Why didn't he call me? I could have lent him money.* The phrases echoed in his head like a mantra.

Fran looked over at her husband. "I guess this is what was on Mike's mind last year when we all noticed how stressed he seemed. You will be able to fix everything, won't you Joe? I can't imagine that Mike would steal from the church. There must be some mistake."

"It doesn't seem likely that Mike would do something so stupid. I hope we can get to the bottom of it. Between Tom and I we should be able to come up with some kind of solution."

Hoping that Mike's problem would be solved, Fran tried to turn her attention to Agatha Christie, but found it impossible to concentrate.

Before long they were ensconced in their beachfront hotel overlooking the inviting gulf. Fran jumped at the knock, opened the door, and gave her brothers a big hug, overjoyed to see them again. Joe sedately shook hands. He poured Tom a Manhattan and a Glenlivet for Mike. Fran found some peanuts and they all sat down to catch up. At first no one mentioned the article in the Courier. They exchanged news of the kids and El Paso. Then Mike made an announcement, "Fran, Joe, there's something I have to tell you." Fran and Joe braced themselves for the embezzlement story. "No, no," he said, "It's not a bad thing. I decided to retire from the priesthood this year. I'm going to move away from

El Paso. I'm going to Alamogordo, New Mexico. A friend of mine, a priest, a chaplain I met while I served in Germany, has a parish there and he said he could use a little assistance." Silence followed his announcement. He wondered if they would fall for the retirement story, realized that he started to lie again. "Holy smokes," he said, "It's not a bad thing. What's the matter with you two?"

Joe, not one to beat around the bush, blurted out, "Mike, there was an article about you in the Courier Post this morning actually—back East."

"Oh!" he paused, rubbed his chin, sipped his Glenlivet. "Was it about my retirement?"

"I'm afraid not, Mike. It was about your embezzlement." Silence blanketed the room, suffocating silence, rendering everyone speechless.

Joe finally broke the void, "Mike, why didn't you ask me for help? I could have lent you money."

"I have a pension," Mike said, "and I'm going to teach piano lessons."

"I didn't mean now; I meant before you embezzled funds. Is there more to this than embezzlement?"

"Can we talk about this later, Joe? I'm just not comfortable discussing this right now."

"If we must. Actually I'm pretty tired right now; we had a long flight. Maybe we should call it a night and meet tomorrow on the golf course. At say about nine o'clock? Is that okay with everybody?"

Tom and Mike left rather quickly. Joe drained his Manhattan, and abruptly switched the subject. "Would you care to join me in another drink to watch the sunset, Fran?"

"I was just about to ask if you would care to join me for a walk on the beach. I want time to think about everything. What do you say?"

"I'm too tired, but you go ahead. I'll still be here when you get back."

Fran picked up her visor, adjusted the strap, checked the angle in the mirror, put the room key in her pocket and left. "See you later!"

Precisely at 9 o'clock the next morning, Joe walked into the pro shop at El Cid. Spotting Tom, he walked over. "Morning, Tom." He scanned the pro shop for Mike unsuccessfully. "Where is Mike?" he asked.

"He got a call last night and had to leave. Where is Fran?"

"She went to the car for her shoes; she'll be right back. But now, when will Mike return?"

"He didn't say, Joe. You know you were right last night. There is more to Mike's problem than embezzlement. Mike doesn't want me to tell you, but I feel compelled to. He's having a rough time, Joe, and he needs your support."

"What could be worse than embezzlement? Tell me what happened?"

"Please keep this to yourself. Not a word to Fran. It would break her heart."

"Okay, okay! I promise! I won't tell her." He glared at Tom.

Tom looked him in the eyes, looked down at his shoes, and scanned the pro shop to make sure Fran hadn't returned. "He has been laicized."

"What!" Incredulous, Joe continued, "Laicized! As punishment for the embezzlement?"

"No. There is no problem with the finances of St. Ignatius. But there is a problem, a very big problem. Apparently he's been leading a double life. He has a wife, twin sons, and a daughter."

"Impossible! He couldn't have!"

Tom noticed Fran entering the pro shop. "Please, Joe, keep this between us. Fran doesn't have to know. Actually, Mike didn't want you to know either."

As Fran approached, Joe picked up a pair of gloves, looked at the price tag, put them back on the shelf.

"Sorry I held you up. What time do we tee off?" Fran scanned the pro shop for Mike. "Where's Mike? Isn't he here yet?"

"He's not coming, Fran."

"Why? What happened?"

"He had to leave. He had some business to take care of. He's moving to Alamogordo."

"Does this have something to do with the embezzlement? Did you take care of everything, Joe?"

"Yes! Yes! Everything is taken care of. Now get into your shoes. We tee off in five minutes."

The next time Fran and Joe traveled to Mexico to escape the frigid weather in the East, Tom joined them, but Mike was noticeably absent. True to his word, Joe kept Mike's double life to himself, but he never saw or spoke to him again. Fran continued to correspond to Mike, not able to understand why he never joined them on vacation.

Atonement

The sooner I leave the better, Mike thought as he shoved his last box of books into the trunk, slammed it shut, and brushed the dust off his hands and the sweat off his forehead. He walked around to the driver's side, opened the door of the T-bird, rolled the window down and his sleeves up, turned the key in the ignition, and put his foot on the gas—all reflex actions, done without thinking. His hands gripped the steering wheel, the same hands that not too long ago raised the sacred Host during the consecration. He looked down at them remembering the last time he held Maria's hand as they kissed goodbye.

Checking traffic in the rearview mirror, he headed for the interstate, moved into the center lane behind a Plymouth then immediately veered off to the left. *Just one more glance*, he thought. *I just want to see them one last time.* He turned around and instead of driving north toward Alamogordo, he headed south to his family. He pushed the pedal, weaved in and out of lanes, passing traffic, barreling toward his goal. As he focused, he slowed down, adjusted his speed to the limit, and drove with purpose over the Rio Grande Bridge. As the hours passed, Juarez became Chihuahua, then Santa Rosali del Camago, San Pedro, Fresnilo, and finally Acapulco. The prairies and tumbleweed gave way to beaches and palm trees.

Images tumbled through his mind: He imagined Rosa and the boys building drip castles on the white sand under the shade of a palm tree, cooling off in the crystal clear water of the Gulf, or chasing monarch butterflies from the bougainvillea. Then, he realized the children were probably not building sand castles or chasing monarchs, they were probably crying, wondering where he was. The thought ripped his heart apart. He wondered what Maria would tell them, what they thought of him. He wondered if these visions would forever haunt him, reminding him of his sin, his human weakness hurtling him into the depths of despair.

He veered to the shoulder as an eighteen-wheeler whizzed by honking. Shaking his head to clear his mind, he switched the radio to a talk show and turned up the volume. Deciding instead to concentrate on the rosary, he pulled the beads out of his pocket and began to pray. The hours passed too slowly and finally he pulled off the shoulder at a rest stop for a bite to eat and a catnap.

Finally, he approached the familiar gated hacienda on the beach. He slowed down, paused for a couple of minutes, then continued to the end of the block. He looked in the rear-view mirror as something like a magnet pulled him back. He shifted into reverse, rolled back, until he was at the house again. He turned off the ignition, turned his head toward the window. Shading his eyes from the blinding sun, he stared through the lush palms, the monarchs pirouetting on the bougainvillea. He hoped to see someone, anyone, through the glass: maybe Maria reading the paper, or Rosa chasing the twins. Tears dribbled down his cheeks onto his shirt as he saw nothing but reflections of palm fronds in the glass, the palms he planted not too long ago. He jumped when he felt a tap on the shoulder. As he hastily wiped the tears, he recognized the guard. He glanced over hoping Carl hadn't noticed the smudged tears. "Carl, it's me Mike!"

"Oh, sir. Just investigating. I didn't realize it was you. I noticed the car, saw it leave and then return, I thought I better investigate."

"You did the right thing, Carl."

"Can I help you, sir?"

"No, no. I was just driving by. I'll be on my way."

"Are you sure there's nothing I can do?"

Mike shook his head and, regretfully, turned on the ignition, then slowly reversed his direction and coasted up the palm-lined street toward Alamogordo, his resolve dissolving into inconsequential bits of despair.

———

One day after the next eventually added up to years and Mike was still absent. She no longer cried herself to sleep or started every time a car pulled into the driveway. She no longer yelled "Mike" when she saw a man his height and stature round a corner. Slowly, she became used to being both mother and father. And sometimes, she still felt his arms wrapped tight around her. True, she didn't live the good life as she had when Mike was home. Her eyes sparkled no more, her chestnut curls became gray around the temples, her lips were framed with tiny wrinkles. But she never doubted the strength of the love they shared. The family had a home, small as it might be, and Maria had been able to put food on the table with her job as a secretary at Papalarama, a three-story retail store chock-full of furniture, glass, ceramics, and jewelry. Now that Rosa, no longer a gangly child, was in high school and Eduardo and Pancho, both taller than Mike, were working in Carmelita's Restaurant, things were a bit easier. She was happy she had been able to keep the family together. Mike would be proud of her.

One night, tossing and turning in her tiny bedroom not able to sleep, Maria came to a decision. She turned on the lamp, picked up her diary from the night-stand, plumped up the pillows, and paged through it, reading entries here and there. Finally, she reached for her pen and began. "If he wasn't killed by the Mafia or during a military mission," Maria wrote, "he must be in Ireland or in jail for gambling debts. I know he would be here if he could. He is my life, my heart, my soul. I know he loved me and the children with every fiber of his being. Yet I also know there is one door to his heart that he would never open to me. I think it's time to find out more about him. Not just for my sake, for his memory is enough to fill my life forever, but the children need to know why their father hasn't come home."

Maria said nothing about her plan to the children as she sautéed onions, chilies, and eggs for their tortillas. But, as soon as she got to Papalarama and checked the mail, she looked through the phone book and called a detective, Emilio Gonzales, and agreed to meet with him during lunch hour.

The clock ticked slowly, but soon it was 12:30 and time for Maria to meet Emilio Gonzales, the man she hoped would find Mike, or at least answer her questions. She hesitated a brief second before she knocked on the door. A receptionist answered and led her into Emilio's office. Maria took one look at the dark wavy-haired man seated behind a disorganized mass of papers and immediately felt that he would answer all her questions. He walked over to her, shook hands, and asked her to be seated. "Now, Mrs. O'Brien, excuse me, but you certainly don't look like a Mrs. O'Brien," said the brown-eyed man scratching his head. "But please, tell me why you need my services."

Maria took the photo from her red imitation Coach bag. "I want you to find my husband."

"Hmm," He studied the photo carefully. "So, he's in the military, looks like a captain in the Air Corps." He looked up. "Now tell me what you want to know about him."

"I want to know where he is. Can you find out for me?" she asked, her eyes watering.

"I can certainly try. A few questions first. Now, when did you last see him? Can you give me the names of any relatives or close friends? And third, do you have any idea where he might be? It would also be helpful if you give me his social security number and perhaps his last place of employment."

Maria answered his questions as best as she could. When she walked out of the office, she was hopeful. More hopeful than she had felt in the last few years.

After several weeks of sleepless nights, Maria finally received a letter. She opened it and read it until her eyes blurred.

"Dear Mrs. O'Brien:

I have good news for you. I have been able to find the information you requested at our meeting on March 8, 1966. Your husband Michael O'Brien lives at 4019 Hoover Avenue in El Paso, Texas. His phone number is Castellano 2-4598.

If I can be of service in any other way, please contact me.

Respectfully yours,

Emilio Gonzales"

Now that she had the information she had coveted, Maria didn't know what to do with it. The information she really wanted, she didn't get, but then she didn't ask for it either. *Why did Mike leave? What forced him to abandon the children and me?* Perhaps she would never know the answers to those questions.

Maria prepared the children's favorite meal, chicken chili, so hot it made their eyes tear. Rosa, Eduardo, and Pancho gulped down the last of the chili before Maria told them her news. "Tonight is a very special night," she said. All three looked at her expectantly.

"Did you get a raise?" asked Eduardo putting down his spoon.

"I bet you got tickets for the bullfight," suggested Pancho.

"I think you found out something about my father," said Rosa blowing on the chili to cool it.

Maria smiled. "You are very perceptive, Rosa. It is news about your father. I hired a private Detective, Mr. Gonzales, and I received a letter today with important information."

"What is it? What did you find out?" screamed Rosa, practically jumping out of her seat. "Where is he? When can I see him?" The boys looked at each other incredulous.

"I have his address and phone number. He isn't very far from us, just over the bridge in El Paso."

"Well, give me his phone number. I'll call him right now," Ed reached for the paper Maria held in her hand.

"Not so fast, Eduardo. I don't know if I want to call. I want to think about it for a while." She held the folded letter close to her heart, paused.

"Mamá, you have to let us call," petitioned Rosa, on the verge of tears. "Perhaps he's been looking for us and can't find us since we moved from Acapulco. If you don't want to know what's happened to him, we just won't tell you. But we deserve to know what took him away from us."

"Perhaps, Rosa, we will never know the answer to that question. But I guess you're right. It's been a long time since we had some answers. Here, Eduardo, dial his number." Her hand trembling, she gave him the letter.

Eduardo dialed. A male voice answered. "Hello." Disappointed, Eduardo knew immediately it wasn't his father's voice. "I'm sorry," he said, "I'm trying to locate a Michael O'Brien." His voice sounded more hopeful. "He's not there? Do you know when he'll be back? Well, is this 4019 Hoover Avenue? I am his son, Eduardo. Hello? Hello?" Eduardo looked at his mom. "The man hung up. Sorry, Mamá." Slowly, he placed the phone on the hook. "I guess we can try again later."

"I've waited so long for this moment." Maria quivered then sighed. She sat down and put her head in her hands and began to rock back and forth.

"Mamá, don't get upset, please. Nothing has changed since yesterday. We're still a happy family. We still had a wonderful father. Tomorrow after school, I will go to El Paso and knock on the door of 4019 Hoover Avenue. I'll peek in the windows and I'll watch the house until I see him. Don't worry," Rosa said. She was adamant.

"No, Rosa, I forbid you to do that. Maybe the detective was wrong. It might be the wrong Michael O'Brien. We'll call again. Maybe he'll be home."

Rosa was true to her word. She took the bus across the border to Hoover Avenue, walked until she found the red tiled roof of 4019. She circled the block a couple of times getting used to the neighborhood. After her third time around the block she took a deep breath, calmed her jitters, and slowly walked to the front door of the white stucco house. She rang the bell, listened, rang the bell a second time, a third time. No one answered. Disappointed and dejected, Rosa walked to the bus stop and waited.

She returned again the next day. Again no answer.

The third day when she rang the bell, the door opened. An older gentleman with a crew cut and pale blue eyes behind wire-rimmed glasses opened the door. "Hello, can I help you?" he asked.

"I would like to see Michael O'Brien," exclaimed Rosa in her best grown-up voice.

"He's not here right now. But who might you be?"

"I am his daughter," proclaimed Rosa loudly.

Tom stared at Rosa, looked directly into her eyes. "That's impossible! He doesn't have any children."

Rosa noticed his eyes twitch and wondered if he was telling the truth. "No! No! My father's name is Michael, Michael O'Brien, and I know he lives here, and I want to see him now," demanded Rosa. Her lip quivered, her heart jumped, her eyes teared.

Slowly, Tom closed the door. It took him a minute to process what had just happened.

He immediately picked up the phone and dialed Alamogordo. "Mike!" He paused for a minute. "What a beautiful girl. There's no denying her Mike; she has your eyes. I'm pretty sure she'll be back again and soon. She's determined to find you. What do you want me to say? What do you want me to do?"

———

Not a day went by that Mike didn't think of Rosa, Maria, and the boys. Try as he might, he found it impossible to obliterate them from his thoughts. Although Tom's call upset him, he attempted to return to his routine with renewed vigor.

He surveyed the avocados, picked up a dark one, almost black, squeezed it gently between his thumb and forefinger. *Too squishy*, he thought. *Maria would never approve of this one.* He reached for another, a greener one, tested it and placed it in his basket. He couldn't help remembering the night he and Maria shopped for their first Christmas together and she showed him how to pick the ripest avocados for chicken relleno. As soon as he thought of her, Mike tried to erase Maria from his mind.

Untangling the past, deleting it, was the key to his sanity. He dropped the avocado in his basket as he absentmindedly turned and walked past the chilies and the arugula and the lettuce. Was that the night he wondered that they turned on the radio and danced in the tiny kitchen, whirling round and round, laughing and singing "La Bomba" at the same time? So close were they that they moved as one body. He could still smell her hair.

"Excuse me, sir."

"Sorry, I…" He looked at the middle aged woman in front of him and immediately recognized her as the mother of one of his piano students. "Oh, aren't you Gabriella's mother?"

"Yes. And you are?"

"Her piano teacher. Michael O'Brien."

"Of course. Of course. I recognize you now. I'm just not used to seeing you in the Walker Market." She offered her hand.

"She has some talent, you know. The way she interpreted "The Minute Waltz" last Wednesday was quite original. You must make sure she practices every day."

"She does. She does. I don't even have to remind her. She sits at the piano as soon as she gets home from school and starts her scales." She clenched the cart.

Mike felt her urgency, "Sorry, didn't mean to tie you up. Bye, see you on Wednesday." He continued down the aisle, then on to dairy.

His days were so different now: attending morning Mass rather than officiating, attempting meditation, praying the rosary, and giving the occasional piano lesson to supplement his pension. As long as he concentrated on praying, his past no longer controlled him.

———

Every day in Alamogordo seemed dreary, not just rainy days. Mike juggled the umbrella, reached into the mailbox, and retrieved an airmail letter: the red and blue bars framing the envelope. It triggered a memory from the distant past. He remembered getting mail from his mother when he was at Villanova. Every week she would write to him and stuff a dollar bill inside the envelope. Small as the amount was, he understood the sacrifice she had to make to send him the money week after week. *Thank God, she isn't here to see my shame, my failure. She was so proud I was a priest.*

He turned the letter over and looked at the return address. *Fran. I wonder what she wants. I hope she hasn't heard that I have a wife and children. It's bad enough that she thinks I embezzled money from the church.* It had been a long time since Mike saw Fran or Joe. Tom visited occasionally, but Joe would never forgive him. Mike knew that for a certainty.

The boundaries of his new life were narrow indeed. *I deserve to live in seclusion,* he thought. *Maybe God, in his mercy, will forgive me someday, but I know Joe never will.* He remembered the passage in his morning reading of St. Augustine. "Trust the past to the mercy of God, the present to His Love and the future to His Providence." He underlined it, wrote it in his journal, and thought of it now, for it seemed to give him peace. Rain seeped inside the umbrella, his shoes were sodden and his pants drenched. He put the letter in his pocket and fumbled with the key, finally opening the door and closing the umbrella.

Balancing the bag of groceries on the Formica counter, he reached for the avocado, the tea, the three boxes of frozen chicken dinners and found space for them in the cabinet and the refrigerator. He grabbed the teakettle, filled it with water, and turned up the burner. From the top shelf, he reached for the Bavarian teacup and saucer and plopped in a tea bag. Remembering the letter, he pulled it out of his pocket. Then he sat at the table, slit it open, and began to read:

Dear Mike,

How are you doing? I miss you and think of you often. There was a time when we were so close I thought I knew what you were thinking. Now you are like a stranger to me, a brother in name only. You no longer come East, nor do you visit when we come to vacation in Mazatlan.

I hope everything is settled as far as the embezzlement goes, and you're enjoying your retirement. Joe said he took care of the problem. Let me know if there is anything else we can do for you.

Mike looked up, rubbed his forehead. He sighed audibly as tension eased. *Thank you, God, for small favors. At least Fran doesn't know the real reason I've "retired."* He focused once more on the letter.

Now for the real reason I'm writing to you. Mikey is get-
ting married this summer and we want you to come. We would
be overjoyed and delirious with excitement if you would marry
them. I'm not so sure you can do that if you're retired, but
let me know. His wife-to-be is absolutely lovely. She's tall
and slender, brown hair and blue eyes, a great combination. The
best part, however, is her personality. She's a very warm, loving
woman and we are so happy she will be a part of our family.

If you can come, I have another favor to ask. Carrie is pre-
paring for a piano competition. She is going to try for a music
scholarship at Curtis in Philadelphia. She has been studying
Beethoven and Bach and has some difficulty with the fugues.
It would make us very happy if you would take her under your
wing and help her out.

Please let me know that you can come back East to cel-
ebrate with us

Love, Fran

P.S. Don't forget your golf clubs.

As he heard the teakettle whistle, Mike jumped up and turned off the gas, and poured the steaming water into the cup. Walking back to the table, he made room for the tea and picked up the letter again. He sat down and stared at the rain dribbling down the window. He blew on the tea, took a sip, and wished with all his heart that he could travel east to be with Fran to celebrate the milestones in her life. *If I could only untangle all these cobwebs in my head*, he thought, *things would be different. Maybe I could tell Fran. If only I had confided in her years ago. I'm so starved for her company.*

He rested his chin on his palms, his elbows on the table. He rubbed his eyes.

As much as he wanted to go, he knew it was impossible, as impossible as rolling back time and beginning all over again. He sank into a funk every time he thought of the people he loved the most, for they were the very people he had hurt the most. Forgiveness was impossible. Alamogordo was his prison.

Found

The boundaries of Mike's world grew smaller and smaller as the years passed. His piano students dribbled away to just a few. Besides his neighbor, Evelyn, who cooked his meals and cleaned his little home, Father Don Monahan, his old army buddy, became his sole companion, his only link to the outside world. He never was able to expunge the images of his family from his memory; those 12 years of his life took on a dream-like quality and always hovered just outside reality.

Guilt aged him quickly. Although his eyes were still noticeable, they seemed dull, lifeless. His curls, now gray and sparse receded from his wrinkled forehead. His frame was rather thin, yet he had a bit of a paunch. There was little joy in his life; his only respite occurred in church when he prayed, or received Communion, or played the organ. He still lost himself in the music, a sense of peace overcame him as he teased his beloved Bach from the keys, sometimes for hours.

Time treated his secret family much kinder. Even though they never found Mike, they never stopped loving him. Gradually their search for him ceased to be their raison d'etre and they put him in the past. Rosa, however, never stopped searching and made it a habit to look up his name in the phonebook anytime she visited a new city. She grew more beautiful as the years tumbled by. She had Mike's eyes, which contrasted sharply with her dark wavy hair and her light skin with the dusting of tiny freckles over her nose. Eventually, she married Pedro, a medical student, she met while working at Wal-Mart. He was mesmerized by her steel-gray eyes; she, his tall lean frame and kind, confident bearing.

———

One day, when they visited Pedro's Aunt Carmen in Alamogordo, Rosa looked up her father's name in the phonebook. As her finger skimmed the listings of O'Briens, it stopped abruptly at Michael O'Brien, 511 Poplar Avenue.

Rosa started to scream and jump up and down. She insisted that Pedro take her to Poplar Avenue at once. When they pulled up to the address, emotion overwhelmed her. Immediately she noticed the T-bird parked in the driveway that her father promised to her when she turned 16. Tears dribbled down her cheeks. She practically jumped out of the sedan and ran through the cyclone fence up the three steps to the door of the tiny cottage. She knocked and knocked again, and they waited and listened and waited some more. Rosa was overcome with emotion.

Finally the door slowly opened. Rosa, shocked, stood planted on the steps, barely able to speak. She managed to say who she was, but little else. Her father looked. He didn't speak. Silent tears spilled down his face. He couldn't stop the deluge. Mute, they stared at each other through a waterfall of tears. Then, just as slowly, he closed the door.

Rosa didn't move an inch. She stood like stone unable to talk, silenced by the impossible. Pedro took her hand slowly led her down the steps, down the walk through the cyclone fence. He held her close, his arm around her shoulder as they walked to the car. He whispered, "He does have your eyes, Rosita, the same sparkle like they're smiling all the time."

"I gave up hope of ever seeing him again, Pedro." She turned back wanting to catch another glimpse of him. Finally they settled themselves in the car and buckled up; Pedro turned the key in the ignition.

"Wait, don't leave yet. Let's just sit here a while. Maybe we'll see him in the window." She stared at the window hypnotized by the reflections of the sun on the glass.

"Now, Rosita, don't get crazy." But he turned off the ignition, and they sat looking at the cottage behind the cyclone fence.

"That T-bird in the driveway is the very car I rode in when I was a child, Pedro. It's not quite so shiny and sleek, but it is the same T-bird. He promised that it would be mine. I used to dream of sitting in the driver's seat of that sleek black Thunderbird, leaning back against the leather seats, my hair blowing in the wind, right hand on the wheel. I remember how my father always took the T-bird when we went out for ice cream. 'Dolce de leche, a double dip, Princesa,' he would say.

'One day when you're 16, this car will be yours.' Now that I have found my father, I don't want to leave. Can we wait for a few more minutes, Pedro? Maybe he'll open the door again."

"I don't think he's coming out again, Rosa. I promise we'll come back tomorrow. Maybe he'll talk to you then." Once more, he reached for the keys; the engine revved up.

"Okay," she mumbled reluctantly. "Do you think he was happy to see me?"

"Well, I think he was definitely overcome with emotion. I really don't know about the happy part. How about you? Are you happy to see him?"

"When I was standing there looking at him, I didn't see the paunchy, balding old man in front of me. I looked at his eyes and saw the handsome laughing young man in a Captain's khaki dress uniform with all the decorations over his heart. My mother would launder it, starch it, and press it until the folds could almost stand up by themselves. Even though we always had housekeepers; this was one job she wouldn't let them touch. I would watch her, thinking maybe one day I would be able to take care of his uniform. I can still see him coming in the door after one of his missions, reaching for me, swinging me around, throwing me up in the air, then giving me a big hug and mumbling in my ear how much he loved me until it tickled and I started laughing. I would grab his peaked cap and put it on my head. Then when he put me down, I would march around the house like I thought a soldier would."

She sat lost in thoughts for a while then punctured the quiet, thinking out loud. "Maybe tomorrow, after he's over the shock of seeing me, he'll talk to me. Wouldn't that be heaven?"

"Ah, my poor little Rosita, I think it will take more than one night for your father to come to terms with seeing you after 20 years. What in the world is he going to do with you now? Certainly, not throw you up in the air and twirl you around."

"I just can't wait until tomorrow. Promise we can come see him again when we visit Auntie Carmen?"

"Of course we can. But be prepared for the door to close on you again."

"Maybe one day he will come visit us. Maybe he will even live with us, Pedro. Wait until Mamá and the boys hear that we found him. Do you think Mamá will ever see him again? Maybe we can be one happy family again sitting around the table at Christmas time singing 'Feliz Navidad.'"

"Dios mio, Rosita! Your father's not even talking to you. Remember, he slammed the door on you, and already you have him moving in with us! Just maybe you'll never see him again. After all, he must have had a pretty important reason for leaving you."

"Pedro, don't ever say that again. Don't even think that."

———

When Evelyn, Mike's housekeeper, unlocked the door and came in to clean up the dinner dishes, she found Mike slumped in his worn leather recliner in a fitful sleep, his head and shoulders jerking spasmodically, the TV droning on, his favorite beef stew untouched. She poked him on the arm a couple of times. "Father Mike," she whispered, "Father Mike, wake up. I'll help you up to bed. Father Mike." After a few minutes, she gave up and covered him with his striped serape, tucking it under his legs. She went into the kitchen, spooned the stew into a plastic container, made room for it in the fridge, washed off the dishes and placed them in the rack to dry. Once more she went over to the sleeping priest but was unable to wake him. She turned off the overhead lights, leaving the lamp on in case he woke up in the middle of the night, and let herself quietly out the door.

———

"Don, this is Mike. Can I come over right now? I need your help!" Father Monahan recognized the tremor in Mike's voice and assured him he would be waiting for him.

Father Don knew about Mike's double life, for he had confessed his transgressions shortly after he arrived in Alamogordo. It might not have been the worst thing Father Don heard in the secrecy of the confessional, but it certainly was one that ate at his insides. In Germany, Mike was an inspiration to him, but these last 20 years had been an uphill battle; Don ached for him. When he first arrived, Mike was in a deep depression. They talked a lot; Mike found it easy to discuss his feelings about both God and his family with Father Don. It wasn't that Father Don knew the right words to heal Mike; it was more like Mike talked so much, he healed himself. Father Don knew that playing the organ helped as well. Mike would come to St. John of God's church almost every morning for the early Mass and then stay and play the organ, a lot of Bach, only a little of Beethoven, for the latter seemed more suited for the piano. As time passed, Mike settled into a rhythm. Until finally, these last few years, he seemed at peace.

Father Don wondered what upset Mike so today. He checked his watch, opened his breviary, and turned to the psalms. He was deep in meditation when he heard the bell. Putting his breviary on the side table, he slowly rose to open the door. He was surprised at the tousled hair, the rumpled clothes, the red eyes. Don put his arms around his old friend as he helped him inside. They walked together into his private sitting room. Mike took his old place in the blue and white pinstriped easy chair while Don went to brew some coffee.

Father Don knew Mike would feel comfortable in the sitting room. Somehow or other the Mexican Madonna and Child hanging directly above the mantel always calmed him. Don hoped he could help him find his way out of the morass that threatened to bury him again.

"Here you are! Black, the way you like it. Mine, of course, is heavily laced with sugar and cream. I still don't understand how you can drink this stuff black." Don could see that Mike had no time for small talk this morning. "So, Mike, what's troubling you?"

"Don, she knocked on my door last night."

"She? Who do you mean?"

"My princesa! She knocked on my door."

"Are you sure? Mike, what are the chances of that occurring after 20 years? Maybe you had a few too many Glenlivets, and it was just someone selling something who looked like your daughter might have looked."

"Don, believe me, it was Rosa. She was beautiful, Don. Her eyes were my eyes. Her long dark hair curled slightly, a sprinkling of freckles dotted her nose.

"Mike, what are the chances of that happening? I mean it's just too coincidental! What did you say?" Don picked up his coffee, blew on it, and took a sip.

"I couldn't talk. I was completely overcome. All of those old feelings returned. Memories kept flipping through my mind: I could see her blowing out the candles on her birthday cake, whacking the piñata until all the candy tumbled onto her head, snuggling up close to listen to a bedtime story, proudly reciting her homework, grabbing my hand to dance the jitterbug, singing 'Tres Ratones Ciegos,' laughing at her brother's silly jokes. Visions just kept repeating like the projector was stuck and the images kept flipping over and over. I couldn't say a word. Tears gathered in my eyes then fell down my face. I didn't know what to do. Time collapsed, reverted 20 years into the past. I couldn't move. I was in a time warp. Finally, I just closed the door and left her standing there. I left her standing outside the door. Don, I don't know what to do!"

Don listened, then waited for Mike to resume.

"I'm getting that empty feeling again, that I'm just a shadow, not fully alive. You've just got to help me. The same old nightmare returned where I'm sitting across from the bishop and then he starts to beat me with a leather thong, and I get up and run away, and he chases me, and then I fall, and I wake up startled to hear myself screaming. Don, I haven't had that nightmare in at least five years. What am I going to do?"

"Is she coming back again?"

"I don't know. Suppose she does! What should I do?"

"Mike, I think it would be unwise to see her. You have made peace with your past. And I think it's best to leave the past in the past. Don't let it torture you."

"Don, seeing her made me realize what a worthless individual I must have been to leave the three children and their mother. How did they ever survive without me? I often wonder if I did the right thing. At the time, I thought I owed it to God to reject my little family as atonement for my sins. I thought it was the right way to punish myself for ignoring my vows. Now, I think God would have forgiven me if I had stayed and provided for my family. The bishop, however, is another story. I will always be anathema to him." Mike took out his white handkerchief, blew his nose. "I did drive by the house in Acapulco a couple of times before I left for Alamogordo, just to see them one more time."

"How about another coffee?"

"Thanks, no, Don. I'm feeling a little better. I think you're right about not seeing her. It's just too painful."

"Have you eaten anything yet today, Mike? We could walk through the park and stop at La Hoya for a sandwich."

"Don, that sounds like a plan. What would I do without you?" Father Don picked up the coffee cups and headed toward the kitchen.

"Say, Don, I think I'll walk into the church to see if God is still talking to me today. When you're ready to go, just come get me."

"Okay, got to run upstairs and get my sweater." Father Don walked slowly up the stairs one step at a time thinking that time spent in prayer would do Mike a lot of good.

Mike knelt before the altar, placed his head in his hands, looked up to the Crucifix and began, "My God."

———

The next day when Pedro and Rosa returned to visit Mike, no one opened the door. They knocked and knocked for at least five minutes, but there was no response. Rosa collapsed again in tears. Again, Pedro tried to calm her but there was no consoling her. They sat in the car outside Mike's house for quite a while trying to figure out what to do. "Pedro, he did it again. He did it again." Rosa repeated it over and over like a mantra. She flashed back to the first time he abandoned her when she was 12. All of the buried emotions rushed to the surface. "Pedro, I want to come back as long as there is a chance, however slight, that he might open it once again." So, they decided to return to knock on the door at least once a year when they drove to Alamogordo to visit Auntie Carmen.

Before they left, Pedro looked at the dusty antique parked in the driveway. "Rosita, that car won't move. It will take thousands of dollars and many months before it will even start. I doubt if they still sell parts for it anymore."

Denial

Amaudlin pall wrapped itself around Fran's shoulders. In times past when she prepared for the trip southwest to visit her brother she was delirious with joy. But today was a different story. It wasn't just that Joe wouldn't accompany her, for he had passed away 10 years ago and she was used to traveling alone. But this time was different, for she was traveling to Alamogordo to pay her respects to her brother Mike.

She received the news of his death after she had sent him an invitation to her 75th birthday party. Fran had been hoping for a positive response from Mike, but instead received a phone call from his housekeeper, Evelyn, with the sad news. Evelyn apologized for not calling sooner but explained that she didn't have Fran's phone number until the invitation arrived. Fran wished she had been in closer contact with Mike these past few years; she wished she had been with him to help him when he needed her. She knew she had to visit his grave, find out from Evelyn the details of his death, see the church where the funeral was held. Fran also realized she couldn't make this trip alone, she needed a companion. Carrie immediately volunteered to go with her, and together they planned the trip.

News of a second phone call from Rosa and Pedro to Joe, Jr., however, stunned Fran: *Outrageous, insulting*, thought Fran when she heard Rosa's story. *How dare this Mexican woman pose as the daughter of Mike, a holy man of God*. Even though she wanted nothing to do with this woman who claimed to be his daughter, Fran reluctantly agreed to meet her, confident she and Carrie could easily reveal her duplicity.

———

As soon as they deplaned, Fran and Carrie rented a car and drove to the Holy Martyr Cemetery to pay their respects. They spent time at the gravesite and said the rosary, then headed for the Best Western to meet with Rosa and Pedro. The directions provided by the gatekeeper at the cemetery were simple and the trip to the motel was quick. However, the Southwest heat and the visit to the cemetery tired her and Fran was looking forward to a rest before meeting Rosa and Pedro.

As the women unlocked and opened the motel door, a waft of hot, stale air affronted them. Immediately, Fran reached for the switch to turn on the air conditioner, then scanned the nondescript room: bland beige walls, beige and brown striped armchairs, a desk, a bureau, a nondescript lamp, and two beds with a bed table between.

The phone rang. Fran wasn't expecting it so soon; she desperately wanted a nap. She glared at Carrie. "Don't answer it. I can't do it. I just can't. I don't want to meet her. I don't want to see her. I don't care what she says. I just don't want to listen to her story. She couldn't be my brother's daughter. It's impossible. He was a good Catholic priest. This Mexican woman must want money or something." The phone continued to ring.

"But, Mom, you agreed to meet her."

"Well, I changed my mind."

"But that's what we flew cross country for."

"Maybe you flew to Alamogordo to meet that woman. I didn't. I came to Alamogordo to pay final respects to my brother."

"You promised, Mom. You promised. It's not easy for me either."

Fran didn't answer, her hand still on the air-conditioner dial. Paralyzed, she stared at the screeching phone.

Finally, Carrie reached for the receiver, and Fran retreated to the motel bathroom. She closed the door behind her, leaned against it, and then rubbed her forehead, wondering why she ever agreed to meet this imposter. She was sure Carrie could handle the situation. Nevertheless, she mumbled a quick Hail Mary and then splashed cold water on her face, grabbed a hand towel, and patted it dry. She put her ear to the closed door, could hear Carrie's voice but couldn't distinguish the words. She waited for silence then edged the door open a crack and peered through, watching Carrie.

———

Slowly, Carrie walked to the motel door, slid the chain-lock, and turned the handle. She pushed the door open and leaned out, straining to see past the row of parked cars. Carrie dreamed, rather had nightmares, of meeting Rosa Santos ever since that dreaded phone call. She always pictured Rosa in a colorful peasant skirt with a white off-the-shoulder blouse and beaded moccasins, thick wavy black hair cascading over her shoulders, and dark eyes dominating a brown face. In her dreams, Carrie demanded proof of paternity, refusing to speak until the Mexican produced evidence.

Standing on tiptoe, Carrie craned her neck, saw a tall lanky gentleman in a gray windbreaker holding the door of the Dodge Dart for a young dark-haired woman dressed in brown pumps, a pencil slim skirt, and an unbuttoned suit jacket over a cream silk blouse. As she approached, Carrie noticed her face, lips, nose, freckles, then the eyes—steel-gray eyes like Uncle Mike's. Gone in one second were all Carrie's doubts. She knew intuitively that the woman standing before her was her cousin, the daughter of her uncle, the priest. Her objections melted quicker than butter on a stack of steaming pancakes as her arms automatically reached out to embrace Rosa O'Brien. Neither said a word. Finally, as they untangled themselves, Rosa smiled. "Hola mi prima." Her gray eyes crinkled.

"Hello, cousin." Carrie smiled, unable to shift her gaze from Rosa's piercing eyes.

The tall gentleman standing beside Rosa cleared his throat and extended his hand hesitantly. "Hi. I'm Pedro Santos, Rosa's husband. She doesn't speak much English, so if there is a problem understanding, I can translate."

"So sorry, please excuse my rudeness," Carrie said gripping his hand tightly. "Come inside. Meet my mother, your Aunt Fran."

Carrie scanned the room quickly, relieved to see Fran walk out of the bathroom, towel still in her hand. Fran, her face deadpan, barely glanced at Rosa as Carrie introduced her. Rosa hesitantly reached for Fran's hand, but Fran continued to fumble with the towel. Carrie wondered if she noticed the eyes.

Fran wiped beads of sweat from her forehead. "Carrie, please turn the air conditioner on. This room is quite stuffy." Then she turned her attention to Rosa and Pedro. "Please have a seat. We have a lot to talk about." She indicated one of the armchairs for Rosa. Pedro perched on the armrest.

Carrie watched her mother sit primly in the striped armchair, hands folded in her lap, legs crossed at the ankles. *I guess she didn't notice the eyes*, she thought and knew the night would be uncomfortable.

Fran looked directly at Rosa. *Now*, thought Carrie, *she'll see the eyes.*

"Rosa, it is almost impossible for me to imagine that my brother was your father. He was such a good priest, so devoted to God and his parishioners." She waited for Rosa's comment. When Rosa didn't respond, Fran continued. "We would get together every February for vacation, my husband, Joe; my oldest brother, Tom; Mike; and I. Before we went to play golf in Mazatlan, we would spend time at St. Ignatius, his church in El Paso." Fran cleared her throat. While Pedro translated for Rosa, Carrie watched her mother, but could tell by the grim look on her face that she hadn't noticed the eyes.

Rosa nodded. "Si, I know now that my father was the pastor there."

When Pedro translated her comment, Fran snapped "He was not just a pastor. He was a well-loved pastor. Every Mass was packed; people spilled out the door onto the steps. After Mass, his parishioners would surround him joking, laughing, shaking hands, and asking for prayers. He raised thousands and thousands of dollars to build an incredible school. Any spare time he did have, he spent in Mexico doing missionary work. So even if he didn't uphold his vows, his schedule didn't leave any time for a family."

Rosa looked to Pedro, listened to his translation; then she turned to Fran and spoke softly, "It's just as difficult for me to realize that my father was a priest as it is for you to understand that your brother, the priest, had a family. I didn't know he was a priest until after he died. I knew him as a wonderful father for 12 years, and then he disappeared. But before he left us, life was heaven. We laughed and played and danced and sang. He called me his 'princesa'; he never used English at home. I always felt valued and loved and protected by both my mother and my father. As a matter of fact, I can't imagine how he had any time for his church."

Her words sound rehearsed, thought Fran as she stared unblinking, listening to Pedro's translation. Still reluctant to believe any scandal about her older brother, Fran started to grill Rosa. "Where did you live? In El Paso, near the church?" Pedro repeated the questions and added, "I don't think she likes you, Rosita."

"No, I never lived in El Paso. We lived in Mexico in three different homes: one in Mexico City, one in Acapulco, and one in Chihuahua."

When she heard the translation, Fran interrupted abruptly, leaning forward with her hands on the arm of the chair. "That's ridiculous! It's impossible on a priest's salary! I know priests don't take a vow of poverty, but that's impossible."

Carrie couldn't understand why Fran was being so relentless, why she was being so antagonistic when it was obvious that Rosa was Father Mike's daughter.

Rosa glanced at Pedro now leaning against the bureau as he interpreted. Encouraged by his slight nod, she took a deep breath, arched her eyebrows. "My father worked for the U.S. military. As an Army Air Corps Captain, he was frequently sent on high priority secret missions…at least that's what we believed. When he wasn't on duty, he practiced the piano at the conservatory, went to bullfights, or just stayed at home with us. When he was on his 'secret missions,' we had absolutely no contact with him. But when he returned, and we were all together again, we celebrated." Fran listened carefully to Pedro as he deciphered the Spanish.

"He certainly must have won some awfully big purses betting on the bullfights." Fran rubbed her forehead concentrating. "Now, just what years are you talking about, Rosa? Because, if I remember correctly, Mike was discharged from the Air Corps around 1950 or 1951. Do you remember, Carrie? We all drove down to that big celebration in Louisiana?" Without waiting for Carrie to reply, Fran turned to confront Rosa.

As Rosa heard the translation she shook her head. "No, no! I was born in 1956, and I was the baby in the family. The twins, boys, are a couple of years older than me. He couldn't have been discharged in 1951or 1952, for he was always in the Air Corps. He would be gone for weeks, maybe months at a time."

As she listened to Pedro explain, Fran grimaced. "But that's impossible. Mike wasn't involved with the Air Corps then. He became the pastor of St. Ignatius in 1952 after he was discharged." Fran, wanting some confirmation, looked at Carrie, who shrugged. She never saw her mother so adamant. She was always a calm, loving, supportive individual. *She must be blinded by her denial,* thought Carrie.

Pedro adjusted his spectacles, gestured to Rosa's leather briefcase, and spoke to her. "Rosa, why don't you show them your photos?" As Pedro explained in English that Rosa brought a few photographs of her family, Carrie hoped the change of subject would soften Fran.

Rosa reached into her bag and pulled out a manila envelope. "I brought some pictures of my family to show you." She smiled as Pedro translated. Carefully, she removed several old black and white photos and passed one to Fran, "This one was taken of my mother, Maria, and my father on their honeymoon." Fran didn't need a translation; she could clearly see her brother in the photo. Carrie, anxious to see, slid to the floor next to Fran. The photo was bent a bit on the edges and quite faded, but they could see that it depicted Mike O'Brien in a light suit, his arm around a smiling woman wearing a silky flowered dress, holding a large bouquet of roses. They were centered under an arch of white gardenias.

"See how happy they look!" Rosa beamed.

"That's definitely my brother," said Fran struggling with the truth the evidence presented. "Is this woman your mother?"

"Si, my mother Maria."

"Maria," repeated Fran. "How do you know it's their honeymoon?"

Waiting for Pedro to transcribe, Rosa said, "My mother told me."

"Where did they get married Rosa, do you know?" Fran continued to fire questions, annoyed with the translating.

"Si, they married in Juarez. That's where they met. My mother told me the story often."

Barely waiting for Pedro to interpret, Fran fired back, "Is there a marriage license?"

"No," said Pedro interpreting as Rosa spoke, "her father and mother married in Juarez in 1952 before a judge and two witnesses but there was no license."

"But that's impossible," Fran insisted. "He was just named pastor in 1952."

"Someday, Rosa, you'll have to tell us their story" Carrie interrupted. "But now, can we see the other photos you brought with you? Do you have any of the twins?"

"They want to see the photos, Rosa," Pedro said in Spanish. Rosa looked through the pictures and pulled another from the pack.

"Here's one of all of us. I remember that day at the beach in Acapulco; we had built a huge sand castle decorated it with stones and twigs. There's my mother and my father and over here with me are the twins—I am about seven, and Eduardo and Pancho about ten." Pedro translated as Fran and Carrie examined the photos

"Adorable," crooned Carrie. "They look identical, and look at your bathing suit, how cute."

Fran grew quiet, unable to refute the black and white evidence in front of her. Carrie wondered what her mother was thinking. She was so close to her brother, this revelation must be difficult. "Rosa, this is just very hard for me. Please, show me what else you have."

The next one, a formal photo of Mike in his Air Force officer's uniform, was very familiar to Fran and Carrie. The identical photo hung on Fran's living room wall. The final photo was one Fran wished hung on her living room wall: the entire O'Brien family in their Sunday best grouped around their parents when Fran, the youngest, was about 6. "Rosa, I never saw this photo before. I love it. Where did you get it?"

After asking Rosa, Pedro said, "Her father gave it to her."

Fran reached for the photo. "Can I see it more closely?"

Rosa reluctantly handed her the old black and white. Fran studied it, ran her fingers over the glossy finish, felt the creases, the torn edge. Carrie knew she would love to have it. "Rosa, do you know who the people are in this photo?"

Pedro replied, "She says that's her grandmother and grandfather and her Uncle Tom and you, Aunt Fran, and standing right behind you, her father."

Fran winced when she heard Pedro say the word "Aunt" with his Mexican accent.

Pedro listened closely to Rosa talk about the photo. "My father often told stories about the O'Brien family, stories of a cottage surrounded by green grass and yellow daffodils in Ireland, acres to play hide and go seek and stick ball, a tiny red brick school house where he learned to read and write. Whenever I asked why you didn't visit, he explained that you couldn't afford the airfare. Of course, now I know there is no truth to this story: he was telling me a fairy tale, but that didn't make me love him any less." Pedro again took great pains to convey Rosa's feelings behind the words as well as the meaning of the words themselves.

Fran shook her head. "He certainly was telling a fairy tale. We came from Canada, St. John's, Newfoundland, to be exact. I can barely remember that summer when the whole family went back for a visit. I was about three or four, Mike at least seven, and Tom almost 20."

Rosa was about to spread the photos on the bed so everyone could see them, but kept searching Fran's face for a sign of acceptance. Fran fingered the photo of her family, unwilling to part with it. "What a wonderful shot of Agnes and Bill, my mom and dad. They were so proud of their son, the priest." So Rosa gathered the photos, shuffled them into an even pile, and slid them into the manila envelope.

As Fran watched Rosa, she wondered how she would ever accept this woman as a niece. "We have to talk more, Rosa; your pictures provide evidence of a life I knew nothing about. Maybe Mike did lead a double life. Please have lunch with us tomorrow, so we can talk more."

After listening to Pedro's interpretation, Rosa squealed, "Si, I'd like that!"

"Why not meet us here at noon and we can decide where to go."

"Si, Si."

"By the way, Rosa," Fran added as an afterthought, "How did you get Joey's number when you called to tell us you were my brother's daughter?"

Pedro, not bothering to translate for Rosa, said, "Evelyn gave it to us when she told us Rosa's father died."

"Oh. I see. Well, goodbye until tomorrow at 12."

———

After Rosa and Pedro left, Carrie hugged Fran. "What a day, Mom. What a day."

Fran stiffened a bit. "I always remember Mike at the piano playing 'I'll be Down to Get you in a Taxi, Honey.' He pounded out that melody like he was being paid a million bucks for it. We would all stand around the piano singing and laughing, swaying with the beat: Julie, Joe, and I. Now, I'm singing and laughing alone; they're all gone."

"He must have been the life of the party."

"He was passionate about everything he did. Playing the piano, saying Mass, building a school. He didn't do things half way. When he got involved in something, he was a whirlwind. He always completed what he started, no matter what it took."

"So what do you think?"

"About Rosa?"

"Yes, about Rosa!"

"I don't know. I can't refute the photos. But perhaps he was just socializing with a Mexican family. Just because he is posing with them in a photo on the beach, it doesn't mean the family belongs to him."

"But, Mom, her eyes. Didn't you notice her eyes?"

"What about her eyes?"

"They weren't brown Mexican eyes; they were gray, steel-gray, Uncle Mike's eyes. Didn't you think you were looking at him?"

"Now, now, Carrie, I'm sure Uncle Mike is the not the only individual on the face of the Earth with steel-gray eyes."

"And her pale freckled face? I've never seen a Mexican with pale freckled skin. How do you explain that?"

"I know intellectually you're right, Carrie. The evidence all points your way, the wrong way. But I'm the only one left who knew Mike inside and out, knew how much he was devoted to being a priest—not just a priest but the most passionate priest it was possible to be."

"Do you think he might have been just as passionate about being a husband and father?"

Fran stared at Carrie, *Was it possible,* she wondered.

———

As they left the Best Western, Pedro put his arm around Rosa; he pulled her close. "Was it worth traveling from Juarez just to meet your relatives? The expense of renting the car? The time off from the hospital?"

She looked up at him. "We had to come to Alamogordo for the court case, Pedro."

"I guess you're right." They walked a bit in silence as they approached the sleek rental. He opened the sedan door and ushered her inside. "Wouldn't it be nice to have a car like this of our own someday, Rosita?" He unlocked the driver side. Then looking back at Room 834, he settled into the rental, turned the ignition, and glanced at her expectantly. "But tell me, Rosita, how do you think everything went? Are you happy about meeting your father's relatives?"

She turned to face him. "Pedro, you know I've dreamed of meeting my father's family for years. I think this meeting has been the most important in my life, except of course the night we discovered my father here in Alamogordo after searching for him for almost 25 years."

"Well, what about the night we got married? Wasn't that pretty important too, Rosita?" he teased.

"Si, Si! Except the night we got married."

"Is your Aunt Fran just the way you imagined her?"

Rosa pondered his question, searching for the right words to convey the mixed feelings she had. "You know he always talked about Aunt Fran. He would lift me onto his knee and tell me stories about her. But tonight I didn't feel any warmth from her. I don't think she wanted to believe Mike O'Brien was my father. I could feel the distance between us widen like the Rio Grande separating Juarez from El Paso."

"But she did invite us to lunch tomorrow. That seemed to me like a good sign."

"I guess so, si. But, you know, Pedro, I was really scared when we walked through the door of the Best Western office. I almost dashed back to the car. I just didn't know how my cousin and my aunt would react. I was afraid neither of them would accept me. My whole body was vibrating. My arms prickled with goose bumps. I think I would have fainted if you hadn't been there." As they drove out of the parking lot, the sun started to sink, and the traffic picked up.

Pedro waited for the light, drumming impatiently on the steering wheel. "I think they liked you, Rosita. How could they help but like you—you are such a sweet woman." He paused, then spoke again. "I wonder if they will help you in the court case?"

Pulling her collar up and crossing her arms, Rosa considered his question. "I didn't want to say anything about it tonight. Perhaps we can mention it tomorrow. What do you think, Pedro? Maybe they would even be willing to testify for us."

"Maybe Carrie would. I'm not so sure about your Aunt Fran."

Pedro veered right then slipped into a parking spot at the crowded Amber Motel. "Well here we are, safe and sound. That didn't take long." He turned off the ignition, and got out, searching for the motel keys. After jiggling the keys for a couple of minutes the lock turned, and he and Rosa walked in. Rosa kicked off her pumps, unbuttoned her jacket, curled up on the recliner and leaned back. "I can't wait to tell Mamá. I wonder how she will react—and my brothers! Pedro, I just can't believe tonight happened! And without your translation, it would have been impossible."

"Anything for you, my love, you know that. Would you like a Corona?" he opened the mini refrigerator.

"Sure! What time do we meet the attorney tomorrow?" She smoothed her skirt and tucked it under her legs.

Pedro searched in the drawer for the opener and then popped the beer. "I think it's 9:30. I have to check my day planner. We have plenty of time to keep our appointment and meet Fran and Carrie later. Maybe you should ask the attorney if mentioning the case to them is a good idea."

"I just don't understand why my father would exclude us from his will. Do you think Evelyn, his housekeeper, forced him to make her the sole heir when he was ill? I don't trust her. There's something about her that I don't like. I wonder what happened to all his furniture and his books. And he always told me that the T-bird was mine from the time I was really young. He would say, 'Princesa, see that snazzy black sports car in the driveway? Someday when you're all grown up, it will be yours.' You know, Pedro, it's hard to believe that it's still parked in his driveway."

Pedro settled his glasses on his nose. "I can't believe that old thing will still turn over. Are you sure the case is worth all we're investing in it? I understand why you are entitled to the estate; after all, you and your brothers and your mother are his rightful heirs. But I'm not sure the estate is worth all the time and money we're investing in it."

Rosa sipped her Corona, pushed her hair off her forehead. "Mi querido, I know you're spending a lot of money and maybe for nil; you are such an unbelievable husband. You are so good to me. I'm keeping my fingers crossed that our efforts are successful. Actually, the most important thing about the case is that the court recognizes the twins and me as Michael O'Brien's children. That would also give us the U.S. citizenship we are entitled to. But, honey, I'm so tired. Let's talk about this in the morning."

Exploring

Waking up from a restless sleep, tangled in the sheets, Fran peered over at her daughter still sound, her journal open next to her. Then, remembering the events of the night before, she ducked under the pillow to wait for the alarm. Her mind was in a muddle. She struggled to understand why her brother deserted his church for some woman and then turned around and deserted her and his children. *I can never forgive him, never,* she thought. She hoped Evelyn would provide some answers today. *Today has to be better,* she reasoned.

As soon as she saw Carrie's eyes open, she fired off the thoughts that were swirling through her mind. "I still can't believe Mike's housekeeper never called me when he died. I'm glad we're meeting with her. I need answers to some questions." She paused for a moment, then began again. "If I hadn't included the RSVP with a phone number on my birthday invitation, I still wouldn't know he was dead." She looked out the window, seeing nothing. "And perhaps we would never have gotten the second phone call, the one from Rosa, the one that set all of us spinning then vacillating from 'what if' to 'no way.'"

Carrie yawned, rubbed her eyes, and listened. Fran leaned on her elbow and continued, "There is absolutely no truth at all in Rosa's claim. You know that, Carrie. I don't care how many pictures she has. It is unlikely, almost impossible, that my brother, a priest, would violate the most important vows of his station." Fran's voice rose as she became agitated. "He was the most devout, the most dedicated priest I knew. No one could steal him from the church. He would rather jump into the burning ash of Mt. St. Helens than violate his vow of chastity." She glared at Carrie, willing her to agree.

"Now, Mom, I know this must be upsetting for you. Just try to keep an open mind. Hopefully, Evelyn will clarify things this afternoon. But to be honest with you, in my mind, the greater sin for Uncle Mike was abandoning his family, not violating the rule of celibacy."

———

Despite the rain, finding Mike's cottage proved easy enough, for the town was well laid out. As they drove up, Fran studied the tiny white stucco cottage surrounded by the cyclone fence. The T-bird was still in the driveway, the same one Rosa mentioned the night before. Carrie and Fran splashed through the rain-drops and knocked on the weather-beaten door. Fran was surprised that a lovely, young Hispanic woman welcomed them, not the stereotypical old, tired, worn housekeeper she expected.

Evelyn invited them into the empty house. It was stripped of just about every-thing—no books, no furniture, no bed, or bureau. The kitchen, minus everything but a table, looked like a trash can: papers on the floor, crushed soda cans in the sink, dishes crusted with dried up food piled on the counter. Fran stole a glance at Carrie who didn't say a word. Fran remembered honey-tone pine furniture with wrought-iron hinges and pulls, terra cotta lamps, a book case crammed with leather bound classics, and of course Mike's leather recliner. She wondered where everything was, sure he would've brought them to Alamagordo.

"Please," Evelyn said, "come across the street to my house where we can sit down and talk. My husband just took the kids to visit their grandmother. There won't be any interruptions, so I will be able to answer all your questions and explain exactly how Father Mike died. I've grown very fond of him these past few years."

Carrie and Fran followed Evelyn across the street, the rain having dissipated, and entered another tiny cottage, but one well cared for and decorated quite tastefully.

They settled into a floral covered sofa and turned their attention to Evelyn. She smoothed her skirt and flipped her long dark hair off her face. "In January, Father Mike was in the hospital with pneumonia, but he recovered. Then one day in June, when he was feeding his cat his foot got stuck on the rug. He fell and was unable to get up. When I went to the house, I found him on the floor and called the emergency squad. At the hospital, the doctors analyzed his x-ray and told Father Mike he had a broken hip and suggested surgery. He refused to undergo any operation. After I promised to take responsibility for him, they gave him some painkillers, and sent him home. His health insurance provided a wheel chair and a hospital bed, and I lent him one of those big La-Z-Boy chairs and a TV."

"How nice of you!" said Fran. "But, I'm confused, didn't Uncle Mike have a chair and a TV of his own?"

"Yes, you're right, Fran, but he needed the chair and TV for his bedroom."

"Oh I see," said Fran, but she really didn't.

Evelyn continued to recount the story. "I had some kind of a beeper system installed and also gave him my cordless phone in case he needed me in the night. Then, I moved one of my twin beds into his house so I could stay if need be. When I cooked for my family, I ran meals over to him." She paused, catching her breath, brushed her hair out of her eyes again and then continued. "Sometimes I even cooked my roast at his house. He liked the smell of a roast in the oven."

Fran nodded, adjusting her glasses. "Evelyn, it is so reassuring to hear how you helped him. How can I ever thank you enough? I only wish I could have helped in some way."

"Well, I really liked Father Mike. Joanna, his former housekeeper, was my sister. She died last year and I took over the job, so I got to know him well in his last few months. He was such a happy man. He always smiled and his steel-gray eyes crinkled up at the corners. I even took my family to his house to celebrate Christmas and Easter. I bought him a tree, a blue spruce, and trimmed it. He was especially fond of my almost-3-year-old. For some reason, he called him Pancho and taught him how to play chess."

This woman was certainly devoted to my brother, Fran thought. *She seemed to go way beyond the responsibilities of a salaried housekeeper.* Fran quickly wiped away a tear dribbling down her cheek. Carrie reached over to squeeze her hand. Recovering, Fran said, "I just don't know how to thank you for taking such good care of him. By the way, was he buried in the church?"

"Yes, the funeral Mass was at St. John of God in town. I bought him a black suit, and his friend Father Monahan provided a Roman collar. All of my family and friends attended—no one else." She paused. "I told the funeral director I didn't think there were any surviving family members."

Fran sighed, her brow furrowed. "Oh I wish I could have been there. Why didn't you call us, tell us of his illness?"

"I didn't know who to contact. I knew Father Mike had a brother and a sister, but I didn't think either was still alive. Then, one day, the invitation for your 75th birthday party arrived. That's when I called." Evelyn crossed her legs and smoothed her hair again.

Fran looked at Carrie. "Tomorrow, let's go to Mass at St. John of God's. I'd like to talk to Father Monahan." Carrie nodded.

"It's not far from here, and I'm sure Father Monahan would like to talk to any friend of Father Mike's. They were pretty close." Evelyn furrowed her brow again, bit her lips, and hesitantly said. "You know, I never knew Father Mike had a family. He never mentioned a daughter or any sons, and Joanna never told me about them. I didn't think Catholic priests married. Then, one day, out of nowhere, I saw this man and woman knocking on his door. They persisted, then they sat in their car for quite a while watching the house. I was curious so I went over. That was when I met Rosa and Pedro. I had no idea who they were, and Rosa had no idea that Father Mike was a priest. I was completely flabbergasted when she told me she was Father Mike's daughter. I didn't know whether to believe her story. She told me they tried to visit Father Mike several times, but he wouldn't answer the door."

"Oh, then they did talk to you."

"Oh yes, several times. I tried to be very nice to them. I gave Rosa his chalice and ciborium, which was inscribed by Father Mike's father and mother. But now I'm afraid they are trying to take all of his property. He left everything to me in his will in lieu of a weekly salary, not that he had very much. And I did take good care of him, especially when he was so sick. Now Rosa and Pedro tell me they are contesting the will. Rosa insists that she and her brothers should share in his estate since they are his children and rightful heirs. I just don't know what to do about it." She glanced at Fran and Carrie expecting some kind of reply.

"We only met them yesterday, and were just as surprised as you were that Uncle Mike had a family," said Carrie. "But, after meeting Rosa, we have to believe that she is his daughter. She has his steel-gray eyes."

Fran looked puzzled and interrupted, "But Rosa never told us anything about a court case. We'll have to ask her about it. I'm confident the court will assess the evidence and come to a wise decision. Have you hired legal counsel?"

"Yes." She nodded. "But I just don't trust those two. I am afraid of them."

Feeling uncomfortable with this information, Fran wanted time to process everything. She felt that Evelyn seemed to be genuinely concerned about Mike, but she didn't want to take sides right now. She recalled the emptiness of Mike's house and wondered where all of his belongings were. She checked her watch. "Evelyn, I don't think we should be placed in the middle of this problem. We need some time to process all of this information you have given us. Carrie and I are deeply grateful that you were so kind to Mike when he needed you."

On the drive back, Fran was unusually quiet, feeling guilty that she was unable to help her brother when he needed her. "I wish I had known. I wish I had known," she sighed. She turned to the window, eyes glazed, and retreated to that place where past and present and imagination and reality intermingled.

Understanding

Carrie and Fran returned to the Best Western with just enough time to freshen up before meeting Pedro and Rosa for lunch. As Fran walked through the door she remarked, "Let's take the Santos to Deming today. It was one of Mike's early assignments and I'm looking forward to seeing it again."

"That would be fun! I'm sure Rosa would like to see where her dad lived. Say! Didn't Uncle Mike marry you and Dad there?"

"He did. His pastor wouldn't give him permission to come home to marry us, so we traveled to Mike. What wonderful memories from that trip! I remember telling your dad I wouldn't marry him without irises, like the ones in van Gogh paintings. So he went out on a mission. When he returned several hours later, he handed me a corsage of delicate lavender violets. From that day on, violets were the only flowers I ever wanted."

"Mom, I think I see them parking. Are you ready?"

"Just about. Grab those sweaters. It might be cold in the mountains." Fran put the toothpaste back in the cabinet and followed Carrie outside. The Santos were thrilled to travel to Deming when they heard it was one of Mike's first assignments.

As soon as they buckled up, Carrie headed west on I70/285 for the two-hour trip through the prairie and sage. Vultures swarmed continuously, and dust balls rolled through the beige landscape until caught by cactus. In the distance were two mountain ranges: the closer of the two, their destination, was snow covered. The heavy sweaters Fran insisted they take would be handy.

The ride was slow and easy and soon the conversation started to flow. Carrie explained to Rosa and Pedro that the family visited Uncle Mike one Christmas many years ago when she was about 12. She remembered Deming as a small town with long one-story beige- and sand-colored ranchers next to a snow-covered mountain and was surprised when she saw the nifty little ski chalets, souvenir shops, and restaurants dotting the main street. "Mom, what a change! It looks just like Vermont!"

They climbed out of the car as soon as Carrie parked, and, very hungry, walked into the closest restaurant, Casa Blanca, a real tourist trap. Earthenware jugs, brightly colored serapes, and a stuffed buffalo head gave a hint of Mexico to the rustic log room.

When the waitress finally came to their booth, she totally ignored Carrie and Fran and spieled off the specials in Spanish. Pedro navigated the menu and ordered chilies and tacos and beer all around.

"How long have you two been married?" Fran asked, leaning forward her elbows resting on the edge of the wooden table. Pedro and Rosa look at each other, then Pedro spoke. "About four years. We met a few years before that working at the new Wal-Mart, actually the first one in town. Rosa was a cashier, and I stocked shelves. I was trying to earn cash while getting my medical degree at The University of Mexico. I needed a job that didn't involve thinking; I desperately needed to rest my mind for those five hours a day."

"Now, Pedro," Rosa said in Spanish, nudging him gently in the elbow. Tell them what you did."

"Sure, Rosita. Don't worry." He turned back to Carrie and Fran, "She wants me to give you all the details, so here's the whole story. Well how could I help but notice Rosa? She was so hot with those gray eyes and that sprinkling of freckles. She had a way of crinkling up her nose every time she laughed, and she laughed often. 'Hey, how's it going?' she would call out with a big smile that put the sunshine in my day.

"I really had to think of some way to get her attention. On my salary and with all of the bills for tuition and books, it had to be creative, not pricey. I couldn't afford to give her turquoise necklaces and bracelets—I didn't even have enough pesos to buy her a burrito. About all I could afford was a cup of coffee. So that's what I did. Every night when I came in to work, I put a cup of Dunkin Donuts coffee by her station. Then I started taping messages to the cup. I started with something like, 'Hola,' then finally, 'How about a coffee at Dunkin Donuts after work today?' One thing led to another and eventually we walked down the aisle together." He gave Rosa a peck on the cheek and patted her hand.

They did seem like newlyweds, Fran thought. "Did you ever meet Rosa's father?"

The waitress interrupted, slapping the chilies, the salads, and the tacos on the table. No one noticed her insulting manner—they were so intent on the story.

"Yes, but not until after we married. Actually, we found him together."

Carrie gulped a huge spoonful of chili and immediately started to fan her mouth. "Water! Water!" She grabbed her glass and chugged the whole thing. "Phew! That's spicy hot and temperature hot at the same time," she said, wiping her burning lips with her napkin.

After Carrie recovered, Pedro turned to Rosa to repeat the conversation in Spanish and asked if it was okay to tell how they found Mike. Rosa nodded. Pedro adjusted his spectacles and told how Father Mike, mute, stared at them, cried, and closed the door.

Carrie and Fran, mesmerized with the story, forgot they were hungry and just toyed with their tacos, taking a bite every now and then. They begged Pedro to continue.

He resumed, moistening his lips. But Rosa, her fingers touching Pedro's arm, spoke quietly in Spanish, telling him how difficult it was to sit in the booth and not know what everyone was talking about. She told Pedro she tried to read faces and saw that Fran and Carrie were riveted to the story, but she felt dumb just sitting there mute. Pedro leaned closer and whispered in Spanish. "Just smile and tell them with your eyes that you love them already, Rosita."

Carrie took a few more bites of her taco, which by now was cold. "Pedro, when did you learn that Uncle Mike was a priest?"

"The day we found out he died. Evelyn told us."

"Oh you poor thing! Rosa, I am so sorry for you." Carrie reached over and touched her hand. "I know what it's like to lose someone you love. My husband just died last year, and it is still very difficult."

Little by little, Fran was becoming attached to this gentle Mexican woman, her calm, unhurried manner and her hint of a smile.

After adjusting his glasses and smoothing his hair, Pedro leaned back in the booth, basking in the spotlight. "Rosa was stunned when she found out her father was a priest, but Evelyn was just as startled when she discovered that Mike had a daughter, twin sons, and a wife."

"Rosa, did knowing your father was a priest change anything for you?" Fran tried to understand Rosa.

After Pedro translated the question, Fran studied Rosa's face to see her reaction. "Rosa says that it changed nothing," Pedro said. "She loves her father without question. It doesn't matter if he was a priest, a concert pianist, or a trash collector."

"What about your mother and your brothers? Were they surprised at all?"

Again Pedro translated. "She said her brothers just laughed. And her mother—she can remember her saying something like, 'Good, then he must be in heaven.' But her mother and father always had a very close spiritual connection, so she guessed it wasn't too surprising. Her mother wondered more about where her father earned his money, how he was able to buy three houses, support the family, bet on the bullfights, and rent the concert hall to practice the piano."

When the waitress cleared the table, Pedro ordered another round of Tocaltas. "You must have been crushed," said Fran. She was beginning to regret that she ever doubted the authenticity of Rosa's claim.

Pedro showed Fran and Carrie how to squeeze lemon on the back of their hands, sprinkle salt on it, lick it, and then swallow the cold Tocalta beer. "Now, Pedro, don't be so fast. What do you do after you lick the lemon and salt?" asked Fran.

"Why you take a swig!" He showed her how. Everyone laughed as Fran quaffed the Tocalta. Pedro and Carrie recorded the event with their cameras.

"But, back to your story now, Pedro. What else did Evelyn tell you?"

"Well she gave us her father's chalice and ciborium, his hat and coat, and the family photo that you saw yesterday. But that was all she offered. She told us he left all of his possessions to her."

"After we left," Pedro said, "Rosa calmed down, but she couldn't understand why Evelyn should receive all of her father's effects. She insisted that she and her brothers were entitled to some of her father's property, especially the T-bird in the driveway. When we were unable to convince Evelyn of this, we hired an attorney and started a lawsuit. Rosa wants you to know that we are contesting his will." Pedro repeated what he said to Rosa.

"Yes, Evelyn told us about the suit this morning. We certainly feel Rosa and her brothers are entitled to a portion of her father's property, but we also think that Evelyn should be compensated for her services. She seemed very loyal, very faithful to my brother. She took care of him when no one else did," said Fran. "Please tell Rosa."

"Pedro," Rosa whispered in Spanish. "Tell them how I used to dream of sitting in the driver's seat of that sleek black T-bird. How he told me it would be mine one day. Then, when I saw it in his driveway, I knew I had to have it. I don't really care about the rest of his property. Pedro, will you explain that we don't want everything—just those things that he promised would be ours? Please, make Fran and Carrie understand that we don't care about his money or the rest of his property. More than anything else, we want to be recognized as his rightful heirs before the law. Pedro, you must make them understand."

"Si. I will, Rosita. Si."

The car was silent on the trip back to Alamogordo, with everyone analyzing the new information. Soon Fran dozed off, cradled by the rhythm of the car.

Adios

The sun was steaming when Fran and Carrie started for St. John of God for the 10 o'clock Mass. Fran was anxious to see the church where Mike's funeral occurred. She wanted to imagine the funeral Mass, the Mass she would have attended if only she had known.

The pink and white adobe church with the rounded arches looked quite foreign, quite Spanish—especially from the outside. Fran and Carrie stepped through the arches into an inviting and crowded circular interior. The carved teak altar was central, the pews arranged like spokes around it. Picking up hymnals, they walked down the aisle paved with tomato-red terra cotta tiles. They squeezed into a pew next to an Hispanic family. Fran bent over and whispered to Carrie, "Don't forget to make your three wishes and say your three "Hail Marys." She took her rosaries out, but couldn't take her eyes off the brightly colored Stations of the Cross and the statues in the niches of dark-haired and dark-skinned figures from the Bible.

Soon the priest entered and a Mariachi band in an alcove on the side strummed the opening hymn. The cantor started to clap, then the congregation clapped and swayed and sang. Fran and Carrie couldn't resist. Carrie began to clap and move and sing. Fran joined in; their voices rose in unison with their new friends. They were one rhythm, one body with the congregation, experiencing a joyous transcendent feeling. As Mass continued, waves of love passed back and forth from priest to people and back again. It was a very special celebration!

"Peace be with you." Fran smiled warmly as she clasped the hand of the attractive Mexican woman next to her. No wonder Mike felt at home in this church. Fran could visualize his funeral. She was so happy he was buried from St. John of God and wished with all her heart she had been part of her brother's final celebration.

For once, Mass ended too soon for Carrie. The last time she felt so intimately involved in a religious experience occurred in the opulence of the Vatican adorned with sculptures of Leonardo and Michelangelo. There, she lost control of her emotions and screamed as loud as she could "Viva La Papa" as Pope John passed by, even though she had vowed to act with proper decorum, unlike the boisterous pilgrims around her. Perhaps she understood just a little bit more clearly what it was in the religious life that attracted Mike O'Brien.

Fran and Carrie walked back through the arches, reluctant to leave the enclave of warmth and love. "I suppose heaven must be like this," exclaimed Fran. "I am elated that Mike was surrounded by this joy, this passionate devotion to God. I would like to talk to Mike's friend at St. John of God, Father Monahan; do you think he said the Mass?"

"He might have. The priest did look older."

"I'm sure the two of them must have talked about Rosa and her brothers. Maybe he can explain why your uncle decided he could straddle both the religious and secular worlds. I don't think I will ever be able to forgive him for breaking the vow of chastity. He broke trust with me."

"Now, Mom, I think I can forgive him for breaking the vow of chastity, but I don't know if I will be able to forgive him for abandoning his family. Even though I gather it is a cultural thing in Mexico for the father to leave the home, find work, and then send money back to support his children., that 'the absent father' is accepted in the culture."

Fran sighed. "Carrie, your uncle isn't Mexican and he didn't support his family. He abandoned his family. She wondered if indeed she had ever really known her big brother.

———

"Rosa, I just spoke to Bruce Jenkins, our attorney. He thinks it would be an excellent idea if we ask your aunt and your cousin to come to court as witnesses on your behalf." Pedro replaced the receiver on the hook and gave Rosa his full attention.

Rosa turned down the TV. "Pedro, I don't want to ask them. If they offer that's one thing, but I just don't feel comfortable asking them." She put the remnants of her tamale on the table.

"It might be the difference between winning and losing. You do want that T-bird, don't you?"

"Yes, but only because it gives me a piece of my childhood: it sanctifies and confirms my time with my father. I need to have the T-bird. Pedro, you just can't imagine what a great father he was."

"But I do know. You've told me before. Many times."

"But did I tell you how he would always listen to his records of Bach, Beethoven, Mozart, or Schubert while he read the newspaper? The sound would fill the entire room. My mother would be in the kitchen rolling out her special dough for her luscious spoon bread tamale pie. Eduardo and Pancho were probably playing chess. Eduardo always won, and Pancho would accuse him of cheating, of course. 'Come on, Princesa,' my father would say, 'let's change the record and cut a rug.' He would put on some rock 'n' roll like 'Rock around the Clock' and we would start dancing. My mother would come out of the kitchen, wiping her hands on her apron, and just watch us, beaming. My father always asked her to join in, and the three of us would get into the rhythm of the moment and whirl around." Rosa jumped off the couch and started twirling around. "He was just something really special. It was always a party when he was at home with us."

"Come, Rosa, sit here, next to me." He reached out to her. She twirled into his arms.

"Lots of times on a clear night, we would go out in the backyard after dinner and look up at the stars. He would point out Venus and Jupiter, the brightest planets; then together we would find the Big Dipper. In the northern sky, we'd trace the outline of Orion, the hunter. Then he would tell me to find my favorite star and make a wish on it. The two of us would find our stars, cross our fingers, close our eyes, and wish. I always wished that he wouldn't have to go on the secret missions, but would stay home with us all of the time."

Pedro looked into her eyes and kissed her gently on the forehead. "I know, Rosita, I know. It must have been difficult for you when he left. He so loved you; it must have been tragic for you. You have such a big heart.; that's one of the things I love about you. That's why we have to do everything Bruce Jenkins asks us. We just have to prove that Michael O'Brien is your father, and that's precisely why we should ask Carrie and her mom to help us out."

She moved away from him. "But we have no plans to see them again before they leave." She shrugged her shoulders.

Pedro scrunched up his forehead and paced from the couch to the TV to the bed and back again for about five minutes. "That's not a problem. I'll give them a call and tell them we want to meet them at the airport to say goodbye. We can discuss the issue with them then. What do you think, Rosita? Do you think it will work?"

"I think that's a good idea. I don't see why they wouldn't want to see us. I'm sure they still have questions about my father. And I want to learn more about his life as well. For one thing, I want to know about his real military life. I want to know what he did to deserve all of those medals on his uniform. Do it, Pedro, call Carrie and Aunt Fran, find out when they leave and tell them we will meet them at the airport to say goodbye. Please, Pedro?"

Rosa gathered the remnants of their tamales, wrapped them in the paper bag, and threw them in the trash. She rinsed out the soda bottles and then flipped on the TV for the weather report. Because the case began on Tuesday, their appointment with Bruce Jenkins was scheduled for tomorrow. Bruce had built a pretty solid case. Rosa's mother found the birth certificates naming Michael O'Brien as the children's father. She was not as lucky in finding the marriage license; however, Bruce felt that the birth certificates were sufficient.

Pedro looked up from the phone shaking his head yes. "Okay, we'll see you at 2 o'clock at the restaurant on level D. Bye till then."

Rosa ran to him, grabbed his arms and started dancing around the room. "You are my hero, Pedro, my zapata. I always knew you would be a perfect husband. Why don't you call Bruce Jenkins? Just to inform him. I'm sure he'll be pleased."

———

Carrie got behind the wheel of the copper Chevy for the last time, waited for Fran to fasten her seatbelt. She started to back out of the parking lot when Fran remembered her watch. She had taken it off to wash her hands and forgot to put it back on. So they returned to the clerk, got the key, and sure enough the Cartier was right on the sink where Fran remembered putting it. This kind of thing was happening more frequently, the forgetting. The women were quiet as they approached the Alamogordo International Airport for both of them were swirling in the immensity of the information they had been inundated with the last couple of days.

"I'm so glad Pedro called to arrange a goodbye meeting at the airport. I still have a few nagging questions," said Fran.

They returned the car, took the shuttle to the airport, and had no trouble finding the cafeteria in Gate D. Sitting at a table just inside were Rosa, Pedro, and an unknown gentleman. As Carrie and Fran approached, Pedro introduced the tall, slender, casually dressed man as Bruce Jenkins, their attorney. Fran extended her hand rather slowly, a bit uncomfortable with his presence. After they sat down, she refused to give the attorney eye contact and kept searching for something in her black leather purse.

"I'm sorry for interrupting your farewell party." Bruce read the body language. He knew he was unexpected. "But I want to cover all bases for Rosa's case, so I think it's important to see you. First," he explained, "I have to establish the fact that Rosa and the twins, Eduardo and Pancho, are actually the heirs of Michael. Then we must prove that Michael didn't intend to exclude them from the will. I'm not sure that I will need testimony from you. In fact, I don't anticipate it, but if you don't mind, I would like to take your names and addresses in case it becomes necessary."

"Sure, we would be glad to help if it comes to that," chimed in Carrie before Fran could even think of a response.

"That's right. You don't have a marriage license for Michael and Rosa's mom, do you? Is that going to be damaging for the case?" Fran wasn't sure she wanted to give this man her name and address.

"No, I think we'll do just fine without a marriage license. Maria is not claiming any of the estate," said Bruce with certainty. "Rosa does have her birth certificate with her father's name on it. That should suffice." After he carefully recorded Carrie and Fran's addresses in his leather notebook, Bruce shook hands and departed.

Fran immediately picked up the menu and studied it even though she wasn't a bit interested in ordering anything. Finally she peered over the top of the menu. "I was surprised to see your attorney here, Pedro; you didn't mention that he would be joining us."

Pedro looked up from the menu, "I could see you were a bit upset. Thank you for providing your address. I promise we won't contact you unless it is absolutely necessary. I just wanted to make sure that our preparation for the hearing was sufficient." He looked into her eyes and patted her hand.

They decided on coffee all around and exchanged addresses and agreed to alternate meetings between Philadelphia and Juarez. Rosa claimed she never dreamed she would meet any of her father's relatives. Forgetting to ask the questions they so wanted to know the answers to, they got lost in saying goodbye. They posed for final pictures, their arms entwined, their faces smiling. More farewells, more hugs until boarding was announced. Carrie and Fran settled into their seats: Fran in the window and Carrie the middle seat. They buckled up and peered out the window to get a parting glance of their newfound family members.

As the tiny Mesa aircraft shuddered to take off against the wind, two Mexicans stood at the gate, one with steel-gray eyes and dark hair whipped by the wind, the other a tall, lanky gentleman with steel-rimmed glasses framing kind eyes. They peered between the black grillwork and waved until they couldn't see the plane anymore.

The two Americans settled in for the six and a half-hour trip to Philadelphia. As soon as the plane lifted off, Carrie stretched her foot under the seat in front of her to locate her backpack and nudged it into her reach, grabbed the leather backpack, unzipped it, and located her pen and journal. As tired as she was, she still wanted to record all of the information she discovered in the last few days while it was still fresh in her mind, for her siblings as well as her children would want a complete report.

As she started to write, she realized they forgot to get the answers to their unasked questions. She chewed on her ballpoint pen, "Mom, where did Rosa say they lived after Uncle Mike disappeared?" Fran didn't answer. Her eyes were closed, her mouth was wide open, and she was breathing deeply.

———

Rosa and Pedro watched until they couldn't see the aircraft anymore. Rosa was relieved that she wouldn't have to wait for Pedro to translate anymore. She promised herself that the next time they met, she would be able to converse with her relatives in English.

"I hope Aunt Fran and Carrie won't disappear from my life the way my father did," cried Rosa quietly as she leaned against Pedro, trying to settle her hair in the wind. "I can remember staying in Acapulco for three years waiting for my father to come home. I would walk home from school every day thinking he would be there as usual. I remember racing home, dashing up the stairs, and bursting through the door to emptiness. 'He's not coming home, Rosa. Just forget him,' Eduardo would yell. 'Just forget him!'"

"But I could never forget him. I was determined that one day I would see him again. I would never forget that I was and always would be his 'princesa.'"

"I remember my mother in the kitchen making tamales for dinner, yet never too busy to give me a big bear hug. I told her I talked to the guard outside that my father hired to protect us until he returned, and he said my father drove by and circled around the property three or four times, and then drove away. I remember asking her over and over 'Why didn't he stop, Mom? Why didn't he stop?'"

"'Now, now, Sweetie,' she said, always making excuses for him. 'Perhaps, he's on one of his military missions again, and he can't stop. We know he would stop if he could. Just remember how much he loved us, how happy we were.'"

"I tried to move on, but I didn't want to live without my father. I knew he loved me, but I wanted to know why he left. What kept him away? What happened to him? Did the Mafia kill him for gambling debts? Did he return to Ireland where he claimed he was born? Was he in an accident? I was just devastated."

"Eventually, we ran out of money and had to sell the house in Acapulco, the one property in Mama's name. We moved to Juarez where my mother hired a detective to find him. Juarez was where my mother met my father so she thought she might find him there."

"It must have been hard for you, Rosita." Pedro wrapped his arm around her as they slowly left the gate.

———

Carrie stopped writing, closed her journal, and slid it in her backpack, zipped it up and, leaning down, shoved it under the seat again. Turning to the window, she noticed that Fran had awakened.

"Did I miss very much?" Fran asked, stifling a yawn.

"No, it is an uneventful flight. Say, what was Uncle Mike like when he was young—before he went into the seminary? Did he date girls a lot or did he ignore them? Was he really holy, always going to church and praying?" The flight attendant pushing the cart down the aisle offered them drinks. Fran had a Coke, and Carrie some tomato juice. She flipped down Fran's tray for her.

"No, I don't remember him being really devout and praying all the time. I mean we all went to church, the early Mass, every Sunday together—your grandmother and grandfather, your Uncle Tom, Mike, and me. Every night we would pray the rosary. We knelt down right in the living room after dinner and my mom would lead us through the decades. There was no escaping it, and we all prayed the Hail Marys and the Our Fathers with the same ardor—or lack of ardor—but Mike didn't seem any holier than the rest of us."

She got that far away look in her eyes; she was reliving the past again. "Mike was a few years ahead of me in high school. He was quite a dancer and quite handsome with his eyes and curly brown hair. The girls were crazy over him. I remember one dance in particular, my mother made him take me. The cafeteria was totally transformed with blue and white crepe paper hung from the ceiling and draped down the walls, just like a circus tent. Blue strobe-like lights blinked off and on while a Jelly Roll Morton record blasted 'Black Bottom Stomp.' He grabbed my hand and whirled me around, and soon everyone was clapping, and then all the girls started to cut in." Fran paused, thought for a moment. "But he never really had one special girl that I can remember, that is, until he met Julie while he was at Villanova." She loved talking about her big brother.

"Sounds like a fun time," Carrie said sipping her tomato juice. "Now did you visit him much when he was in college?" The flight attendant interrupted again with pasta.

After Fran peeled the cover off her food, she continued, "You know I did. He went to Villanova. What sister wouldn't visit as much as she could, especially as a junior and senior? He lived there in the dorms. You do know that your dad was his roommate," she replied drumming her fingers on the tray. "So I had an ulterior motive every time I visited him."

"Exactly when did you start going out with Dad?" Carrie heard the story about the "bet" many times before, but she always enjoyed hearing her mom tell it. She always liked the way Fran's eyes danced when she talked about Joe.

"That started when I went to Temple. One weekend your Uncle Mike brought his roommate home. He was handsome with his blonde crew cut, his blue crew neck sweater, and saddle shoes. We were sitting around the dinner table after devouring your grandmother's special meatloaf before the rosary began, and I started to razz Mike and Joe about the upcoming football game: Temple versus Villanova. At any rate I bet Joe a dinner in Philadelphia that Temple would win.

Sure enough, Temple won! I called him the next day and asked when he was taking me to the Bellevue for dinner. He was a bit surprised when I said the Bellevue, but he lived up to his side of the bet. And you can be sure I never took my eyes off him. I remember borrowing my best friend's silver fox stole to wear that night. Your father didn't really have much of a chance after that. A few years later your Uncle Mike married us in Deming, his first assignment."

"Mom, where did Uncle Mike get the money for Villanova? I didn't think Grandmom and Grandpop had much money."

"No, they didn't have a lot of money. But by that time, Tom was a lawyer, a very distinguished Philadelphia lawyer, and he helped support the family. Mike also got some money, a partial scholarship for the piano. He was excellent, you know. He actually studied the piano at Villanova, but then he decided to go into the seminary."

"Well, I guess Uncle Mike must have had some kind of religious awakening during those years he spent at Villanova—Mom, I'm glad we came, aren't you?" Carrie reached over to pat her hand.

"It's all so complicated, so difficult to understand. But yes, I'm glad we came." She smiled, leaned back in her seat, and closed her eyes one more time.

Carrie rummaged in her backpack again, this time for *Pillars of the Earth*. She opened it, then pushed her seat back to read, but she just couldn't concentrate. She reread the same sentence at least five times. Finally she shut the book, leaned back, and surrendered to memories. She remembered walking through the huge wooden door of the Basilica of Saint Peter and Paul holding her father's hand staring at the light as it filtered through the stained-glass windows—the purple, green, ruby red panes of glass reflecting on the sculptured figures of the saints. High above the altar, the gold stars sparkled in a blue ceiling. Then the seminarians from St. Charles chanted the Easter service. Their voices filled the holy spaces, every niche of the ornately wrought cathedral. They permeated her soul, lifted her to heaven. Suddenly, she realized that she had always been mesmerized with the rituals of the church.

But she never associated Uncle Mike with those rituals. She visualized him at the piano, making it sing, at the dinner table, his gray eyes smiling, in his pressed dress khakis and cap, in his backyard among the roses barbecuing. Even though she had been to his Masses several times, she always thought of him as her uncle, never a priest. She remembered very clearly that photo of him in a white chasuble holding up the Host before a multitude of men in khakis underneath the palm trees in the Philippines, but other than that photo, she never pictured him in vestments.

And the more Carrie listened to Rosa's stories, the more difficult it was for her to understand how her uncle could have abandoned his family. Perhaps she was thinking of her own family, her children whom she loved dearly and her husband whom she recently lost. She couldn't imagine how the bishop forced her uncle to desert his wife and children to live a life bereft of both his church and his family. She wondered if she would ever understand, but more importantly, she wondered if her mother would ever forgive.

Results

"Rosa, Pedro," Bruce Jenkins, confident in his camel cashmere jacket, shook hands with his clients. "So glad you could come in. Have a seat, please."

Rosa and Pedro sat in the mahogany library chairs in front of his cluttered desk. "How can we help you, Bruce? What else do you need from us before the trial?" Pedro unzipped his windbreaker and as best he could settled into the uncomfortable chair.

"Well I want to go over the evidence. Make sure everything I have is correct. Now, Rosa, you told me that you want to establish the fact that you and your brothers are indeed Michael's children and are therefore entitled to his estate. Is that correct?"

"Yes, Bruce. That's most important to me." Rosa, relieved to be speaking in her native tongue, knew she could articulate her desires clearly. "However, there are some of his personal effects that I also want. I understand Evelyn's claim, and I don't object at all to sharing the estate with her, for I know my father promised her compensation for his care. I want her to have everything that my father owes her, but at the same time, my brothers and I think that we are entitled to a portion of his estate as his heirs."

Bruce listened, nodded, and made a notation on his yellow pad.

"By the way, Bruce, have you found out where my father's effects are?"

"I did, yes. Evelyn packed everything away to keep it all safe."

Rosa paused and then continued, "You know, Bruce, more than anything else I want to become an American citizen because as his children, my brothers and I, also, are American citizens."

"Now we do have your birth certificate, which lists Michael O'Brien as your father. I don't think the judge can fail to acknowledge you as Michael's daughter even though your father hasn't signed the document."

"My mother told me my father missed all of our births. My aunt Alma would take my mother to the hospital and stay with her. She and my mother were and still are very close. Since my aunt is childless, she was especially happy to be with my mother at such momentous times."

"Do you know why your father wasn't present at your births?"

Rosa crinkled her nose and thought for a few minutes. "Of course we know it isn't true today, but my mother told me that he was on secret military missions. A week or so before we were due, he would tell her that the Air Corps needed his expertise. He told her to call Aunt Alma if she needed anything. 'There was nothing I wanted more than to be at your side when our babies were coming into the world,' he supposedly told her, 'but I had to obey the military.'" Pedro leaned over and touched her arm.

"I see. How do you feel about that?" asked Bruce.

"I'm not really sure. Maybe being a priest had something to do with it. He must have felt really conflicted because I know he loved us very much. But I'm not angry because I know by his every word and every action that we were very dear to him."

"Yes, I see." He studied his yellow pad then asked, "You have also given me several pictures of you and your brothers with your mother and your father that I can display as exhibits for the jury to assess. I was just wondering if you have any other legal documentation."

"What kind of documentation do you mean?"

"For example, income tax returns listing you as dependents, maybe your parent's marriage certificate?" He paused.

"I would guess my father did the income tax returns since he was the American, so no I don't have any. My mother doesn't have a marriage certificate either. She does remember some kind of paper, but it doesn't exist anymore." Rosa hesitated, glanced at Pedro who fidgeted with his wire rim spectacles again. "Actually, now we don't even think they were legally married. My mother said my father hired the judge, and after a brief ceremony everyone signed a document: my mother, my father, the judge, my grandmother, and my Aunt Alma. But it just quietly disappeared. As a matter of fact, now, we even doubt that the judge was authentic."

Pedro leaned over and gave her a hug. He turned to Bruce, "Will this weaken our case?"

"No, no, I don't think so. I am simply trying to gather as much documentation as I can. Thank you for being so honest with me." Again Bruce made a notation on his pad.

"Do you have any other questions?" Pedro asked, leaning forward.

"No, I think I took up enough of your time today. Again, thank you for coming in. I'll see you in the court house and, don't worry, we have a strong case." He stood, walked around the desk, and shook hands. "Tomorrow." He gave them a thumbs-up sign.

"I hope you're right, Bruce. We've planned a big celebratory dinner with Auntie Carmen for tomorrow night." Rosa slipped her hand through Pedro's elbow as they exited the office. "Pedro, you were rather quiet this afternoon."

"Do you forget, Rosita? I have been translating all weekend for your father's relatives. My voice is worn out. I need a nap before dinner tonight."

"Poor Pedro, I am forever indebted to you."

———

Judge Alvarez looked around the table at Rosa and Pedro seated next to Bruce Jenkins and then to Evelyn and her attorney, Juan Alcala. The judge cleared his throat, "Rosa, Evelyn, I have studied the briefs prepared by your lawyers, listened to their arguments today, examined the exhibits, and I have come to a conclusion. The court finds:

"1. That Rosa O'Brien Santos, Eduardo O'Brien, and Pancho O'Brien are the children of the decedent Michael O'Brien.

"2. That all parties have agreed to divide the estate in half, less costs of administration and debts owed to creditors.

"3. That personal effects are not included in the division of the estate."

Rosa frowned, pinched Pedro's arm, eyes glued to Judge Alvarez. Judge Alvarez continued his pronouncements. "It is therefore ordered that:

"1. Rosa O'Brien Santos, Eduardo O'Brien, and Pancho O'Brien shall choose the personal property they want.

"2. Any remaining personal property will belong to Evelyn Sanchez.

"3. The estate will be equally divided between Evelyn Sanchez and Rosa O'Brien Santos, Eduardo O'Brien, and Pancho O'Brien."

Rosa jumped up wrapped her arms around Pedro. "Pedro, Pedro, we did it! We did it! We won. We proved that Mike is my father and the father of Eduardo and Pancho. I am so happy! What a crazy week this has been. Now all we have to do is get my father's birth certificate, and we are citizens of the USA."

"Okay, Rosita, okay. Calm down now, calm down. We are still in the judge's chambers, remember."

She reached across the desk to shake the judge's hand. Then she looked at Bruce Jenkins. "Bruce, I knew you could do it. How can I ever thank you?" She offered her hand, but changed her mind, wrapped her arms around him and gave him a big hug.

"That's what I'm paid to do." He grunted, then extricated himself from her grasp. "Now we have to set up an appointment with Evelyn so you and your brothers can choose whatever personal effects of your father's you want, and then the remainder of the estate will be divided equally between Evelyn and you and your brothers."

"Does that mean that we each get one-fourth?"

"No, it means that the estate is divided in half. Evelyn gets one-half and you and your brothers each get one-third of the other half. Now when will you and your brothers be available to decide which personal effects you want?"

"How about around two o'clock on Saturday? My brothers could drive up in the morning, and we could all return to Mexico Saturday night or Sunday morning. Ooooooh! Bruce, I just can't wait to sit inside that sleek black T-bird again. Pedro, do you think it still runs?"

"We'll find out soon enough, my wife, daughter of Michael O'Brien, Air Corps Captain, priest, husband, father."

Bruce conferred with Evelyn's attorney, who agreed with the day and time. After confirming the appointment with Rosa, Bruce collected his yellow legal pad, all of his exhibits, shoved them into a manila folder and into his worn leather briefcase. "I'll see you and your brothers on Saturday. By the way, as soon as you get your father's birth certificate, give me a call and we can start to process the forms for citizenship."

"It's a dream come true, Bruce. Please, join us for dinner as we celebrate with Auntie Carmen."

"Thanks, but I have a parent-teacher meeting in a half hour."

———

"Hey, Rosita, Are you almost ready? We don't want to be late. Our reservations are for 6:30 and we have to pick up Auntie Carmen." Pedro checked his hair in the mirror and adjusted his tie, happy, he threw it in the duffle bag at the last minute.

"Go start the car. I'll be with you in a sec." Rosa uncapped her lipstick and carefully applied the burgundy color. She stepped back to judge the effect. Satisfied, she capped the tube and placed it in her cosmetic bag. "Okay—finished I think." She checked her pencil thin black skirt in the full-length mirror, smoothed it over her hips one last time. Then she dashed out to the car. "Sorry, Sweetie." She smiled as she slipped into the rental.

The drive to Carmen's was a quiet one. Pedro and Rosa were emotionally and physically drained after their weekend of meeting with Michael O'Brien's relatives. They looked forward to a very tasty and very relaxing meal. Pedro pulled up to an adobe rancher in the affluent section of town and rolled to a stop. "Just wait here, Rosa. I'll go in and get Auntie Carmen." Rosa pulled down the visor and checked her hair in the mirror. Satisfied, she flipped the visor up, leaned back in her seat, and closed her eyes for a second. The next thing she heard was Auntie Carmen's hearty giggle.

"Auntie Carmen, you don't know how happy I am to see you. I can't believe we've been here in Alamogordo all weekend and are just getting to spend some time with you. You just look so svelte and snappy!"

"It's always wonderful to see the two of you—and looking so well. Now you will have to tell me everything you have been up to. It's been quite a while since I've seen the both of you," Carmen replied, sliding into the back seat.

In no time they were settled into a comfy booth at La Hacienda. They ordered chicken enchiladas, black bean and feta cheese burritos, and shredded cheese chimichangas with black bean and corn salad. Not until they started to sip their margaritas did Rosa and Pedro begin reciting their odyssey. Auntie Carmen couldn't contain herself. "Now, dears, I want to hear every single thing about your meeting with Michael O'Brien's relatives."

Rosa beamed, "I just can't explain how easy it is to love my prima and my tia. It is as if I have known them all my life. The most difficult thing for me was to convey to them how much my father loved us. They couldn't seem to understand why we weren't angry because Michael O'Brien had abandoned us; I tried to show them the bigness of his heart. And then of course, there was the language barrier. I had to depend on Pedro's translations so every conversation took so much time."

"I am so happy that the meeting was satisfying for you."

"I told them how I remembered my father coming home from one of his alleged military missions with chocolates for Mom and lollipops and gummy bears for all of us. He would pick us up and swing us around and snuggle and tell us how much he missed us and how much he loved us."

Auntie Carmen gave Rosa her rapt attention as she fussed with her scarf.

Rosa absentmindedly placed the brightly colored linen napkin on her lap. "I can remember him coming into my bedroom at night after we were all tucked in. He would sit on my bed, open a new book he just bought especially for me and read to me until my eyes closed. My very favorite was *El Mago de Oz*. I never tired of listening to his voice; his Spanish had a lilt to it. I could easily visualize the Tin Man, the Lion, and the Scarecrow and their adventures with Dorothy."

"What wonderful childhood memories you have, Rosa. It's no wonder you loved him so."

Once Rosa started talking about her father, there was no stopping her. The words tumbled out. "In the morning he would make pancakes with maple syrup, an American treat, then drive us to school. If he wasn't away, he always came to watch the plays I was in. He would sit in the audience next to my mother. They would hold hands and beam anytime I spoke. Afterward, we would always go for helada frito."

"We should look at the menu, Rosita. I'm getting rather hungry," mentioned Pedro when Rosa paused to take a breath.

"Si, si, Pedro. Just one more thing, Auntie Carmen, he never, ever became angry or cross with us. He always listened to our point of view. If I had a problem—didn't matter how ridiculous—he would listen then tell me what he thought. He was just the most perfect father anyone could have. And now I guess I know why. He was, after all, a priest." She sipped her margarita. "I remember one time he took all three of us to the aquarium. We spent the whole day there. I remember sitting next to him watching the wall-size fish tank. He would make up stories about the sharks, the angelfish, and the bristle nose catfish. I laughed and laughed. It is one of my favorite memories." Rosa reached for the menu.

"I guess in a way you were lucky," said Auntie Carmen. "You only had your dad for 12 years, but apparently those 12 years were enough to last you a lifetime."

"Si, si," Rosa agreed.

"I wonder what it was that prompted his leaving. Could it have been related to his superiors in the church?" Auntie Carmen questioned, not expecting a response.

Pedro could smell the burritos before the waitress set them on the table. "These really are the best in town."

Now, Pedro, my dear boy, how is your research at the clinic progressing?" Auntie Carmen asked her nephew.

Pedro explained that it would be many years before he would be able to find a way to slow and perhaps stop the ravages of Alzheimer's disease. He had a personal stake in his research project for his mother had died from complications of the dreaded illness.

"Someday, Pedro, I'm going to read about you in the newspaper." Carmen was especially fond of her nephew.

Debriefing

Shortly after Rosa, Pedro, and the twins returned from Alamogordo where they had divided their father's estate, they gathered on Ed's patio, behind the adobe rancher to debrief and explain the trip to their mother.

A gentle breeze moved the palm fronds even though the sun was noon high.

The whole family gathered around a circular table under a giant multi-colored umbrella. "Mia Madre, it's so wonderful to see you." Rosa exuded.

The smell of hamburgers grilling on the fire tantalized the hungry group on the patio. "Hey, Eduardo, "What's keeping the burgers? Did you forget how to grill? Make mine rare, will you?" Pancho teased his twin.

"Keep a lid on it, brother. Do you want the spatula?" Eduardo yelled to Pancho.

"Eduardo, Pancho, hush now," said Maria. "We have more important things to talk about than how fast the burgers are cooking. Don't keep me in suspense, Rosa. I want to know everything about Fran and Carrie," Maria said. "Now, tell me every little detail. Don't leave anything out and begin at the beginning."

"Mamá, I thought our first meeting would be strained. I thought I would have to show Carrie and Aunt Fran the photos to prove that I was my father's daughter. But, Mamá, I was just shocked when Carrie threw her arms around me the moment I saw her. She told me I had my father's eyes. Aunt Fran took a bit longer to accept me, but she is exactly like my father said she was—warm, friendly, willing to try anything, pleasant, happy. She is just wonderful."

"Here's your burger, Pancho," interrupted Eduardo. "Sweetie, can you bring out the salad and tortillas now?" he asked his wife. "Who else wanted burgers? Mom, how about you? Rosa, Pedro, come on up here and get yours. I'm not serving you." He winked.

Pedro adjusted his wire rims and teased, "Who do you think you are? The homeowner? Hey, how about another cervezsa? Come on, Eduardo, you'll lose your title as 'hostess with the mostess!'" he joked.

"Mamá, we do have pictures. Here, you can look at them while we eat. And please take whatever ones you want. I have copies."

"Oh my, I never imagined a red-headed relative. Someday, sooner than later, I hope I meet them."

"She has two red-headed brothers as well," Rosa said as she took another bite.

"You know what else Mamá? They can't understand why we aren't angry that my father left us. They are shocked that we don't hate him."

"Well, there were some very hard years, but they were overshadowed by those 12 wonderful years we all had together. And without him, I never would have had you three exceptional children. Now, I understand that you have some things of your father's; exactly what did you bring home?"

"We took several books: *The Confessions of St. Augustine, Seven Story Mountain,* and a few others, most of his music, the leather jacket I remember him wearing several decades ago. The china, which I believe was his mother's. It's really very dainty, tiny yellow daisies ringing the plates. I think he bought it when he was stationed in Germany. I also grabbed a photo album, the Oriental carpet that used to be in his study in Mexico City, and several smaller items."

"And of course the T-bird."

"Well, yes and no. The T-bird won't move. So Pedro hired a mechanic to figure out if it makes sense to repair it."

"For some reason, your father really didn't want us to find him. But I'm sure deep in my heart that he still loved us." Maria closed her eyes and shook her head.

"I am too. I'll never forget the way the tears poured from his eyes when he answered my knock in Alamogordo. Maybe someone discovered that he had a family and reported it to the church. I bet his bishop made him leave us. It must have torn him apart. I wonder if we'll ever find out the real answer. Talking to Carrie and Fran did give me some ideas though."

A Frisbee game was in progress in the shade under the palm trees. Maria smiled approvingly as the grandchildren interacted with their father and uncle. "Now, Rosa," she said, "I understand you have proved that you are Michael's daughter. What's next? When do you get your citizenship that you have wanted for so long?"

"That should be easy, Mamá. All I have to do is give our lawyer, Bruce Jenkins, my father's birth certificate. And that's it. It is automatic. Do you have his birth certificate?"

At this point, little Rosie came running to the patio sobbing. She fell onto Maria's lap. "Abuelita, Abuelita," she shrieked, "look, my knee. It's bleeding."

"Now, now! What happened?" Maria calmed her granddaughter as she pulled her up onto her lap and patted her back. "What happened?" She rocked her back and forth.

Calming down, little Rosie blurted out between sobs, "I was running for the Frisbee, really fast; and I saw Daddy running too, and then I tripped. I fell on the stepping stone, and it's all Daddy's fault."

"Now, now, you'll be okay."

"Mamá what about the birth certificate?" Rosa interrupted.

"Rosa, did you forget? We thought he was from Ireland. I never saw a birth certificate." She frowned. "Hmm…we didn't even have to produce one for our wedding."

"No worry! I know where he was born; I copied it from his gravestone. Bruce Jenkins explained that all I have to do is write to Trenton, New Jersey, and Trenton will send the certificate to me immediately. He even gave me the address. I am so happy that I will become a citizen of the United States of America, my father's country!"

"Hmm…I don't know…It just sounds too easy to me, Rosa." She took another sip of her iced tea. "Much too easy. But you have my blessing. I think I would like to have American children and American grandchildren. And I would very much like to meet my husband's American family."

Philadelphia

Carrie heard the ringing, thought it was signaling the last class before summer vacation. Then as she opened her eyes in the semi-darkness, she realized it was the phone. Peering out of the blankets, she flipped on the light and reached for the phone. "Hello," she mumbled. "Who? Could you repeat that, please? Oh, Rosa, how are you? It's so good to hear your voice!" Now fully awake she realized something must be wrong. Rosa had never called her before. "Your husband!! Oh, Rosa, I am so sorry. When did it happen? Where were you? Did he have a heart attack? But he was so young. Are you okay?"

Carrie couldn't believe Pedro had a heart attack. *Maybe I haven't awakened,* she thought. *Maybe this is some nasty dream.* Because Pedro seemed so young and healthy when they were all together in Alamagordo some years ago, Carrie had difficulty believing exactly what Rosa was saying. And although her English had improved since they last met, she was still difficult to understand over the phone. As best as Carrie could figure out, Rosa was going to use the insurance money from her husband's policy to come to the states in search of her father's birth or baptismal certificate so she could finally become a citizen. Pedro's cousin, Emilio, who lived in Virginia and spoke English fluently, was meeting her at the Philadelphia airport that afternoon.

Carrie was so delighted, she immediately invited them for dinner, and Rosa promised they would drive directly from the airport.

When Carrie finally looked at the illuminated clock on the night table, she shuddered. After she saw 4:30 am, she fumbled in the bureau drawer next to her bed and pulled out a sleep mask, adjusted it over her eyes, then snuggled into the blankets again, hoping for a few more hours of sleep. Planning dinner would just have to wait.

Pedro's death was not the only change in the years since the cousins met: Fran was in a nursing home now, the Alzheimer's having progressed. Most of the time she was perfectly lucid, but sometimes she would get up in the middle of the night thinking it was day and wander around the house, turn on the stove to cook breakfast and forget to turn it off, or leave the house to walk to Mass, then wait on the church steps in the dark until the doors were unlocked. As much as Carrie hated to admit it, Fran needed 24-hour supervision. Although the transition was difficult for Fran at first, she seemed to have adjusted.

In the next morning, Carrie jumped out of bed, dusted, vacuumed, shopped, set the table, and started to prepare dinner. Only her good china and silver were suitable for Rosa's first visit to the states. Carrie often wondered how things would have been different if she and Rosa had grown up knowing each other. She wondered if they would have been closer now, if they would have laughed and teased each other, shared secrets, sunbathed on the Gulf or the Atlantic? The cousins did correspond on a regular basis but hadn't seen each other since meeting in Alamogordo. Carrie wished she could invite Rosa to stay, but when Fran moved to Chandler Hall, Carrie sold the family home in New Jersey and moved into a one-bedroom row-house in Philly.

Carrie invited her brothers and their families to dinner to meet Rosa, but most of them already had plans: back-to-school night, baseball games, theater tickets, and illnesses. Joey was the only one without a prior engagement.

He was the O'Brien who received the call from Rosa when Mike died. He was also the one who called the O'Brien clan with the news about Uncle Mike's digressions. He along with most of the O'Briens, including Carrie, refused to recognize the truth in Rosa's claim. The phone lines buzzed for several days as Fran and the children discussed the possibilities, as well as the ramifications, of Uncle Mike's double life. Few of them were ready to welcome Uncle Mike's "supposed" family into the inner circle. Fran, of course, was quite upset and refused to discuss the issue. To this day, she hadn't forgiven him for betraying his God and his family.

Just as Carrie slid the chicken into the oven, she heard the doorbell. As she ran down the stairs to open the door, she untied her apron. Wondering if Rosa had changed, she unlocked the front door. All she could see was Rosa's smile, full of enough warmth to melt an Alaskan iceberg. Carrie's arms reached out to encircle her, to hold her close. She was overjoyed to see that the years hadn't changed Rosa at all. She still looked lovely, still dressed in that understated classic style: a lavender striped suit and white pumps. The biggest difference was Rosa's grasp of the English language. She was now able to express herself more clearly. "Carrie," she began, "please meet my cousin, Emilio. He lives in the States and will help me find my father's records." Carrie immediately liked Emilio and shook hands.

Carrie barely had time to give her guests the abbreviated house tour when Joey arrived. "Rosa, I'm so happy to meet you," he smiled warmly, clasping her hand. At last, he understood why Carrie knew intuitively that Rosa was Uncle Mike's daughter. Her eyes were identical to his. "I've heard so much about you." He greeted Emilio, and they moved into the living room. The arpeggios and chords of Beethoven's *Pathetique* filled the room. As Carrie walked over to turn the volume down, Rosa remarked that it was always her father's favorite.

Joey popped a bottle of champagne. After filling everyone's flutes, he stood in the center of the Oriental carpet and raised his glass to toast his cousin. "Rosa, welcome to our family. Emilio, nice to meet you." Rosa and Emilio sat on the burgundy settee, Joey opposite them on the blue velvet armchair while Carrie brought in a tray of brie and grapes. They chatted about the weather, about the flight, and about Emilio's job. In flawless English, he explained that he worked for the government at Langley Air Force Base doing research for NASA. He explained that he wasn't in the military but employed by the military. Because of this connection, he felt confident he would be able to help Rosa on her journey toward citizenship.

"Just how do you plan to find Uncle Mike's baptismal certificate?" Joey asked after they sat down to a roast chicken dinner with risotto, string beans, and Caesar salad.

"We are going to begin the search in Camden, where my father grew up. While there, we'll visit every parish in the area until I find it-St. Mary's, St. George's, Sacred Heart, the Cathedral, St. Anthony's, Our Lady of Mount Carmel, and Joan of Arc. So far it has been impossible to prove he was a citizen since neither Harrisburg nor Trenton has any records of him." With a little help from Emilio, Rosa was able to speak for herself in English. "If we can't locate the baptismal certificate by Wednesday, on Thursday we intend to travel to Washington. We want to search the military records, for they also are an acceptable proof of citizenship. Then we shall drive to Trenton to find out how to proceed."

As Rosa talked, Carrie sensed the urgency in her voice. She realized that gaining citizenship meant much more than it seemed on the surface. Perhaps it served as an affirmation of her father's love. Without really thinking, Carrie blurted out, "Rosa, I'd really like to help you some way."

"I welcome all the help I can get."

"I have an idea. I have a whole folder of information about Uncle Mike. Why not come back here before you go to Trenton? We can share what we know and explore the Internet. We are bound to discover something. Then, I'll drive you to Trenton. Together, I think we have a better chance to succeed." Carrie hoped Rosa would agree.

"Well that certainly sounds like a well-thought-out plan." Joey put down his fork, wiped his lips with his napkin, and waited for Rosa's response.

"Carrie, you're an angel! Let's do it."

"I think that calls for another toast." Joey raised his glass again. "Say, Rosa, now that that's settled, do you mind answering a few questions? Perhaps you have discussed this with Carrie, but I was wondering if there ever was a time you thought your father might be a priest?"

"Never. We thought he was in the Air Corps, but we even feared he might be connected to the Mafia because he seemed to have an endless supply of cash."

"How about after his housekeeper told you he was a priest. Did you believe her? What did you do then?"

"I think I did believe Evelyn because she had his chalice and ciborium that was inscribed by his parents. Pedro and I also went to the church where he was buried and talked to the priest there. Father Don Monahan was his name, if I remember correctly. We spent several hours talking to him. He and my father were very good friends. He seemed to know that my father had a family, but he told us he couldn't divulge anything he knew under the seal of confession. 'You must be a very holy woman if you are the daughter of a priest,'" he told me."

"Were you raised Catholic?" Joey wanted to know. "I don't mean to pry, but I am curious. Don't feel you have to answer."

"Oh, I don't mind. Neither my brothers nor I were raised Catholic. We hardly ever went inside a church. But our family was a very Christian, a very loving family. Both my mother and my father had a great love of God. My father didn't go to church when he lived with us, unless he did it without anyone realizing it. Perhaps he left on Sunday mornings to go into El Paso to say Mass. I just can't remember. But how about you? How did you react when Pedro and I called and told you that your uncle had a family? Did you believe us?" Poor Rosa was talking so much her food was getting cold.

"To be truthful, I didn't," Joey admitted. "Actually, I thought the whole thing was some kind of a money-making scam. But based on Carrie's story and now seeing you in person, I know for a fact that my uncle had a double life: a loving family and a thriving parish. By the way, how did you know my phone number?"

"My father often talked of Uncle Tom and Aunt Fran and Uncle Joe. I really thought I knew a lot about his family. After we found out about my father's death, I just wanted to get in touch with my relatives. So Pedro and I went to the Alamogordo library and looked up Uncle Joe's phone number. We knew he was a physician like you. Later we discovered we had found *your* number since Uncle Joe had died several years before. Rosa turned to Carrie. "Carrie, what did you think when you heard that your Uncle Mike had a family."

"Like Joey, and probably most of the family, I thought the chance of my uncle having a family was non-existent. That is, until I saw you. And you were there for that story. Intuitively, instantaneously, beyond any shadow of a doubt, I knew that you were my cousin. Your eyes gave you away." She paused, then continued. "There is another thing I've been wondering about: Did you ever visit his church, the school that he built at the same time that he was living with you, your brothers, and your mother?"

"Yes, Pedro and I drove to El Paso one vacation and found his church. I looked at the adobe house where he lived. We walked around the high white fence, looked in the yard, tried to look in the windows. We walked into the church. I got an eerie feeling thinking that I was following the footsteps of my father. I liked walking where he walked. I liked the church. It was quite modern yet very warm with large windows letting the warmth of the sun blanket everyone. I sat in a pew and tried to imagine listening to him preaching a sermon. We went back to the rectory and I knocked on the door. An older priest answered. I didn't quite know how to approach the subject, but I first asked if he knew my father. Because he had assisted him many years ago, he remembered him. He called him 'a very holy priest.' He just couldn't believe what I told him. He kept shaking his head." She paused and then abruptly changed the subject.

"Carrie, this has been a very delicious meal. I loved the roasted chicken, and the tomatoes in the risotto popped as I bit into them. And it has been so wonderful meeting another of my father's relatives; however, we are really tired and must think of leaving soon. We rented a motel room in New Jersey so we could be situated close to my father's early childhood homes."

Rosa and Emilio came back for dinner the next night, and the next night, and the night after that. Unfortunately, Rosa was not successful in Camden. None of the parishes in Camden had a record of Mike's baptism. The records were either thrown away, stored in another site, damaged by flooded basements, or burned.

So Rosa and Emilio traveled to Washington and researched the military records. They encountered more bad luck from the National Archives; Thousands of military records were destroyed in the fire that swept the archives center in St. Louis, Missouri, on July 12, 1973. The sections from "H" to "Z" were burnt beyond recognition. There was no record of Mike's birth or nationality. However, Rosa learned that he was discharged as a captain and awarded several medals. Discouraged by her failure, Rosa called Carrie and asked if she would help her search the computer before she traveled to Trenton. She vowed not to return to Mexico without proof of her father's citizenship.

———

After a leisurely breakfast of sausage; apple pancakes; and an orange, banana, cantaloupe, blueberry and strawberry fruit salad; orange juice; and coffee, Carrie and Rosa were ready to start. They got out their notes and pens, turned on the computer. Before they started their search, they reviewed the material they already had. They discovered they had quite a bit of documentation, but not the documents needed to prove that Mike was a citizen of the United States. They had his death certificate with definite proof of his Social Security number along with his place and date of death, and his date of birth. They had a facsimile of a page from the 1910 census where he was listed as residing in New Jersey. They also had Xeroxed pages showing he was listed in the 1920 and 1930 census. They also had proof that he was listed as an American on the passenger list of the *Pomeranian* returning from a trip to Newfoundland..

"Surely, this material was evidence that Uncle Mike was a citizen of the U.S.!" Carrie shuffled the papers on the table.

"No, unfortunately. I have already sent all of these documents to Trenton. The naturalization bureau replied stating that none of them were eligible as proof of citizenship. Only the following documents were acceptable: a birth certificate, a baptismal certificate, a passport, or a copy of discharge papers from the military." Rosa took a deep breath. "And Carrie, we don't have any of them."

"I can't believe that his death certificate with his birth date is not acceptable. Well, let's start with the military. Maybe we can find something there that might help. Where are the documents you and Emilio found in Washington?"

"We did find some interesting stuff." Rosa shuffled through the papers in her folder and pulled out a Xeroxed document from the National Archives. "Look at all of these medals awarded to my Father. The Presidential Unit Citation, The Asiatic Pacific Campaign, three bronze Service Stars, the Philippine Liberation Medal with one bronze Service Star, a World War II Victory Medal, a Service Lapel Button, the American Campaign Medal, and a National Defense Service Medal."

"Isn't it ironic that someone who received so many medals for defending this country can't even prove his citizenship? What did he get the medals for, Rosa? Do you know?"

"No, but I do have some of them. Evelyn gave them to my brothers and I after we won the court case."

"Maybe we can find out why the medals were awarded. The only things I remember about Uncle Mike's service in the military were from photos. Several show him saying Mass outdoors in the Philippines to a very large group of Air Corps enlisted men on folding chairs, and there's a photo depicting him sitting in front of a huge dark metal rectangular piece of equipment with a lot of dials referred to as a 'ham radio.'" Carrie turned back to the computer and opened Google, which referred her to the "Grunt" website. "Rosa, look here, read this:"

The Presidential Unit Citation is awarded to units of the Armed Corps of the United States and co-belligerent nations for extraordinary heroism in action against an armed enemy occurring on or after 7 December 1941. The unit must display such gallantry, determination, and esprit de corps in accomplishing its mission under extremely difficult and hazardous conditions as to set it apart and above other units participating in the same campaign. The degree of heroism required is the same as that which would warrant the award of Distinguished Service Cross to an individual.

"Why didn't I ever know this? Was I just too young to be curious? I'll have to ask my mother about all these medals." They continued to read the information.

It is awarded for participation in the Philippines' liberation from 17 Oct 44 to 3 Sep 45, if personnel: 1) participated in the initial landing operations on Leyte or adjoining islands from 17 Oct 44 to 20 Oct 44. Personnel are considered as having participated in such operations if they landed on Leyte or adjoining islands, were on ships in Philippine waters, or were crew members of airplanes that flew over Philippine territory during the period. 2) Participated in any engagement against the enemy during the campaign on Leyte and adjoining islands. Personnel are considered as having participated in such operations if they were members of or present with units actually under enemy fire or air attack, or were crew members in an airplane under enemy aerial or ground fire. 3) Service in the Philippine Islands or on ships in Philippine waters for at least 30 calendar days during the period 17 Oct 44 to 3 Sep 45. Persons who meet more than one of the conditions above are authorized to wear a bronze service star on the ribbon for each additional condition under which they may qualify."

Carrie scanned the remainder of the description. "Service seems to be the sole requirement for the remainder of the decorations." Not wanting to admit defeat, Carrie continued to pore over the material they had amassed. As she looked more closely at the document from the National Archives, she noted Mike's discharge listed as occurring in 1951 at Shreveport, Louisiana. It triggered a memory. "Rosa, Shreveport, Louisiana, rings a bell. I remember looking through some old photo albums when I was helping mom clean out the family home. I distinctly remember one photo because it was so unusual. There was a lake in the foreground, the sun sinking in the distance. In the center was a blond curly headed toddler holding a bottle of beer—can you imagine—as two huge black labs hunkered behind. There were also photos of the Carlsbad Caverns."

Rosa shook her head, "Couldn't be Carlsbad Caverns. They're in New Mexico, and 750 miles of Texas separates Louisiana from New Mexico. The distance just doesn't work."

"Maybe it was the Luray Caverns in Virginia. That would make sense. I still remember the photos of the vast underground rooms with the towering columns, the stalactites and the stalagmites. The only thing I've seen to top it are the caverns in China, Guilin, to be exact, where red, purple, orange, blue, and green lights cast shadows of the stalactites and stalagmites into the unending gloom and dance on the mirrored surface of the still pools."

Getting a bit impatient with Carrie's memories, Rosa interrupted. "Well, let's get back to work. Do you remember any photos of my father?"

Carrie picked up a document, studied it for a couple of minutes. "Look at these dates, Rosa. He was released from the military in '51, and he married your mother in '52. There's not too much time between the two events. When do you think he returned from Germany? Did your mom ever tell you how they met?"

Rosa nodded. They realized, as with everything else in life, the more they knew, the more questions they had, and the more they wanted to know.

———

The trip to Trenton proved to be disappointing. Without the proper documents, the cousins were unable to convince the Immigration Board that Mike was a citizen.

"No, Carrie, it wasn't a waste of time. Granted, we weren't able to prove that my father was a citizen. But look at all we accomplished. I discovered a lot of wonderful facts about his real life in the military. I visited the city of his birth. I met another relative. I saw your wonderful home and spent a lot of time with you."

"I bet a lawyer would be able to get some results." Carrie looked both ways, then accelerated when the light turned green. She was disappointed the trip to Trenton was a failure, and couldn't understand why Uncle Mike's past was so elusive. "Well, what will you do now," she asked her cousin?"

"I just have to consider all options at this point. I think I'd like to settle in El Paso where my father lived for so many years. I could probably apply for a green card and find a job. Maybe my mother would come and live with me." She paused as she tried to figure out how to reinvent her life. Absentmindedly, she scratched a spot on her beige pants, looked out the window thinking that everyone she saw was a citizen of the US, so many of them. *Why not me*, she wondered.

"I haven't been in El Paso since I was a kid. I'd love to visit, especially if I could meet your mother. Let's make some plans when we get home."

El Paso

A year passed before the cousins finally arranged to meet in El Paso. Carrie was waiting for Rosa and Maria to arrive at the Hotel Camino Real for lunch. After an hour of pacing on the marble floor of the Camino Real, monitoring the sliding glass doors every time they hissed open, Carrie checked the time and finally realized that Rosa and her mother were definitely not meeting her. It was an hour past the appointed time and there was no message, no Rosa, no Maria, and therefore, no lunch. Carrie was flummoxed, for the lunch took several weeks of planning. The cousins exchanged many emails organizing Carrie's trip to El Paso, where Rosa and her mother had moved. Just before Carrie left Philadelphia, she confirmed the necessary details and the name of the hotel through email.

The excitement of meeting Maria quickly dissolved into a conundrum of epic proportions. She plopped into the nearest armchair and fumbled in her purse, pulling out her room key, wallet, reading glasses and finally her worn leather-covered address book. Thumbing through it, she located Rosa's phone number. Stuffing everything back in the purse, she scanned the lobby for a phone and marched toward it, her heels clicking on the marble floor.

After dialing, she waited expectantly for Rosa's voice, but heard instead, "This phone is out of order at the request of the customer." She hung up and tried again, pausing after each number she dialed. The result was the same. Totally upset, she closed the address book and took it to the desk clerk where she patiently waited to be noticed. When the young blonde finally looked her way, Carrie said, "Hi, would you mind dialing this number for me? I think I must be dialing incorrectly because every time I dial I get a message stating that the phone is out of order. I'm not sure I'm getting an outside line."

With an arrogant tilt of the head, the clerk said, "I'd be happy to help." She picked up the address book with red lacquered nails.

Carrie watched intently as the number was dialed. She studied the clerk's face for signs of being connected.

"Sorry, I'm afraid this number has been disconnected. But, if you have an address for this party, I will gladly get a cab for you."

"Would you do that please? I think it's my last resort."

As Carrie sat in the cab for the 40-minute ride, her mind went haywire. She imagined all sorts of things. Perhaps Maria decided she didn't want to meet her after all. Maybe Rosa and Maria were evicted and had to leave the city. Maybe Maria had a medical emergency and went back to her son's home in Chihuahua.

As she looked out the window, the high-rises and large hotels surprised her. She hadn't been to El Paso since she was a teenager and drove cross-country with Uncle Tom and her brothers, Joey and Mikey. What a trip in that old Studebaker! She could still remember the sweat dripping off her chin and the perspiration staining her shirt as it got hotter and hotter each day closer to the destination. What a delight to be riding in an air-conditioned cab.

The taxi glided to a stop under a huge palm tree in front of a modern stucco building. Carrie paid the driver and asked him to return in two hours. She rummaged for that address book again and walked through the courtyard until she found 307A.

Not knowing what to expect, she took a deep breath, crossed her fingers, and then rapped on the door. She listened closely, but detected no sound. Just as she was about to knock again, the door opened.

A happy Rosa appeared before her. "I am so glad you finally came!" She wrapped her arms around Carrie. "I've been waiting for hours."

"You've been waiting for me? But I've been waiting for you. Didn't you get my last email?" Carrie realized that Rosa knew nothing of a two o'clock lunch at Camino Real. She was unaware of all of the consternation she had caused, and instead had been wondering why Carrie was so late.

"No, I never got that email because I discontinued my account about a week ago, for I no longer have a computer. When you were so late for lunch, I thought you might have decided not to come, but now, I am overjoyed to see you directly before me." She ushered Carrie inside the sparsely furnished room devoid of any decorative touches, the walls bland smudged with the outlines of furniture no longer there. Carrie tried to mask the surprise she felt at the paucity of the tiny apartment. In the corner, sitting on an old threadbare sofa against an empty wall, was Maria, the partner of Father Mike.

"Please, meet mia madre."

Carrie immediately approached Maria, who insisted on rising. Trembling, she reached for her walker and slowly pulled herself up, tears welling in her eyes and gently sparkling on her cheeks like sequins. She moved the walker aside so they could hug. She seemed to be in her eighties and frail, but quite alert. As her arms encircled Carrie, her shoulders shuddering with the effort, tears fell in torrents. Then she pulled back and looked right through Carrie into her heart where she read warmth, acceptance, and love, and hugged tightly again.

Finally, she took Carrie's hand and patted the empty seat beside her and they sat down. Maria continued to stare.

"My mother is so surprised, for you don't look like my father at all," explained Rosa.

Carrie fumbled in her purse for her photos and pulled out one of Fran. Maria shook her head smiling. "Si! Si!" She held the photo to her heart.

"Please keep it. I want you to have it. You must come visit my mother. I know she would love to meet you."

Maria knew very little English, but Rosa's language skills had improved so much she was able to translate for her mother. Before they sat down to lunch, Rosa opened a photo album, which included the black and white 8x10 formal photo of the O'Brien family that Rosa had shown to Carrie and her mother several years ago. Maria turned the pages one by one, smiling as she pointed to her treasured photos, turning to see Carrie's reaction as she showed her family one at a time: the twins, Eduardo and Pancho, and Rosa. Carrie reached over for her hand again, and fingered the delicate tissue-thin skin.

Rosa explained that Maria never exhibited any anger over her husband abandoning her and the family; Rosa said she knew deep in her heart that if it were humanly possible he would have remained with them. "My mother feels only the depth of his love," Rosa said.

When Maria talked about their first dance, her eyes sparkled as she swayed back and forth remembering. From a worn leather pouch, Maria took out some letters she had saved. Two were from Fran to Mike, discussing Mazatlan vacation plans; the third, from Mike addressed to Maria, the only letter he ever wrote to her, dated in 1960, was taped together and preserved in a plastic sleeve. Very carefully, she removed it from the sleeve, pressed it to her lips, unfolded the creases, smoothed it open, and handed it to Carrie.

"Thank you for sharing this, Maria. I can tell you treasure it dearly." Rosa translated for her mother.

As soon as Carrie looked at the letter though, her face registered disappointment, for she was unable to understand the Spanish. Perplexed, she turned to Rosa. As Rosa prepared to translate, Carrie held her breath. Finally, she thought, she would hear the words her uncle used to proclaim his love for Maria, the mother of his children. Her eyes were glued to Rosa as she began to read.

Dear Maria,

I hope you are in good health. How are the children? Doing well, I hope.

I have a favor to ask of you. Please send me 20,000 pesos from our joint account. I am at the Mayo Clinic and must have the money for the removal of a tumor. Please send it addressed to me at the clinic.

Thank you.

Mike

"Thank you for reading the letter to me, Rosa." *How disappointing*, thought Carrie, *I hope my face doesn't show how upset I am. This is the one and only letter Maria has from my uncle and it reads like an electric bill. I don't think he deserved her devotion.* Carrie reached over to touch Maria's hand.

Rosa served lunch on the card table as if she were entertaining Evita Munoz. The first course was chicken tacos and chili mixed with a pico de gallo so hot it made Carrie cry. She was extremely embarrassed as she drank several glasses of water trying to dilute the scant forkful she ingested. However, the rice seasoned with sour cream was perfect for her American palate. For dessert, Rosa served a yummy homemade chocolate cake with coconut frosting.

Carrie heard the taxi honking outside. "Rosa, tomorrow I want you and Maria to come to my hotel, El Camino Real, for lunch so we can continue our conversations."

"Thank you so much, but I must work tomorrow from 10 to 6."

"Oh, were you able to get your citizenship?"

"No, but I have a green card and I'm starting the process of naturalization."

"Oh, well then, you will be a citizen soon. But, I so wanted to see you again." Carrie's eyebrows knitted in a frown. "Well, do you think your mother would be able to visit Fran someday? Could she manage the flight?"

Maria vehemently nodded as Rosa translated for her. "Maybe when she gets a bit stronger. I know she would love to meet your mother."

After a final tearful hug, Carrie departed, waving to Maria until the taxi rounded the corner and she couldn't see her anymore.

———

There were two more stops on Carrie's agenda before she left El Paso: one, St. Ignatius, Uncle Mike's church; and two, Juarez, the meeting place of Uncle Mike and Maria.

As she taxied to St. Ignatius, Carrie was surprised by the busy highways and strip malls, but as she neared the church, the surroundings seemed more familiar. Traffic gave way to empty streets bordered with adobe ranchers set back on dusty grass plots. Soon after driving by the chain-link fence of Fort Bliss, she arrived at her destination. Asking the taxi driver to return in an hour, she stepped out of the cab to explore.

She walked around the rectory several times and peered over the white stucco fence. Immediately, she recognized the red-tiled roof and envisioned the barbecue where Uncle Mike cooked hamburgers for her lunch. The small shrine to Our Lady was still situated in the center of the lawn, her blue mantle faded to gray. Although she hadn't planned to, Carrie unlocked the gate and walked up the cement path. Not knowing what to expect, she knocked on the door. Knocked again and again. Relieved that the door remained closed, she decided to visit the church. Before crossing the street to the church, she snapped several pictures. In the empty church, Carrie studied the statues, the altar, the stained glass windows, the Stations of the Cross, and tried to imagine Uncle Mike at the pulpit.

She genuflected and sat in a pew. Carrie's mind was whirling with all that had transpired since she last sat in this holy space. Then, she picked up a church bulletin and absentmindedly perused it. Staccato footsteps on the terra cotta floor interrupted her reverie. Carrie looked up as a beautiful Mexican woman walked past her and knelt before Our Lady's altar. She lit a candle and remained several minutes in prayer, her head bowed. Carrie watched in silence, wondering if the woman knew her uncle. Not wanting to let the opportunity slip by, she decided to find out. As the woman crossed herself and stood, Carrie did the same. She followed her to the door and tapped her on the shoulder.

"Excuse me! Pardoname!"

"Si? I mean, yes?" The woman turned to face her.

"Hola," Carrie offered her hand. "I am visiting El Paso from Philadelphia in Pennsylvania." The Mexican continued to stare, but hesitantly shook her hand.

"I love your church. It has been a long time since I've been here, but this used to be my uncle's church. He was the pastor here. He built the school. I was wondering if you might have known him."

"What was his name? I was baptized, made my Communion and confession here in St. Ignatius. Got married here too. In fact, my father built the school himself, with his workers, of course. I might have known your uncle."

"He was Father Michael O'Brien." Carrie held her breath, wondering how the woman would react.

The woman's face brightened, her eyes light up, she smiled. "I loved, I mean my whole family loved your uncle. He was one of my father's best friends. He built the school for your uncle. He played golf with him, always beat him, too. Afterward he would eat dinner at our place."

Carrie's breath came out in a sigh. She clasped her hands under her chin. "I'm so happy to hear you say that."

"My name is Pilar, Pilar DelGado was my maiden name. My dad's name was José. I was thinking of Father Mike, inside there, as I prayed for Mom and Dad. I just lit a candle for them. They died in a car crash three years ago today. And as I was praying for them, I thought of your uncle and the fun we used to have around the dining room table when he visited."

"I'm so sorry, Pilar."

"Thank you. But please tell me what happened to your uncle. My husband, Rafael, and I had scheduled our pre-Cana conferences with him, and he seemed to disappear like a big black hole swallowed him up or a band of angels came down and wafted him off to heaven—we never heard from him again. None of us heard from him. It has always been a mystery."

Carrie didn't know what to say to her. She didn't want to tarnish Pilar's opinion of her uncle, but on the other hand, she felt that Pilar deserved the truth.

"You know there were a lot of vicious rumors circulating around back then. In one version, Father Mike was a thief and robbed from the church. However, there was an article published in the El Paso Times exonerating him. Then there was another vicious rumor accusing him of fathering children. There was a faction of us who felt there was no truth to the rumors, but it would be nice to know what really happened." Pilar's eyes begged for truth.

"Pilar," Carrie began not sure which version of the truth she was about to tell her. "We're just trying to put the pieces of the puzzle together ourselves. I wish I could tell you more, but I just can't," she finished.

―――――

Carrie pictured Juarez as a romantic place across the border where dark-eyed, dark-haired men and women wore sombreros and serapes, silver and turquoise. It was easy to imagine Uncle Mike and Maria dancing in a quaint hotel and falling in love there, that is, if he hadn't been a priest.

But as she neared the bridge to cross the Rio Grande, the scenery changed. The streets were littered with trash; the storefronts needed paint; seedy-looking unkempt Mexicans begged for pesos or tried to lure her to purchase second-hand goods. The bridge itself was pulsing with pedestrians and bumper-to-bumper auto traffic, the smell of gas fumes stifling. Carrie told herself it would be worth it when she crossed the border into the romantic Mexico she envisioned, so she pushed on. To her dismay, the scene only worsened as she continued. After five blocks of one shabby building after another, she decided to turn around and return to El Camino Real in El Paso. She much preferred to envision Maria and her uncle dancing in the Juarez of her imagination than the Juarez of today.

1996

Peace

Even though the maple bureau and night table and the velvet brocade armchair are hers, and even though she has adapted to the ever-present urine smell, Fran feels like a prisoner in her one -bedroom home, like a character in *Days of our Lives* desperately wanting someone to switch the channel. Today, these thoughts fade as she anticipates her afternoon guests.

Jeremy opens the door to the bathroom, helps her into the wheelchair, and pushes her before the mirror, the one she has looked in for the past half century.

"Oh, Sweetie, how lovely you look in that raspberry jacket and the skirt with all those tiny rosebuds. Getting all dolled up to meet your visitors, today?" Jeremy asks.

"My visitors? Oh, yes, my visitors. I want to look extra special today." She studies her reflection wondering how it has wrinkled so. "Can you fluff up my hair? I can never reach the back. Then my lipstick, my hand shakes a bit and I can't get a straight line."

"Sure, Darlin,' I'll make you look like the queen herself. Nothin's too good for you, Sweetie, you know that."

"You always say that, Jeremy." She watches his hands as he runs them through her hair and then smoothes the stray strands with her brush, the faded silver monogrammed brush her mother gave her when she turned 16.

She tilts her head from side to side. "Fluff it a bit more over here on the right, please."

"How's that, Darlin?"

"Good, good. Thank you."

"Shall I roll you into the atrium, now? Maria and Rosa will be here soon."

"Who? Did you say Maria and Rosa?"

"Yes, Rosa, your niece and her mother."

"That's right. Please, let's go."

Her caretaker moves her through the halls into the glass-enclosed room. "I'll park you right here so you can look at all the lovely flowers and watch the entrance at the same time. Your visitors should be here soon." Jeremy brakes the chair, pats her on the arm. "Smile, sweetie, you look absolutely lovely." He leaves her alone, all alone with her thoughts.

Fran follows the path of the sun as it rests on the deep purple leaves of the hydrangeas lining the entrance to Grand View. She remembers her mother's hydrangeas, faint pink darkening toward the stem. She and Mike would often scramble under its bushy branches to play with his army men, advancing and retreating until one of them declared a truce.

How simple life was back then, thinks Fran. Nothing ever came between her and her older brother in the growing up years, but complications multiplied as the years passed. Even now, ten years after his death, she can't find it in her heart to forgive.

Ever since being faced with Mike's secret, she struggles with the awful truth of his double existence. But being denied entrance to his "other" life hurts far more than the knowledge of his sins against the church they both loved. *How could he slam the door on Rosa, that lovely daughter of his?* She shakes her head, sighs, and flicks a fly from her fingers, wishing she could flick away the resentment she feels toward Mike. Footsteps echoing on the tiled floor shatter her thoughts. She turns toward the brown-eyed, brown-haired woman rushing into her arms, the daughter of her brother the priest,

"Hola, Tia Fran," calls Rosa, as she closes the distance for a hug. "I'm so happy to see you. And I'm even more thrilled that you will meet mia madre." On her walker, Maria advances slowly to meet her sister-in-law. Her heart wants to bounce, but her body only permits walking, walking very slowly.

She appears shrouded in a blur of brown: pale beige dress almost touching the tightly laced oxfords, the copper skin, chestnut eyes, pale waves framing her face pulled back in a knot at the nape of her neck.

The smile dominating her face is warm, welcoming, inviting, but the space between the two women is uneasy. Fran has moved from the notion that Maria stole her brother from the church, but not quite far enough. Once the formalities of meeting were dispensed with, there would be time for conversation. Questions Fran rehearsed in her mind for the past ten years would finally be answered, that is, if she remembers the questions, and remembers to ask them. She studies Maria's face for clues as her halting gait inches her closer and closer, her brightly colored raffia bag swinging from the walker.

Fran remembers the photos of Mike with his arm around Maria that Rosa showed her when they first met; the black and white evidence that forced her disbelief to dissolve into a wary acceptance. Since then, she has become quite fond of Rosa: so fond, that she is unable to forgive Mike for deserting his family. She watches Maria, hoping to discover why Mike loved her.

"This is mia madre, my mamá, Maria." Maria extends both arms. Fran reaches for her hands. Their eyes lock, their tongues still, emotion fills the void.

"Hola. Mike's sister—I never thought I would live to see this day. So many times I asked Michael to bring you to our house." Her smile is saturated with joy. "He talked about you all the time. I knew he loved you very much, so every birthday, every Christmas, I would beg him to invite you. Every time I asked him, he answered in the same way. He would tell me you lived in Ireland and couldn't afford the airfare. Of course, I know the truth now, but I didn't know it back then."

Fran listens. She stares at Maria as Rosa translates. Finally, she unclasps her hands and motions for her guests to sit down. *So this is the woman my brother married. Just an ordinary looking Mexican grandmother. Nothing special. I wonder what attracted him? I wish I had met her before when we were both younger.* The thoughts muddle through her mind.

"Tia Fran, are you okay?"

"Yes, yes, just thinking." She shoos another fly away. "Rosa, will you close that window, please? The flies are bothersome today."

"Of course, of course." Rosa jumps up to fulfill Fran's request. She didn't expect the meeting to proceed so slowly. She can feel and see tension in Fran's face and doesn't know how to erase it.

"I love your jacket, Tia Fran. Raspberry, isn't it? It looks lovely with your hair." She sits down again.

"Thank you. It's one of my favorites." Fran closes her eyes remembering the past, wishing she could return to the days when she and Mike were best of friends.

Maria wipes the perspiration from her forehead with a white handkerchief edged in lace, the smile still planted on her face.

"Is Carrie coming to have lunch with us today?" Rosa's question startles the silence.

Before Fran can answer, Jeremy saunters in. "Afternoon, ladies. I'm comin' to get my darlin'. Don't she look real good today? If you follow me, I'll roll her into the dining room. I requested a special table for you ladies. It's in the corner, very private, so y'all can have a real gabfest. Are you ready, Darlin?" Fran nods.

"What about Carrie?" asks Rosa.

"The office will send her to the dining room," remarks Jeremy as he slowly pushes the wheel chair.

Once Carrie arrives, tension eases. Sometimes it is difficult for Fran to find the exact words she wants to say and it troubles her. Meeting Maria for the first time is emotional enough without worrying about conversation at the same time. As lunch progresses, Fran and Maria grow closer. Before long, they are jabbering away, Maria speaking in Spanish not understanding English, and Fran speaking in English not understanding Spanish. When Rosa and Carrie understand what is happening, they start to giggle. Soon Fran and Maria also start laughing as they realize what they are doing.

"Mom, Rosa will translate for you. Just tell her what you want to ask Maria."

"I really want to know how she can still love my brother after he deserted her. I can't forgive him for that. I want to know how she can."

"She says his love still touches her every day. Every time she looks at her children and grandchildren, she sees his face, hears his voice. She knows beyond a doubt that my father would never leave her and the children unless something he couldn't control forced him to leave. She wants to know why you can't feel his love and forgive him as she has." Fran watches the light in Maria's eyes and thinks of Mike.

Maria reaches into her raffia bag and pulls out a package swaddled in tissue paper tied with a blue ribbon. "This belongs to you," she says.

Fran takes the gift, unties the ribbon and peels apart the paper. She gasps as she looks at the gift in her hands. Then she looks at Maria. "Thank you. Thank you." She runs her finger over the inscription *"All our love, Mom and Pop."* A tear escapes and rolls down her cheek as she presses the chalice to her heart. "Thank you, Maria, for giving my brother back to me."